Wind of Fate

The MacIntyres – Part II

Novel

Barbara Eckhoff

Translated from the original Version
Der Wind in meinen Federn
Copyright @2019 Barbara Eckhoff

BOOKS BY BARBARA ECKHOFF

Um uns herum die Dunkelheit (German Edition)

Der Wind in meinen Federn (German Edition)

Wenn Liebe Zweifel sät (German Edition)

When Love grows doubt (English Edition)

Wind of Fate (English Edition)

Barbara Eckhoff
Wind of Fate
The MacIntyres – Part II

ACKNOWLEDGMENTS

I sincerely thank Joanne and Renate, who once again had a good eye and weeded out quite a few of my mistakes.
Without both of you, this book would certainly not have been published.
Thousand hugs and kisses to both of you.

Prologue

Wyoming 1862

Relentlessly, the wagon train pushed on mile after mile through the endless expanse of the prairie.

With the hopes of many travelers, for the fulfillment of their dreams of a better life, which until then had been marked by poverty and despair.

In the year 1862, a mixed group of people from all social classes headed west. Aristocrats and businessmen side by side with people whom they would have allowed near them only as serfs and servants. But here, in the new world, everything was different.

Here, it was not a person's origin that counted, but who he was himself. People had to support and help each other and everyone had to contribute. That was the only way they could make it to the end, to Oregon. This trail was hard and relentless and would claim its victims, if they did not stick together.

They had seen plenty of evidence of this along the way. Skeletons of dead cattle, overturned covered wagons that were slowly rotting or even crosses, which stood at the side of the road. Each of them knew the risk and yet it had not deterred this group, with their belongings, cattle and horses, to face the challenge. Thirty covered wagons rolled in the already warm spring sun, on a predetermined path, across the prairie.

They had been on the road for weeks and were

now on their way to Fort Laramie, where they wanted to replenish their provisions. It was the last opportunity before they came across the Rocky Mountains into Oregon. Robert was also on this trek with his family. But unlike all the other travelers among them, he was not heading toward an uncertain future, but knew what awaited him at his destination. He made this trek already for the second time and had known exactly what hardships he would put his little family through.

Twenty years ago, at the age of ten, he was with his parents in just such a trek to Wyoming. At that time, it had all been exciting and thrilling for him. He had previously read books about cowboys and Indians in his home country of Scotland and was eager to see some for himself. His parents, both members of the Scottish aristocracy, had made their way to Oregon with their fortune, where they had dreamed of building a large horse breeding operation. They hadn't made it all the way to Oregon. They had stayed near Fort Laramie because they had found the land there which had been ideally suited for their project.

Besides, they had speculated that the Army would always need new horses. The plan of his parents had been unusual but it had worked out. Eleven years later, they were the proud owners of the finest and largest horse breeding farm in Wyoming. They had built a large farm from nothing, and it had grown over the years. In the meantime, several other families worked and lived on the ranch. Robert was looking forward to seeing what had changed in his absence. Eight years he had been away from home, but now it was time to pay a visit and introduce his wife and young son. He had sent a letter with a family photo of them ahead of their visit and fervently hoped that it had reached its recipient. What had been exciting twenty years ago, was beginning to grate on his nerves. For weeks they were on the road and every day it was the same scenery.

In the morning he lined up with his wagon and saw nothing but the covered wagon in front of him all day long. They tried to keep the connection, until in the evening, when they put the wagons in a circle and went to rest. Comfort did not exist. The wagons were simple and protected only provisionally against the forces of nature. Dust, heat, rain and wind tore at the forces. There was still no other way to cover the long distance.

A railroad line in this direction did not yet exist and carriages did not drive yet either, since there was a lack of intermediate stations. How much easier it was to travel in Europe. This boundless expanse could almost drive you out of your mind. He admired the people here, who, full of anticipation and zest for action, set off again every morning into the unknown. He would never have chosen this step. In the meantime, he felt at home in Scotland. In the last eight years, he found his fulfillment there and so this visit to his parents would also be a farewell because he had no intention of going down this road a third time.

In the meantime, it had become noon and his wife sat with her son next to him on the coach box. Moira, as his wife was called, was a gift from God. He had met her seven years ago at a ball. With her elegant appearance and the radiant smile with which she had been introduced to him, she had immediately captivated him. Her lovely nature and the beauty with which she had been presented, had quickly convinced him that she was the woman of his life. Now they had been married for almost seven years and she had always been by his side until now. About five years ago, she had given birth to his pride and his son.

Somewhat sleepy, he sat cuddled up next to him on his mother's arm.

"Dad will it be a very long time before we see

Granny? And can I ride a pony there, too? Please yes?"

Robert had to grin. His son already seemed to be developing into a real MacIntyre. In this family, lay the sense for the most beautiful animals in the world. For horses. His father had an extraordinary feeling for these creatures and he was also very good with them. Apparently, this gift had been inherited just like the bright blue eyes.

"In two days we should have reached Fort Laramie and then it's another two days to your grandparents. Grandfather will take you for a ride and grandmother will bake her delicious cookies for you. It's going to be a good time, son."

"Did you hear that, Mom. I get to ride with Grandpa."

The little boy had become quite excited and beamed at his mother.

"Yes, I'm excited too. Your dad has always told us so much about the ranch, that I can hardly wait to go." Lovingly, she wrapped her arms around her little boy and had to realize once again that his radiant smile warmed her heart. At five years old, the little fellow was already very headstrong. He developed a strong will and could charm her with his smile. Just like his father, she thought silently and looked over at him.

Robert had immediately caught her eye, when they had met for the first time. He had looked so breathtakingly handsome in his black suit. With his tall, slim figure, he had towered over many other men. His black hair, which shone like velvet in the sun, had been a stark contrast to the bright blue eyes that smiled warmly at her. Even now she noticed tingling through her body when he caught her gaze and smiled at her. She loved this man like the first day and this love for him together with curiosity had made her expose herself to these hardships. But she was also feverishly awaiting the end of the journey.

"Indians!"

Suddenly things got restless and panic broke out. Again and again the trek leader shouted the word as he dashed past all the wagons at a sharp gallop. The front wagons now drove faster and the leader came back at a wild gallop and ordered them to build a wagon fort.

"Oh my God, Robert! Indians! What are we going to do?"

"Both of you get in the back and lie flat on the ground. Get my cartridges out of the box , and then take cover."

Moira quickly climbed inside the wagon with her son. Through the rear opening she could see that all the others behind her were trying to keep up with their speed. She pushed her son to the floor and gave him a sign to stay there. Quickly she looked for the box with the cartridges and handed them to her husband. Then she lay down close to her son on the floor.

The speed of the galloping horses shook the wagon hard. From outside she could hear the war cries of the approaching Indians. Fear rose up in her. Quite unconsciously she pulled her son closer. She heard the trek leader yelling commands again and immediately noticed how the wagon was going in circles. All the wagons managed just in time to form a circle, which they kept so tight that no one could get through.

Then the pandemonium broke out. A huge horde of Sioux Indians attacked the wagon train. With a great roar they galloped around the wagons. Quickly, the people of the trek made their way to safety.

Children and women were sent into the wagons, while the men, armed, lay down under the wagons and waited for the command to attack. This was not long in coming. When the first arrow hit one of the wagons, the leader gave the order to fire. The first volley of rifle fire was immediately followed by a rain of arrows from the

Indians. After the first losses, the Indians changed their tactics and started shooting incendiary arrows at the wagons, which immediately caught fire.

Women and children inside forced their way outside to safety from the flames, where they were met by the arrows of the Indians. The horrified men shot what their rifles could give. The midday sun shone down on a scene of horror. Shots and screams of death would not end. Moira rummaged out of a pocket a small bag and gave it to her little boy. In the sack was a small amulet, which she had received from Robert.

This amulet contained the pictures of her and Robert. Furthermore there was a photograph, which showed them all three together and the little teddy bear that Robert had received from his mother. She hung the bag around her son's neck.

"Take good care of it. If anything happens to us, go to grandmother, do you hear? I pray to God that we will survive this."

Moira tried to suppress the tears that were welling up inside her. Her son needed her strength. Frightened, he crawled closer to his mother. She was still on the floor in her wagon and could hear from outside the screams of the people who had been hit. Suddenly, her wagon began to burn as well. If they did not want to burn alive, she had to get out of it. Quickly but carefully they both crawled to the exit.

She shouted for Robert, who immediately came out of hiding and pulled his son down to him. He gave him the hint to lie flat on his stomach under the car. Just as Robert was about to help his wife, an arrow flew in his direction and he was just able to take cover before it bored into the wood in front of him. Immediately he put on his rifle and aimed at the next Indian who galloped past him. He pulled the trigger and saw the Sioux fly off his horse. That second was enough for him to lift his wife off the wagon as well.

But just as she wanted to crawl under the wagon, she was hit by an arrow right into her heart. She collapsed before the eyes of her son.

"No!" cried Robert in horror. In his pain, he no longer thought of his son and took the rifle, firing without taking cover himself. He took down three Indians before he himself was killed by another arrow in the back. Little MacIntyre sat shivering under the wagon of his dead parents. He buried his face between his knees and closed his ears with his hands.

He only vaguely heard the last death throes of the other passengers. The Indians' cry of victory drowned out everything else. All at once it was silent. No more shots were fired, no more screaming could be heard. Only a small whimper came from somewhere. Should he dare to come out from under the wagon, or should he rather stay there. He was as quiet as a mouse and did not even dare to take a breath.

How long he had sat still he did not know. Just as he was about to breathe a hand grabbed his arm and pulled him out from under the car. Horrified he cried out and looked into the war-painted face of the Sioux before he felt the cold blade of his knife against his neck.

Chapter 1

Wyoming 1877

Still lay the silence of the night over the prairie, but on the horizon one could already see the first signs of the new day. Slowly the darkness gave way to the deep orange of the rising sun. The night had been starry but the small glittering dots in the sky were fading fast. The harsh winter was over, but there was still an icy wind that swept across the endless expanse.

The rising sun would soon bring the first warm rays that would make the prairie blossom and change into a green landscape dotted with wildflowers.

With eyes open, you could see the harbingers of spring everywhere. Small tender buds on the trees, a first tentative green on the earth and also the animal world got up from the winter sleep. The air smelled of several well stoked campfires.

Around them stood the tents of the Cheyenne. Except for a few warriors who sat wrapped in blankets around the fire and kept watch, it was still quiet in the camp. Horses grazed quietly nearby. It would not be long before it would be daylight and life would awaken in the tents.

The two men, who were watching the actions in the village from a hill, sat silently on their horses. Both wore long brown suede pants with fringes on the outer seams. Matching long-sleeved suede shirt embroidered with colorful beads. Their feet were in buffalo skin lined moccasins. To protect themselves from the cold, they had blankets embroidered with rich Indian patterns, around their shoulders. The long black hair was braided into two pigtails each, held together by a small leather band. Around the forehead they wore a simple band of snakeskin, in which an eagle feather was stuck at the back of the head.

Perfectly calm, man and animal stood on the hill and only the hot breath from the nostrils of the horses, which was visible in the cold air, betrayed that these were living creatures and not statues.

"My brother knows he doesn't have to go."

Without taking his eyes off the village, he had addressed his friend. The other man remained silent long before he finally answered:

"I know, but it is better this way."

"My brother has been preoccupied with many new thoughts, since the great chief has gone to the eternal hunting grounds."

"Mantotohpa will fill the void well and lead the Cheyenne warriors wisely."

"Then why does my brother want to go away? What will Hon Avonaco say to this?"

"She has known since yesterday and understands."

"Honiahake is sad to lose his friend. He has been like a brother to him."

"I will miss Honiahake too, but I have a mission to accomplish."

"Let me go with you."

"No, I have to do this alone and the tribe needs you."

"Will you come back one day?"

"I don't know yet."

"Your place is here, and whatever the outcome

of your search, you will be welcome."

"I know. It will be time. May Manitou protect you, Honiahake!"

"May Manitou protect and help you with what you have to do."

They both raised their right arms and made a sign of farewell. Then he took one last look at his village, before he steered his horse into the adjacent forest and was swallowed up by the darkness.

Only Honiahake remained, sadly steering his horse down the hill back to the village.

Chapter 2

The bright bell of the little schoolhouse rang out for the conclusion of Sunday worship. Reverend Charles Duncan bid farewell to each of his small congregation with a handshake. Every other Sunday he held his church devotions at the Hunts' cattle ranch.

He had known William Hunt since the day he came to the ranch. With a lot of courage and confidence, and a handful of cattle he had come west and had bought land near Fort Laramie. William Hunt had intended to build up a large ranch to supply the area with cattle and meat. At that time, the fort had been only a small outpost with a few soldiers.

It was the last station, occupied by whites, where man and beast found a safe rest before making the arduous journey westward across the Rocky Mountains. Since then Fort Laramie had developed into a large military base and housed several cavalry garrisons.

In the meantime, a small town with stores, saloons and even a small hotel had formed in the immediate vicinity of the fort. Charles' pride and joy was his own little church, which was located on the outskirts of the village. From Monday to Friday he gave the children school lessons there and every second Sunday the bell rang for devotions.

The other two Sundays of the month he rode to the Hunt Ranch, which was a good day's ride from the fort away. William Hunt and his wife Gloria had been regular visitors to his little house of worship until they had built a small chapel on their own land and asked him to hold his devotions there as well.

By now the ranch was in its second generation, because James, the forty-five-year-old son of William and his wife was now the boss. His father had retired after the death of his beloved wife three years ago and had left the business in the hands of his son. In the past, both had made the ranch the largest in the area and had become respected citizens of Laramie.

If James had inherited his father's skills and could be a tough guy about his business, he became quite tame when his pretty daughter Isabella, was near him. She was his pride and joy. Charles had baptized Isabella eighteen years ago and a year later had to provide assistance to the family when James' wife and Isabella's mother died of pneumonia.

It had been a difficult time then, but Isabella had grown into a young, smart and confident woman thanks to her grandmother Gloria and the two men. After the death of her grandmother three years ago, she was the first woman in the house and made sure that everything worked in the household. She was a hardworking girl and mastered despite her youth the tasks with bravura. The only place where she got help, from the wife of the first foreman, was the kitchen.

The ranch employed about twenty men, almost all of whom wanted to be fed.

"Reverend Duncan, don't you want to come over to the house before you start on the long journey home? Louisa baked some fresh apple pie early this morning. and I know you like it so much."

The Reverend was brought back to the present by

Isabella's question.

"That's sweet, my child. Perhaps a slice. I really can't resist freshly baked apple pie. Your grandmother always knew that."

Laughing, she hooked the arm of the Reverend

"Well, then, why don't you come with me?"

They both set off on the short walk from the chapel to the main house. This consisted of a two-story log house with a wide porch around it. Two steps led up to the front door. On the porch stood two wooden rocking chairs, in which her grandfather had liked to sit with her Grandmother. Isabella often sat on evenings with her grandfather and listened to his stories from back then. In front of the house, several wooden stakes had been driven into the ground, to which one could tie horses or carriages. Today only the horse of the reverend stood there and waited patiently for his master.

"How's the development of your school coming along? Are you making any progress?"

"Yes. Right now I have three students aged five and seven, and two nine-year-olds whom I teach three days a week here in the chapel. I enjoy it very much and wish I had more students. But at the moment there are no other children on the ranch, except for two little babies. And until the two babies are ready for school, the first students will already be done with it."

"I think it's remarkable that you started the school on your own initiative. People entrust you with their children. That is not easy, especially when you're as young as you are."

"Everyone should have the opportunity to be able to read, do math and write and I have been very fortunate that my grandmother was of the same opinion and taught me all this and now I just want to pass on my knowledge. Unfortunately, I only have time to teach three days a week. The housework and the ranch's bookkeeping leave me little time for that."

"Your father should be very proud of you, Isabella. He couldn't have had a better child."

"Sometimes I catch myself thinking, if it wouldn't have been better, if he'd had a son instead of a daughter. He could be more of a help to him than I can be. He works hard and could use help. I will never be able to give him a hand as a son could have done."

"Isabella, you mustn't think like that. You were and are your father's sunshine. If God had not called your mother to him so early, you would probably have a whole crowd of brothers and sisters around you, but God did not want it that way."

"What are you two dawdling about, Charles get inside, the apple pie is waiting."

Isabella and the Reverend had just reached the first step to the porch, when the door opened from inside. Isabella's grandfather appeared in the doorway. Laughing, they both hurried, and while Isabella scurried past her grandfather, Charles stopped in front of William.

"William, I was just in company and wanted to enjoy it a little longer."

"You old charmer. Come on in or the coffee will get cold."

Laughing, they both went inside the house.

Chapter 3

Isabella had exchanged her Sunday dress for her riding costume. It was such a glorious spring day that she wanted to steal a few hours and venture out for a ride.
It was the first, since the long winter, and it would do her and her mare Tipsy good to get off the ranch.

After the Reverend had been invited not only to the apple pie, but also for lunch, he was now on his way home, and Isabella had a little time to kill before she had to see to dinner. She had agreed with Louisa to be back on time. Quickly she slipped into her brown winter riding skirt, which was made of heavy wool.
Along with it she wore a white blouse with long sleeves and high collar. Against the still fresh temperatures, she put on her moss green jacket made of warm winter wool, which reached her hips and had a longer peplum towards the back. Her appearance was completed with warm, wool-lined, brown riding boots, black gloves, a jaunty lime-green scarf, tied around her neck and a cowboy hat that did not quite match her elegant style of dress, but was very practical and under which she hid her long, chestnut hair.

With a last, satisfied look in the mirror, she left her room and made her way to the stable. Normally, she did not make such a fuss about her appearance, but today was a beautiful day and she was looking forward to her ride. So why not dress up for a change?

The opportunities on a ranch were not very often available. With a smile on her lips and a little melody in her head, she arrived at the huge barn.

The stables were part of a large barn complex located near the main house. One barn housed the horses used for ranch work. Just behind it were several paddocks where the horses now grazed and quite a few small and larger paddocks where the cowboys could break in new horses or drive cattle in for branding.

In one of these small paddocks, a bit off to the side, stood a black stallion that watched her with attentive eyes. The ears pricked, he followed every move she made. Isabella thought about it and paused briefly before turning to the animal. Slowly, she walked toward the small paddock. Immediately the animal started to move and ran restlessly around. Her father had caught the wild mustang a week ago and brought him here.

He wanted him for himself and would have long ago ridden him but the animal was the devil in person. As soon as someone tried to approach him, he rose threatening. When Isabella came closer, the stallion started to snort, tossed his black mane wildly back and forth and pranced on the ground. Isabella stopped. She was only a short distance away from the fence and could see the diabolical eyes of the animal.

It was a beautiful animal, but unfortunately unrideable and she wondered, as she turned around and went back to the stable, what her father was going to do with him. Well, today she was going to spend some quality time with her own horse. Her chestnut mare was already neighing happily when she heard her coming down the aisle. Tipsy was a good-natured horse, that Isabella had bought as a foal for her fifth birthday. Since then they were one heart and soul and understood each other blindly, when they rode out together.

"Well beautiful? Shall we go for a ride today? It's so beautiful outside. You'll like to let the wind blow through your mane."

The mare joyfully rubbed her nostrils against Isabella's arm and neighed approvingly, as if she had understood what she had just heard. It was not long before Isabella had saddled her horse and left the stable. Skillfully, she swung herself into the saddle and steered her mare in the direction of the main house, since her grandfather had just come out of the front door.

"Do you want to take a little ride?"

"Yes, it's lovely today and I haven't been out for a long time."

"Don't ride too far, though. Did you bring the rifle? Just in case?"

She reached up to her right thigh and pulled the rifle stock out of the holster a little so that her grandfather could see the weapon.

"It's all there, I'll be back in a couple of hours. See you later."

She slid the rifle back into the holster, tapped her hat in salute and gave her mare the command to trot. Joyfully they both trotted off.

The sun was shining brightly from the sky and not a single cloud clouded the weather. First she rode a good distance along the fence of the cattle pasture and had seen several of her father's cowboys at work. The ranch was located in a kind of high valley.

In the distance you could see forests, hills and high mountain ranges to the right and left of the ranch. In between far-reaching pastures. Later she had made a small but sharp gallop over the endless expanse of the adjacent prairie which had led into a stop on a hill. She looked around. From the hill she had a breathtaking view of her home. As far as the eye reached, she saw small black points grazing on the prairie. They were her father's cattle. The ranch house could no longer be seen. "That was lovely, wasn't it Tipsy? Come let's ride on."

Happily, she patted the animal on the neck and Tipsy snorted in satisfaction. She steered her horse into the adjacent forest and rode slowly into it. All too far, she did not want to ride more, since she had promised to be back on time, but they both enjoyed the ride so much that she decided to extend it a bit more. She loved the smell of the forest. The delicate, lime green buds of the new leaves. Her horse carried her safely along the small trail around the trees.

Somewhere above, sat birds singing their spring song. She was briefly startled when two rabbits jumped out of the bushes in front of her, but Tipsy didn't let that upset her. Cheekily, the two rabbits sat down on the forest floor in front of them and watched the approaching hares, before they suddenly disappeared with a leap into the undergrowth. Laughing, she rode on.

A deer appeared in the undergrowth and immediately disappeared from her view. All of nature had awakened from its long winter sleep.

She enjoyed the peaceful atmosphere that prevailed here. How gladly she would have stayed longer but she had to make her way home. Isabella knew her way around here well. How often had she come along this path. Only a short distance, then the forest would open up and a small trail would lead down the embankment, where she could ride along the forest on open prairie back to the ranch.

Suddenly Tipsy stopped abruptly and began to neigh nervously. Isabella looked around, but could see nothing suspicious. Reassuringly she tried to talk to the increasingly nervous animal.

"Calm down, Tipsy. What is it that makes you nervous? Come on let's ride on."

But the animal did not move from the spot. Instead, it began to neigh loudly and prance nervously on the spot. Isabella slowly pulled the rifle from the holster and inwardly prepared herself to fire a shot. Whatever was around her, she had to try to steer Tipsy out of the woods. She had not quite finished this thought when, out of nowhere, a cougar jumped on her horse and bit the animal in the neck. Tipsy reared up wildly in pain, shook its neck convulsively and tried to shake off the beast. Isabella had cried out in horror when the cougar jumped onto the horse in front of her.

The moment of shock had lasted until she had recognized the situation, had used the cougar to bite the horse's neck firmly. She couldn't shoot, the cougar was too close for that, but she tried to knock him off his horse with the butt of her rifle. With all her strength she hit the animal, the cougar let go of the horse's neck and now clawed his one paw deep into her thigh, while he came closer to her body with his sharp teeth.

Painfully she cried out and panic-stricken she continued to hit the cougar with the rifle. At that moment Tipsy started to move, to escape the cougar. But the cougar had bitten into her neck again. With great difficulty she managed to stay on the horse and at the same time tried to shake off the beast.

Tipsy was going faster and faster. Isabella held at the same time the reins in one hand and the saddle horn to give herself support, while the other hand tried to hit the cougar with the butt of the rifle. Crouched, so as not to be lifted out of the saddle by the branches of the trees, she saw the end of the forest coming. She had to make it as far as the open prairie, then she would be able to move better, but until then endless time seemed to pass. Finally Tipsy had reached the embankment and galloped down at a wild pace. Isabella was in danger of losing her footing. She was a good rider and had been in the saddle since childhood, but she had never been prepared for this extreme situation.

She clawed her thighs against the horse's body and was glad when they arrived on level ground. But instead of Tipsy riding toward the ranch, she swept along the prairie in the opposite direction. Now she was able to stand up. She tied the reins around the pommel of the saddle so she wouldn't lose them and took the rifle in both hands. With the remaining strength she still had, she took a swing with the rifle and hit the cougar on the head with full force. The cougar finally let go of the animal, snarling, and with a second blow immediately following, the cougar flew off the horse in a high arc. Inwardly, Isabella breathed a sigh of relief.

She had managed to shake off the dangerous beast. Isabella quickly stowed the rifle in the stock under her thigh and took up the reins again, while she tried to calm down Tipsy and steer her in the direction of the ranch. But the animal was in such a panic that it did not respond neither to the reassuring words of her nor to the rein aids. On the contrary, now on the open terrain, the animal gained even more speed. They moved away at a murderous pace mile after mile more from the ranch and the environment became more and more unknown to her.

On the hill he reined in his horse. The forest was behind him and now gave him a clear view of the breathtaking landscape below him. He had been on the road for a long time with his mission, but he had not made a single step forward. Somewhat undecided as to, where he should turn now, he stood on the hill and let the magic of nature fall upon him.

Between the small ridge on which he stood and the deep ravine that opened up a few hundred yards away from him lay green prairie. His gaze wandered to the left, where he saw that the canyon widened and the prairie ended. There, he would only get further if he could find a way down and the gorge allowed him to ride in it. To the right, the terrain looked as if he could continue his way. Just as he wanted to steer his horse in this direction, down the hill, a cloud of dust on the horizon caught his attention. What could it be that was coming at him at a seemingly rapid pace?

A herd of buffalo? No, the dust cloud was not big enough for that. He had seen many buffalo herds before, and when they came, the ground shook and the dust clouds were huge. His trained sharp eyes suddenly spotted a single rider, but what drove this rider into this area with such speed? Slowly he gave his horse the command to descend the hill. He did not want to reveal himself too early to the oncoming rider.

When he reached the bottom, he took cover behind a bush and could observe from here that the rider had not reduced his speed and, from his point of view, was dashing along the precipice in an extremely dangerous manner. The rider had to be insane. He could plunge into the abyss at any moment with a misstep of the horse. When the horse was at his eye level, he realized that the rider was a woman, who had apparently lost control of her animal.

Without hesitating, he slammed his heels into his horse's flanks and galloped wildly after the rider. The horse was fast, but it was no match for his mustang and so he made up ground yard by yard. The rider did not seem to have noticed him, nor was she aware of the danger she was in. At any moment she could lose her balance, or her horse could fall with her, into the ravine. Glancing ahead, he saw that they were nearing the end where the ravine joined the ridge and the grass ended. The rider's animal continued to dash towards it without stopping. He recognized the panicked look in the horse's eyes and knew that he had to get the woman from the animal. With the Indian words that he whispered into his horse's ear, the animal immediately stepped up its pace once again. He shifted to the left of the panicked animal and now rode almost level with it.

At that moment, the woman caught a glimpse of him and widened her eyes in fear. Just as she was about to draw her rifle with her right hand, he steered his horse right next to hers, bent over to her, wrapped his right arm around her delicate waist and lifted her with a skillful grip from her saddle. He threw her directly over his animal's neck. Quickly he yanked the reins and let his mustang run out for a few more yards before he brought the animal to a halt.

Elegantly he let himself slide off the horse and pulled the woman kicking in front of him off the horse. Because she flailed wildly and he let go of her at that moment, she lost her balance and landed on her rear end. With a cry, she tried to pull herself up, but her legs failed cooperate and she landed on the floor again. Desperate and driven by fear, she slowly crawled away from the frightening Indian, who was now standing calmly next to his black stallion and watching her closely.

Chapter 4

Oh God, she was lost! The cougar alone would had been bad enough, but now she had to deal with Indians and she knew from her grandfather's stories that these creatures had no pity for women. She also knew that the warriors raped women, took their scalps and then often killed them or just left them with the severe injuries until nature finished its work. Whatever she faced now would be gruesome and would cause her death. Isabella looked around in panic. At the moment she saw only him. Where were the others?

An Indian usually never came alone. But so far she could only see him, and he was standing very quietly beside his big, black horse and watching her. He made no move to approach her. What was he up to? What was he waiting for? Was it going to be some kind of a game? Stirring up her fears, was that the incentive he needed to carry out his gruesome work on her?

Isabella tried to calm herself. It did her no good if she continued to panic. So far she could only see him and maybe she could somehow escape. If she got back on her horse again, then she might have a chance, because there was her rifle on the saddle. She looked around, but couldn't see Tipsy. Where had her horse gone? Sobering, she had to realize that far and wide only the Indian with his horse and she were here.

Could she manage to outsmart him, to steal his horse? As tall and proud as he stood there, watching her, she did not really have confidence in her idea.

He seemed young, only a few years older than herself, and his outward appearance showed her that he was quite muscular under his Indian clothes.

He would probably be nimble and strong and would not let her touch his horse easily. There had to be another way. Isabella who was sitting a small distance away from him in the grass , tried to get up again, when a sharp pain went through her thigh where the cougar had injured her. Immediately she sank to the ground with a cry. She must have hurt herself.

But she couldn't possibly check her leg here, where she would have had to lift her skirt to get to it. With a pained face, she crouched on the ground and watched as the Indian turned to his horse, took a blanket and a small leather pouch from it, and walked toward her in slow steps. Quietly she prayed to God to assist her. Whatever would happen now, she would not surrender without a fight. And if it was the last thing she would do on this earth, it would also become hell for him.

Until the bitter end. She braced herself inwardly for an attack, but the Indian stopped just before her and spread the blanket on the grass. Then he pulled her onto the blanket with a quick grip that came as a total surprise to her and caused her to let out a cry of fear. She was just about to escape his grasp when he knelt down next to her. He unsheathed his long knife and gestured for her to be quiet.

Completely intimidated by the sight of the knife in front of her body and the energetic look of his strange steel-blue eyes, a sudden rigidity set in, so that she could not move. But when he started to lift her skirt at the place where the pain was, her calmness was over.

Isabella struck at him and tried to escape from

his grip. But it all helped nothing, he exposed the spot on her thigh and they could both see that two deep bites and a long scratch were causing the pain. The cougar had bitten her thigh and had torn open the skin with a paw. In her panic, she hadn't noticed that at all.

The Indian reached into his small leather bag and took a few herbs from it. He handed them to Isabella and indicated that she should put them in her mouth and chew on them. Slightly skeptical, she did not want to do this but the warrior did not give in and so she reluctantly put the herbs in her mouth. They tasted bitter and it was strange to chew on them, but the longer she did it, she had the feeling as if the pain in her leg became less.

In the meantime, the Indian had taken a strip of cloth from her skirt with his knife and cut a bandage from it. Now he held his hand in front of her mouth and gestured her to spit out the herbs.

She followed with interest how he applied the salivated herbs, now like a sticky mass, distributed on the wounds and then firmly fixed with the bandage. After that, he rose again, pocketed his knife and brought the bag back to his horse. Isabella did not know what she should think about it. He had helped her. Up to now he made no signs that he wanted to hurt her.

Could it perhaps be that she had judged him too quickly and had done him an injustice? She had no experience with Indians, did not understand their language and knew only the stories she had heard from others. But this behavior did not fit at all into the bloodthirsty picture, the one that had been shown to her so far.

Calmly waiting, she sat on the blanket and watched, as he whispered something in his animal's ear and then walked past her to the abyss. She turned around and saw that he looked into the depths. He walked a little along the precipice and then slowly descended until he was no longer visible. Now she was alone with the horse.

It would be her opportunity to run away. But something made her sit on the blanket as if subdued and look in the direction of the canyon. What was he up to? It took quite a while until she heard something from his direction. The first thing she saw, was her saddle and then she saw him coming up the ravine with her rifle.

Where had he gotten Tipsy's saddle and where was her mare? Slowly she realized that her horse had fallen into the ravine. Quickly she pulled herself together, ignoring the pain in her thigh and hurried over to the precipice. He was just able to drop her saddle and rifle and catch her as she fell into his arms, stumbling and sobbing on the precipice. With his strong arms, and she pressed close to his body, he held her tightly and made her look over the precipice into the depths. At the bottom she saw her beloved animal lying shattered.

"Tipsy, no," she called down to the dead animal and then broke down in tears. In her grief for the animal, she didn't even realize that the warrior's strong arms had carried her back to the blanket, where he had settled her again. The Indian had gone back to fetch her things, had put her saddle and the rifle on his horse and had returned to the blanket, where he sat down next to her to wait for her to calm down. He did not know quite how he should behave.

This woman was so different from the Indian women he had known so far. She showed her feelings openly and seemed to be very attached to the dead animal. Moreover, she seemed to have totally forgotten her not exactly insignificant injuries.

It had been a cougar that had left those marks and he had seen her horse, whose neck had been deeply gaped. The animal would also have had no chance of survival if it had not been thrown down the gorge in panic. Somewhere this young woman had to have come from and maybe she could show him the way, because then he would surely bring her home.

It was already late and darkness began to dawn. They should be on their way. He straightened up, lifted the completely distraught woman in his arms and took the blanket with him. Carefully he put her in the saddle, stowed the blanket and swung himself behind her on the horse. Holding the reins in one hand, he held the woman tightly against his chest with the other arm. Thus he followed the tracks that her horse had left behind.

Chapter 5

In the meantime, it had become dark and on the ranch there was a lot of excitement. Isabella was long overdue from her ride and not only James and William were out looking for her, but also the cowboys of the ranch had formed search parties.

Louisa had stayed at the main house, in case she should turn up and try to pass the time with food preparations. When the men came back, they would all be hungry. God, she hoped the girl would be alright. Neither James nor William would survive, if anything happened to their only child and grandchild. But something must have happened. It was not Isabella's way to be late.

The girl was always dependable. Hopefully the men would find her, and just as she was finishing the thought Louisa heard hoof beats in front of the house. Quickly she hurried to the door and wrenched it open just as James and William and the rest of the cowboys got off their tired horses.

"Did you find her?"

"No, I'm afraid we didn't. We have searched the entire surrounding area but found nothing so far and now it's dark and we can't see anything anymore.

"Come on in for now. I have food on the stove and a good coffee to warm you up again. You can take your time to plan what you want to do next."

"Yeah, maybe you're right. Men, we take a rest, the animals need a rest too!"

With these words James and William went ahead with worried looks and the cowboys followed them.

During the meal, everyone was thinking, and it was probably the most silent meal that had ever been eaten in this house. When all had finished their meal and were sitting at the table with only their coffee cups, Malcolm, Louisa's husband and the foreman of the workers, said to James, "I know it sounds hard, but I don't think we have a chance to find her tonight. It's already dark out there and we've been able to follow the trail all the way to the forest. But we can't do anything in the forest tonight and I think we should start again tomorrow at sunrise. Our chances are better then. What do you think?"

William looked at James expectantly, and if it was his granddaughter who had to be found, he inwardly had to agree with his foreman. They had searched everything and found nothing of her until dark. Tomorrow morning they would have a better chance. James looked at him and recognized in his father's look the same answer that he had to give with a heavy heart. "You're right. We can't do anything tonight and we will continue the search first thing in the morning. Go and use the hours to sleep before we leave again."

The cowboys said goodbye and James said to William, "I hope I'm doing the right thing. I'm terribly worried. I don't know what I'll do if something happens to her."

"Don't think of the worst right away. Isabella is smart and not a child anymore. She will spend the night out. She can take shelter and she has a rifle with her. You'll see, tomorrow we'll find her. Maybe she's just lost and will wait until the morning so she can find her way back home. Do like your men and try to get some sleep." With these words he pushed his son almost up the first steps on the stairs to the upper floor.

Isabella woke up to the smell of leather and horse. It took her a while to realize that she was still sitting on the horse of the Indian which carried her safely through the dark night. She must have fallen asleep, because the last thing she remembered was him lifting her onto his horse and riding with her in the direction she had come from.

Isabella noticed that she had snuggled up against him and her head was resting against his broad chest. Immediately she lifted her head and moved a little away from him. With this abrupt movement he automatically strengthened his grip around her waist and held her tightly against him, at the same time trying to calm her down.

"Shhh!" carefully he stroked with his hand over her soft hair. Isabella was startled a little at this tender gesture and realized that she was no longer wearing her hat. That piece was dangling loosely on the side of her saddle, for he had taken it from her so she could snuggle up to him. Slowly she calmed down again and allowed him to pull her back to his chest. She tried to relax, which, oddly enough, she didn't quite want to do.

She had never sat so close to a man before. Had never felt before a man's body through her clothes. Through the movement of the horse and the closeness to him she could feel every one of his muscles.

His chest was muscular and the arms strong. In the darkness she couldn't see his face, but he had very distinctive facial features with pronounced cheekbones, which she had noticed earlier. The most interesting thing about him, however, were his eyes. She had never seen a person with such bright blue eyes and they somehow magically captivated her. In the meantime, she no longer had the feeling that he wanted to do violence to her.

32

But where he rode with her, she did not know.

She wanted to ask him but how should she communicate with him. She did not speak his language, and whether he understood her, she did not know since he had not yet spoken a word with her.

"Where are you taking me?" She said more to herself than addressed to him. Nevertheless, he reined in his horse and stopped. Isabella straightened up. Repeated her question and looked him firmly in the eyes.
"Where are you taking me?"

There was no answer. He looked at her, but did not understand what she was saying. She kept trying.
"What's your name?"
She tapped her own chest with her hand while saying, "Isabella."

This she repeated a few times, until it seemed that he had understood, because he suddenly answered in a deep, extremely masculine voice:
"Chágha tho"
"Chágha tho?"
He nodded in agreement.
"I am Isabella and you are Chágha tho."
She beamed and suddenly warmed his heart and he smiled back slightly. Secretly, Isabella had to grin. The first step towards international understanding was made. Slowly, she noticed how the cool night temperatures were creeping into her bones, because she began to shiver. He, too, must have felt this because he suddenly reached behind him and pulled out the blanket on which she had been sitting earlier and put it around both of them. Grateful for this gesture, she snuggled up closer to him again and pulled the blanket tightly around her. Somehow she could not explain it, but she was no longer afraid of him. He was a stranger to her and she did not know what he was up to. She could not communicate with him, but something reassuring emanated from him.

Until now, he had made no effort to show that he was up to no good. Secretly she hoped that he would take her home and not to his people.

Where he rode, she could not see in the darkness, but he seemed to know exactly the way. She had no idea how he managed to find his way in the night. Totally exhausted and tired the gentle rocking of the horse let her fall asleep.

Chágha tho held the white woman tightly against him so that she would not fall off his horse. She was shaking like a leaf and cold all over. By being close to him and the blanket around them both, she would hopefully warm up a bit again. The attack of the cougar, the loss of her horse and the injury tore at her body and he noticed how she kept nodding away. He followed the tracks of her horse and would take her home.

Even if, for some inexplicable reason, he found it a pity to have to let her go. This woman was not an Indian and belonged to one of her own kind. She had to live here somewhere. He didn't think she lived all that far away. She was not dressed for a long ride and did not give the impression that she had been on the road for a long time. What man would let his squaw ride through the wilderness alone like that?

If she were his wife, then......he was surprised at himself. Had he ever thought about taking a wife before? Why did he come up with this thought? Maybe it was because it felt good, as she sat there leaning against his chest, in front of him. Or maybe it was the scent of her hair that rose to his nose. Her hair smelled like a wildflower meadow in spring and it was so soft.

When he had touched it earlier, he would have liked to have his fingers roam through her hair. She was beautiful. Her facial features were so fine and the green eyes could sparkle menacingly.

He found that she was a mixture of a shy deer and a wild cat, and he liked that. Earlier, she had been very afraid of him and he had seen that she was a fighter. He had known that she would defend herself to the bloody end and that had impressed him.

However, she seemed to have put aside her fear towards him and he didn't know if he thought that was good or bad. On the one hand, he enjoyed that she slept on his chest. On the other hand, it also frightened him, because he suddenly developed feelings that he did not know or understand. He could probably handle her better if she continued to be afraid of him.

It was about time that he got rid of her again. To the right, a wooded area had opened up and he decided not to ride into it, but to follow the wooded area in the open. In the darkness it was easier and safer.

It was not long before he could make out small black outlines in front of him. When he came closer, he saw that they were cattle, which were fenced in some distance on the prairie. This had to be her home., he was almost sure about it. He followed the fence and arrived with his horse at the ranch gate. Except for cattle, he could see nothing. A house was not to be recognized from here. Nevertheless, he would deliver her here.

They would help her, if it wasn't her farm she lived on. He stopped his horse and gently shook Isabella awake. She woke up, looked around and saw that he had brought her home. Without another word, he got down from the horse, lifted her off and put her on the ground. But her injured leg gave way and he was just able to catch her before she would have fallen to the ground.

He put her down, took her saddle from his horse and indicated her to sit on it. He would leave her here. It would be too dangerous for him to ride on the terrain.

After all, he was an Indian and the whites were not really friendly towards them.

He was sure that she would not sit here for long and so he got on his horse without another gesture and was about to ride away when Isabella jumped up and tried to grab his reins.

"I know you can't understand me, but I still want to thank you. Thanks for bringing me home.

I have had no experience with Indians before and I don't know how you would say it, but I will say it to you in my language."

She grasped his hand and looked him firmly in those insane ice-blue eyes that now looked at her inquiringly. A feeling of affection flowed through her.

"Thank you Chágha tho. Thank you, very much."

She slowly let go of his hand and was about to say something when she heard hoof noises behind her. The Indian must have heard it, too, because he formed an Indian greeting with his hand, digged his heels into his horse's flank and dashed toward the forest. Isabella watched him until he had disappeared into the woods. Somehow she was sad that he had left, as absurd as it sounded. But this sadness did not last long, because she was joyfully received by the arriving troop, led by her father and grandfather.

"My God, Isabella, what happened? Where is your horse? Are you hurt?"

"Oh dad!" with these words she threw herself into the open arms of her father, who had already jumped off his horse and was coming towards her. He lifted her onto the animal and gave one of his cowboys a sign to take the saddle and the rifle. Together they rode back to the main house. From a safe distance, Chágha tho had watched the scene. For a reason inexplicable to him, he had stopped on a hill to watch the arrival of the riders. He had become curious. What kind of people lived there and could they perhaps help him with his mission?

Chapter 6

"Come, child, eat the hot soup and drink the coffee. You must be frozen to death."

Louisa put the steaming food in front of Isabella's nose and immediately her stomach began to growl. Smiling she took the spoon and tasted the deliciously smelling soup. At the table, and full of expectation for her story, sat her grandfather and father. They could hardly wait, but Louisa had given them to understand in a stern voice that the girl should first get her strength back.

After Isabella dutifully had a plate of soup, some bread and a hot cup of coffee, and feeling herself getting warm again, she began to talk.

"Well, I was just going to do my little round yesterday, but when I was in the forest, a cougar attacked me..."

"A cougar? My God, child, are you hurt?"

"It's not so bad, Dad. The cougar attacked Tipsy and I didn't manage to get him off the horse. I couldn't shoot and tried to knock him off but it took me some time before I managed to get him off Tipsy.

Tipsy was in such a panic that she ran in the wrong direction and I could not control her. She had a murderous pace and I had my hands full trying not to fall off. In the process, however, I no longer paid any attention to where she was riding. Suddenly an Indian appeared next to me and pulled me off my horse..."

38

"An Indian pulled you off your horse? My goodness, are you sure nothing happened to you? What did the bastard do to you? Where is he?"

Isabella put her fingers on her father's hand to reassure him.

"It's all right, Dad. He didn't hurt me. On the contrary, I think I owe him my life. Because he got me off the horse before Tipsy fell into a ravine. Dad she is dead, my beloved Tipsy is dead.... "

Isabella sobbed. At the memory of yesterday, tears were running down her cheeks. Louisa stroked her back tenderly. The girl needed rest. She had been through a lot. Thoughtfully, James and William looked at each other. Both seemed to think the same. Indians! Here in their area? They hadn't been seen for a long time. These were disturbing messages.

"What else happened?"

"Well, he fetched the saddle and my rifle from the ravine and fixed my leg, and..."

"He touched you? The son of a bitch will get to know me," immediately James jumped up and was about to go to the door, when Isabella held him back by the arm.

"Please dad. He didn't do anything bad. The cougar hurt my leg and he put a bandage on it. Then he brought me home. That's all. I must admit that I was very scared at the first moment. I thought he might kill me. Grandfather had told me all these terrible stories, but he didn't do anything reprehensible."

"Where is he now?"

"I don't know, he left before you came and rode off toward the woods."

„Were there more of them? Did you see other Indians or had the feeling that there were more?"

"No, I didn't see any, and I think he was alone."

"Good, my child. You should go upstairs. Louisa, would

you please check the injury on her leg?"
"Yes of course. Come my dear."
James waited until his daughter had disappeared with
Louisa, before turning to his father.
"What do you think of this?"

"Well, it's strange. An Indian who travels alone
on the road, I've never heard of that. So far, the red
devils have only appeared in hordes. Maybe we should
send out a squad and see if we can find any traces of
them or if we can find him. He can't be far."

"Yes, and then I would like to have a look at the
place of the event, see if we can find any clues. Not that
I distrust my daughter but maybe she didn't observe or
witnessed everything. Caution is called for here. I'll tell
Ben to put together two squads. One is to see if he can
find the Indian, and the other one goes with me to look
at the canyon."
"Okay, but I'm coming with you."

"I think it's better if you are here with the rest of
the people, in case the red devils are up to something and
want to attack us. We should be on our guard and be
prepared for anything. I don't trust them with anything"
"Okay, that's what we'll do."

It was not long before James and his men were
divided into two squads and left the farm in different
directions. Chágha tho had left his place and could
follow the events on the ranch from a slightly higher
part of the forest. He watched as a small group of riders
made their way towards the ravine.
Probably Isabella had told them what had happened and
now they wanted to see for themselves. The other troop,
he counted six men, came galloping in his direction.
Were they after him? He would keep an eye on them.

Actually, he should have moved on, but somehow he had become curious about the people down there.

He took his horse, led it into the woods and looked for a place from where he could watch the riders arriving, without them seeing him right away.

"Hey, guys! Here's something. It looks like someone's been sitting here. The redskin has been watching our ranch. Spread out and search the area. But be careful. We don't know how many we're up against."

The cowboys poured out in all directions and scoured the forest. It was getting dicey for Chágha tho. They had not seen him yet but he was surrounded. He had to sneak through their ranks. Carefully and without making a sound, he crept through the forest on his horse. Just when he thought he had shaken them off, he heard a shout close behind him. They had discovered him and rushed towards him.

"There he is. After him."

Two of the cowboys rode after Chágha tho, while the other four tried to cut him off from the right and left, which they succeeded in doing. Now they had him surrounded in a small clearing and drew the circle around him ever tighter. Chágha tho whispered a few words in his stallion's ear, then threw himself at the first cowboy and took him down from his horse. In a flash he had drawn his knife and held it to his throat, holding the others at bay. Immediately the others drew their pistols and aimed at the Indian.

"No men, the boss wants him alive."

"Boy, give it up, it's no use, we outnumber you."

But Chágha tho pulled his hostage back with him, step by step. The cowboys followed at a proper distance. Just as he was about to disappear into the forest with his hostage, one of the cowboys became nervous and fired his pistol. Chágha tho was able to dodge the bullet but it grazed his arm. The knife which he had held in this hand fell to the floor and that was the second that was enough for his hostage to elbow him in the stomach and then pounce on him. The Indian fought back best he could, but against the now rushing five cowboys he was powerless.

With a well-aimed blow to the Indian's temple, the cowboys sent him into dreamland. Tied up tightly with their lassos, they put him on his horse and set off for the ranch. The boss would be satisfied, they agreed.

Chapter 7

Louisa drew open the heavy curtains in Isabella's room and let in the afternoon sun. Immediately, Isabella awoke in her bed. She felt refreshed. A few hours of sleep had done her good.

"Well, there you are. You slept like a stone, but now you look rosy in the face again. I thought I'd check on you, before I dedicate myself to the preparations for dinner."

"Oh is it that late? I've been asleep for a long time. I'll get dressed in a minute and help you."

Isabella slipped her feet out from under the covers and was just about to get up when Louisa gently pushed her down again.

"You stay in bed today. Tomorrow you can go back to work. I'll take care of everything."

"Where's my father?"

"He was in the canyon with some people and has just come back. Probably he is now in the stable with the Indian."

"Indian? What Indian?"

"Well, I suppose the one who brought you here. Steve outsmarted him in the woods earlier with a couple of men and brought him here. He wanted to kill Matt and that's when they captured him."

Horrified by what she was hearing, Isabella jumped out of bed and grabbed her clothes. Regardless of her aching leg, she ran while buttoning her blouse, down the stairs. She did not hear the shouts of the surprised Louisa behind her. She grabbed her coat and hurried over to the stable. A little out of breath, she arrived there just as she heard angry voices from inside. She tore open the barn door and could see her father among some of his people, standing in front of the Indian who had been tied to a pole.

"Open your mouth and talk, you redskin. Who are you and what are you doing here?"

Furiously, he hit the Indian brutally in the face. Just as he was about to land another blow Isabella's voice behind him made him stop.

"Father, no!"

Isabella pushed the surprised cowboys aside, ran past her father and stood protectively in front of Chágha tho. Horrified, she realized that he had been brutally beaten up and was bleeding from the arm.

"Isabella, this here is nothing for you. Go back to the house. We'll talk later."

Angrily, he pointed his arm toward the house.

"No! I will not let you treat him like this!" she shouted to the men. And further without looking at her father's angry face, she yelled, "What has he done to you that justifies this?"

"Isabella, I will not tolerate you behaving like this. This is a man's business and women have no business here."

"With all due respect, father. But I will not leave. Not until this stops. What has he done that warrants this treatment?"

"He touched you, and he's an Indian. That alone is enough."

"He didn't touch me, he saved me. And I don't care if he's a white, a black or an Indian. Look at yourself. You are standing here with seven men around a defenseless man and you are enjoying yourselves by

44

inflicting pain on him. And it doesn't matter what the color of his skin is. He is and remains a human being and I think it is time to approach these people instead of always condemning them. What will become of this country if we do not finally try to get along peacefully with each other."

"Isabella, that's enough. You have no idea what you're talking about. If you had seen the deeds of this red plague with your own eyes, you wouldn't be talking such nonsense. They´re murderers, rapists and arsonists."

"There is evil with them just as there is evil with us. Not all of them are the same. Father, please. He didn't do anything. He would have had an easy time with me. He could have raped me, scalped me, mutilated me and thrown me out there to the hyenas. He could have dragged me off to his camp and no one would have ever seen me again. BUT - he didn't. He left me here safe and sound on the doorstep."

It had become quiet in the stable. The cowboys had quietly backed off a bit and James looked at his daughter thoughtfully. Isabella, on the other hand, paused in her plea and looked at her father pleadingly.

"Please father. I would not be standing before you, if he hadn't been there. He brought me back to you. I owe him my life and YOU should also be grateful to him and not keep him here to punish him for something he didn't do. Untie him, please. His wounds need to be taken care of."

James saw in his mind the ravine in front of him where he had found Isabella's mare earlier. The animal had had a gapped neck and he had immediately recognized that the animal had no chance of survival after the attack of the puma. The animal must have gone mad with pain and had then raced into the abyss. He wanted to block out the images he had seen of his daughter when he was with her horse. He had imagined how she, too, had fallen there. Lifelessly lying down there with a broken neck, and yet he was glad that she stood before him so alive.

All the time that Isabella had been protecting him, he had not dared to move. Now he lifted his battered face and tried to recognize her father from his swollen eyes. He had not understood the words she had said, but the gesture was unmistakable.

She had come to defend him. A woman stood up for him. How good, that the warriors of his tribe could not see this. He would have been exposed to their ridicule and scorn for some time. And probably he would have had to prove himself anew. But besides the disgrace he felt, there were other feelings in him.

She fought for him and no one had ever done this before. Chágha tho could see the father struggling with himself. He seemed to be torn inside. On the one hand, he did not want to embarrass himself in front of his daughter, and on the other hand, he seemed to be weighing what he had heard. Finally he answered, "All right. You may be right. Maybe we have overdone it here. But we have to find out if he is alone and who he is."

"Thank you, Father." relieved, she wrapped her arms around him and kissed him on the cheek.

"By the way, his name is Chágha tho."

Stunned, James looked at his daughter.

"How do you know that? Can he understand us?"

Immediately his voice became more aggressive again.

"No, he can't understand us, but we got the name together somehow. Maybe there is someone in the Fort who speaks his language? We'll bring him over to the house and then I'll take care of his injuries and you could send someone to the Fort who can translate for us."

"Boss! If you don't mind me butting in?"

One of the cowboys had stepped behind the two and saw two pairs of eyes eagerly directed at him.

"From what I understand, Malcolm speaks a few words. At least he was a scout with the army and may be able to help, shall I go and get him?"

"Yes, Willy, go and get him. It's worth a try," and turning to Isabella he said, "He won't come into my house. He'll stay here in the stable. You can take care of his injuries here, and two of my men will stay here too to guard him. Do we understand each other, young lady? I can't believe I let you twist me around your finger but your mother could be just as stubborn when she set her mind to something."

James ordered two of his men to stay with Isabella and gave them instructions to untie the Indian and take him to a vacant box in the back. A short time later, Isabella was sitting with a bowl of warm water, a sponge and bandages and cleaned the wounds on Chágha tho's face and arm. Malcolm had joined them and was watching from outside the box. The two men were standing next to him when James returned to the stall.

"Malcolm, have you been able to find out anything yet?"

"Unfortunately no, he refuses to answer. Or he doesn't understand me. Well, it's been a while since I last spoke Algonquian."

"Keep trying. It's probably a little bit of everything. He's not going to be very cooperative after the treatment we've given him. Which tribe do you think he belongs to? Sioux or Shoshone?"

"Neither. I'm sure of that. He is a Cheyenne."

"Cheyenne? Really? That's not their territory here."

"I'm absolutely sure of it. From the Indian markings and the feathering he's definitely Cheyenne. The name would also fit. I don't know if I can get him to talk, the only one he seems to have a little trust in is your daughter."

"Mmm. Isabella?"

"Yes father?" Isabella looked out of the box.

"Do you think you can encourage him to talk to Malcolm to have a conversation."

"I can try."

Isabella finished her work and was putting her medicine together when their eyes met. Ice blue eyes tried to catch her gaze. She smiled at him and in a calm voice she talked to him as if he could understand her.

"Speak to us. Please Chágha tho. Tell us where you come from. This is my home."

She spread her arms to either side of her and then formed a kind of tent. And repeated the sentence and the gesture again. "Where are you from?"

Suddenly he formed a tent with his hands and pointing into the distance and saying an Indian word, which she did not understand. But Malcolm had followed the matter closely and recognized the word.

"He said that he is Cheyenne. And with the gesture he implied that his tents would be far away. That's right. The Cheyenne do not have their hunting grounds here."

Now Malcolm tried it himself. He addressed Chágha tho in his own language. At first it seemed as if the Indian did not want to speak, but Isabella unconsciously squeezed his hand and encouraged him to answer. Malcolm sat down in the straw across from him and repeated his question in somewhat halting tones.

Finally Chágha tho answered. A short time later, Isabella, James, and the men marveled at how Malcolm seemed to be able to communicate with the Indian. Isabella was detached by her father to help Louisa in the kitchen with the meal preparations. Somewhat reluctantly, however, she complied with her father's instructions.

"Well, what does he say?" James had been impatiently pacing back and forth in front of the box.

Malcolm stood up and walked toward him. Both left the barn, leaving Chágha tho to the supervision of his men.

"As I suspected. He is a Cheyenne, but he is alone in these parts. Why - I could not quite find out. Probably it is something like a test. The young warriors are often assigned by their tribes with some kind of test of courage and have to prove themselves.

That is probably why he is alone and so far away from his people."

"So you mean there's no danger from him?"

"Not the one we're thinking of, anyway. There will be no attack, and we should feel as safe as before."

"So what do you think we should do?"

"I would let him go. He has done nothing wrong and the Army doesn't like to see any problems in that regard."

"Yeah, you're probably right about that. Let's let him stew a little longer and tomorrow morning, he can go."

"Okay, boss. I'll talk to him tomorrow."

"So, what did he say father? Did you learn anything?"

Isabella immediately rushed toward her father as he walked in the front door.

"He's Cheyenne, just as Malcolm suspected.

He's here alone without his tribe. Malcolm thinks he must be on some kind of a test of courage from his tribe and that's why he's so far away from his own people. Tomorrow he can go."

James joined Louisa in the kitchen and took the hot coffee pot from the stove. With a filled mug he sat down at the dining table. Isabella hugged her father, pressed a kiss on his cheek and disappeared back into the kitchen to continue helping Louisa. James, on the other hand, was not sure if his decision was the right one. Something seemed to bother him, but he did not know exactly what it was.

Chapter 8

The sun had not yet risen properly when Malcolm joined Chágha tho in the stable. The two guards stood at the entrance and greeted their man.

"You go into the house to eat. The Indian may go."

"Okay, he hasn't slept a wink all night, just sat in the corner and stared at us. It was pretty creepy."

"Did he do anything else?"

"No, he was peaceful. His horse next door was, too."

"Ok, go and fortify yourselves. Afterwards we'll have our hands full again, since we had to leave work for almost two days."

The men went on their way and Malcolm continued on his way to the Indian. He stopped at the stall of his horse. It was still standing with the Indian halter at the head, in the box and ate straw. Chaghá thos weapons, his knife and bow lay in front of it. Malcolm took these things and went to the last box, in which Chágha tho was still sitting on the floor just as he had left him last night. If the Indian had any emotion toward him, it was not noticeable. It was as if he was seeing through him. Nothing stirred in the man's body or face. Malcolm stopped in the opening and addressed him in his language.

"Here are your weapons, you can go."

He held the things out to him, but the Indian remained sitting still. Malcolm was about to repeat the sentence

when the man replied:
"Why?"
"Why? Well, you didn't do anything. You are free."

"Chágha tho didn't do anything before, either and yet he was captured. So why let him go now? Whites and Indians are not friends."

Malcolm scratched the back of his head, placed the weapons next to him against the wall and sat down opposite the man. So the young man wanted some explanations.

"Whites and Indians have their differences. Yes - but we are peaceful. Have lived here for a long time without having any problems. The father was afraid for his daughter and may have misunderstood the situation. But he realized his wrong and let you go."
The daughter is brave. Chágha tho only saved her from death, but he understands the father's fear and accepts his apology."

With that the Indian jumped up and Malcolm was surprised at the speed with which he had done it. If he had made an attack against him now, he would have been hopelessly lost. But the Indian reached past Malcolm and picked up his belongings, went to his horse and untied it. Without another word or turn, he led his horse out of the stable, jumped on its back, uttered a bloodcurdling scream and galloped away.

Isabella, who had observed this scene from a distance, got goose bumps at the scream. Immediately she thought of the minutes when she had seen him for the first time. How he had stood with flowing hair and a proud face next to his horse and she had been terrified of him. He was certainly a dangerous man, who should not be underestimated, but she had also seen a side of him that was tender and sensitive. But now he was gone and she would not see him again and this certainty left her with a strangely sad feeling.

Chapter 9

Four days later, the ranch had long since returned to normal. The cowboys had gone about their work and had begun to round up the cattle on the prairie. After the harsh winter it was important to get an overview of how many animals had not survived. In addition, they wanted to separate the pregnant dams and the cows with already young calves from the rest of the herd, so that the calves would grow up close to their mothers and it would be easier to give them their brand in a few weeks.

After that, the herds would be reunited. William, as the old head of the ranch, was no longer involved in the regular work, but he was still often with the cowboys and helped them. As long as he could still mount a horse with his old bones, he would be out there helping.

Even though he had cut back a bit lately, the ranch was and remained his life. He had always been an outdoorsman, preferring to be out in the fresh air and lending a helping hand than to be in the office doing paperwork. This was now the job of the new boss and James was more talented at it than he had ever been.

He was proud of his son who was moving the ranch forward. Isabella had been teaching her students again for the last four days. Her small wooden schoolhouse, which also served as a church for the Reverend, stood only a few yards from the main house. It consisted of a single room, with benches on the right and left side in which her students sat during the school day and on Sundays the residents of the farm sat to join the service. On the far wall was a blackboard, in front of it stood her desk. In one corner was a cupboard containing books and other school supplies.

Her piano, on which she played during church services, was right next to it. The room had two windows through which the spring sun was already shining quite strongly. When the class had ended for the day and the students went home, she left the school building shortly afterwards and went over to the main house.

The wounds on her thigh had healed quite well, so that she no longer had any difficulties when walking. All at once Dan, one of the cowboys, rode past her at a wild gallop over to the main building. Arriving there, he yelled, "Boss, boss the Indian is back."

He was just about to storm up the stairs, when the door was yanked open from inside and her father appeared on the porch. As she approached, Isabella heard him ask, "What did you just say?"

"The Indian is back. We saw him sitting up on the hill in front of the woods. He even started a campfire."

"How long has he been there and what does he do?"

"I don't know exactly how long he's been there. We were working in the pasture nearby. He is just sitting there and seems to be watching us. Does not bother to stay hidden. I just thought I'd let you know right away."

"You did that right. Go find Malcolm. Tell him to get over here right away. I want to know what's going on. This whole thing doesn't sit well with me."

"It's okay boss, I'm on my way."

With that, he mounted his horse again and set off to find Malcolm. Isabella had overheard everything, and hurried after her father, who was about to go back into the house.

"What are you going to do?"

"I'm going to ride with Malcolm and ask him what he wants. I don't want him sneaking around here."
"Are you going to capture or hurt him again?"
"I hope it won't come to that, but if there's any trouble, I won't hesitate to do something."

Chapter 10

After leaving the ranch four days ago he had ridden south. He had wanted to go further on the search.

But on the following day he had seen a settlement in the distance. Curious, he had ridden up a hill and from up there had a magnificent view of the prairie below. However, he had also seen the large number of houses of the whites. He had never seen so many buildings and people walking through the streets. His tribe had already been large, but compared to this number of whites, they were a minority.

On the outskirts of the village he saw the fort of the Army. Large and well guarded, it stood there. From his position he could clearly make out the eight watchtowers and could observe what the soldiers were doing. His father, the chief, had told him and the young warriors of his tribe, again and again, about the battles of the soldiers with the Indians. He had believed that one day the white man would be gone again.

But when Chágha tho saw this fort and the many people who were living there, he was no longer sure that the old chief would be right. Having become thoughtful, he had watched the goings-on down in the valley for a whole day and the next day he had seen how a wagon train with many cars had been cheered by the soldiers and the town.

Something was bothering him as he watched the scene.

He just couldn't put his finger on what it was. Since Chágha tho had left his tribe and spent many days on his own, he had become very thoughtful. Lately he caught himself more and more thinking about the future and what it would bring him. He had often prayed to Manitou and tried to figure out what he had planned for him. In his opinion, the problem between white and red was that each did not understand the other.

If he spoke the language of the whites, and he was sure that he could learn it, he could explain many things to them and vice versa. Chágha tho looked into the distance, lost in thought. He did not understand himself at the moment. In the past, such thoughts had been unknown to him. It had been always enough for him to be the son of the chief and that he had his place within the tribe. But nothing had been the same for a long time. The old chief was dead and he had left the tribe and would probably never return.

Now alone by himself, it seemed important to him to learn everything he could about the white people. But he was neither stupid nor reckless. He knew that if he rode down there he would be a dead man or at least a prisoner of the Army.

If he really wanted to learn something about the whites, he had to start out smarter. And so he had made the decision two days ago, to ride back to the ranch. Although they had not exactly met him with open arms there either, something nevertheless drew him back there. Maybe he could make a deal with the daughter's father. It was worth a try, he thought, and so he set off on his way back.

Now he sat back in the same spot where he had been captured by the cowboys four days ago. He did not want to remain hidden and make it easy for them to see him. With the campfire, which he had lit, it would not be long before they would notice his presence and from then on

it would become clear whether Manitou would protect him or whether he would find death here. The cowboys were busy with the cattle. He could see them herding and rounding up the animals among the bushes and fir trees in the vast, unmanageable area.
Why they were doing this, he did not understand, but he followed the action with great interest.

It took longer than he had thought before he could see cowboys paused in their work and looking in his direction. Shortly after, one of them galloped over to the main house. Now it would not be long. Chágha tho took the reins of his horse and held them in his hand. His weapons lay ready to hand beside him. Sitting by the campfire, he awaited the arrival of the ranch owner. For of this he was sure, this time he would come in person.

"He is up there, boss. That boy is either mighty stupid or he's got guts. After all that he'll come back and put himself in danger again."
"If I only knew what he was up to."
"We'll soon find out."

Malcolm and James drove their horses up the mountain and came out of the woods sideways toward the Indian. Chaghá tho was sitting peacefully by the campfire when the two men appeared. He made an inviting gesture for them to join him at the fire. James looked a little puzzled over at Malcolm, who was already getting off his horse.
"Boss, get off and come to the campfire. Take the rifle with you, but put it over your arms so it's not a threatening gesture."
He saw Malcolm do the same, and then strode over to the fire, where Malcolm sat down and laid the rifle on

the grass beside him. James settled down as well and looked the Indian briskly into his eyes. He did not want to be intimidated by this young fellow.

The wounds he had inflicted on him days ago had almost faded, and so he saw for the first time that the young man had distinctive facial features. His high cheekbones and the straight nose gave him almost an aristocratic appearance. The long hair, which was braided into two pigtails, was as black like coal.

His skin was only slightly darker than his own. But probably the most striking feature about him were his sky-blue eyes. Such eyes he had seen only once in his life and that was a long time ago. Now he noticed how this pair of eyes was watching him closely. They had been sitting in silence for a while. Each tried to size up the other, but now Malcolm opened the floor to the Indian.

"What are you doing here?"

"I'm watching you and learn."

Somewhat taken aback by the answer, he first looked at James, who looked at him questioningly, and then back at the Indian.

"What is it Malcolm, what did he say?"

"Give me a minute, I'll have to question that again. You are here watching us? Why? That I don't understand."

"I have seen the many people and the Army Fort. Chágha tho wants to understand the whites. Learn their language and see how they live. That's why I came back."

"Mmh"

"Malcolm what's he saying?" impatiently James looked at him.

"A strange thing boss. He says he has been to Laramie and now he wants to learn the language from us and also wants to see how we live."

"What, I never heard that before. Why would an Indian

want that?"

"Let's ask him. Chágha tho, why do you want to know?"

"Chágha tho thinks that if he speaks the language of the white people and how they live, he can understand them better, and that is his wish."

"Well, he actually wants to learn the language and everything we do so that he can understand us better. That's kind of interesting. Maybe we should grant him that wish."

"You can't be serious, Malcolm. We take an Indian out to the ranch with us? How would that work. There would be friction between the men and him."

"Well, maybe it would depend on trying."

And again he addressed the Indian.

"How do you picture it. What should we do?"

"Chágha tho is strong, can help with the cattle."

He pointed his finger at the cattle herds in the valley.

"And in the process he can learn and understand."

Malcolm scratched his two-day beard with his fingers. Personally, he thought the idea was unusual but not nearly as bad as his boss probably did. Somehow the boy had guts and that impressed him.

"Boss, he's asking if he can help with the work."

"Malcolm, let's face it, how would that work. The boys down there aren't exactly thrilled that there's an Indian lurking around and now I'm supposed to take him to the ranch and let him work for us. Can you imagine what fuss that will make?"

"I don't think it would be that bad. I personally could take him under my wing and teach him everything he needs to learn. Besides, we'd have him under better observation than if he's up here sneaking around us."

James thought for quite a while before answering and Malcolm thought he was going to say no

"Ok let's try it. But if it doesn't work out, then he has to go, and I want him to know that up front."

"That's fair. I'll tell him."

Malcolm translated what his boss had told him and the Indian nodded. All three men rose almost simultaneously. Chágha tho extinguished the fire and swung himself onto his horse. Together he rode with the two white men down to the ranch. It was an uncertain future he was embarking on, but he was sure Manitou was with him.

When the three horsemen reached the ranch, the cowboys and the rest of the ranch residents came across the small group. Curious, they left their work and followed the small troop at a safe distance. In front of the barn, James stopped and turned to his people, who had formed a semicircle around them. Men, women and children, all had gathered. The news that the Indian was back had spread quickly. Now everyone stood in front of the three and were looking at the Indian curiously.

"Hey boss, did you catch that one again?" resounded from the crowd.

"No, he's here of his own free will this time. He's going to stay with us for a while and help out."

A murmur went through the crowd and people looked at each other in disbelief. Had they understood that correctly? A big man, a little older than James, stepped forward.

"Did we get that just right, Boss? You want the Indian to stay with us at the ranch?"

Immediately, all pairs of eyes turned to James and they eagerly awaited his answer.

"Yes, you all got that right. He wants to learn our language and get to know us better. For this purpose, he will live and work."

"You're not serious right now! The red devils steal

horses and cattle, they pillage, murder and rape. They are deceitful and treacherous and one thing they certainly don't do is work. I don't want to have anything to do with such a red brood."

James had expected resistance, nevertheless he could not let Carl, his cowboy, get away with this hostility. He had to show him who was boss on this ranch.

"Carl, he may not understand us, but I don't want anybody around here using that kind of name anymore. His name is Chágha tho, and if you have any problems with him being here, then you should learn to get a grip on them as soon as possible. I have decided that he will help us and as long as he is here he will be treated properly. Are we clear on that?"

Without a facial movement, he looked from one to the other and then stopped with his gaze fixed on Carl. While the others nodded silently, Carl stubbornly maintained his attitude and gave no sign that he would back down.

"I hope I have made myself clear now. Then, the show is over and you can go back to your work."

After the crowd, including Carl, had dispersed again, James turned to Malcolm.

"Carl could be trouble. We're going to have to keep an eye on him. I don't want him stirring up the other guys."

"Mmm, you might be right about that. I will keep an eye on it. Where should we put him up? With the single cowboys, I don't think that's a good idea right now."

"Maybe he can sleep in the barn tonight? I'll figure something out for the next few days. Can you tell him that?"

James got off his horse and gave the reins to Malcolm.

"Please take care of my horse and I'll see you in the morning."

"You got it, boss."

A little later Malcolm and Chágha tho were alone in the stable tending to the three horses.

"The white man does not want Chágha tho here."

"You mean Carl? Well, he'll come to terms with it. Everything takes time. You'll see."

He tried not to let on but he would have to keep a close eye on Carl. The man was not so easily dissuaded from his opinion, he knew him too well for that.

"You can sleep in the straw until we find something better."

"Chágha tho need nothing else. The stable is good."

"Okay. Then I'll see you tomorrow for work," with that Malcolm left the Indian alone.

After dinner, James joined his father on the porch. When the weather was good, William liked to sit outside in the evening and smoke his pipe. Isabella often kept him company when James was still busy in the office. Tonight, the two sat in front of the house in the two rocking chairs. Isabella had taken some patching material outside and wanted to mend a few holes in her father's pants. William drew on his pipe with relish and watched her. It was a beautiful evening.

The night was clear and you could see the first stars shining in the sky. Lights were shining in the cabins of the cowboys who lived with their families on the ranch. Here and there, in the distance, one could hear the mooing of isolated cows. Nature became quiet and slowly laid itself to rest. It would not be possible to sit out here for long now, the cold would quickly creep into their limbs as the night temperatures in spring were still quite cold and damp. William enjoyed letting the days end like this. The door opened and James joined them. Lost in thought, he walked past them and leaned on the wooden balustrade. His gaze went over to the barn. Isabella paused with her tamping work and looked at her grandfather, but she said nothing. He made a thoughtful face. When James turned around and leaned back against the railing, the grandfather addressed him.

"I hope you didn't make a mistake today. That boy is going to be trouble."

James massaged the back of his neck.

"I know, but they'll suck it up."

"You sure about that? Carl won't give it a rest. He's stubborn and intransigent."

"Yes, unfortunately."

"You know Carl lost his ranch, his wife and his little daughter in an Indian raid?"

"Yes, I know that, but that was over twenty years ago. At some point you have to be able to forgive and forget, and the boy wasn't even born then."

"Carl never got over that. He hates Indians with a passion, and you bringing him here isn't going to make it any better."

"I know, Father. But right now, this is the best solution. I don't know what he is up to, and I'm better off keeping him under control here than having him sneaking around the ranch every day. That would make everyone nervous. I can't take Carl's feelings into account when it comes to the ranch. We have to find out why he's really here, and we can best do that, when he's around. Malcolm will take care of him, since he's the only one who can talk to him and we'll see how fast he learns our language."

"Maybe you're right." William pulled at his pipe again. Isabella, who had listened to the whole thing in silence, said to her father, "I could, I can give him language lessons."

Threateningly, the father pointed his index finger at his daughter and answered in a sharper tone than intended, which made Isabella back up a bit, frightened.

"You, young lady, stay out of this! AND - you keep your distance from that Indian. I don't want you near him. If there is any trouble here, then I don't want to see you in the middle between the two. Have I made myself clear?"

"Yes, Father," she rose, annoyed and disappointed.

"I am tired. Good night," she took her needle work, and went into the house. William looked at his son.

"Was it necessary to tell her off like that?"

"It's better to let her know right away, so she doesn't get any ideas. She's stubborn sometimes, like her mother was."

William laughed. "And you loved her."

"Yes, good night father."

"Good night, son."

The shadow that was leaning against the outside wall of the barn looking over to the house, had observed the scene. He had been standing there for quite a while, watching the movements on the porch.

Now he saw how Isabella had gone into the house and, a short time later a room on the first floor was illuminated by a glow of light. So this was her room. He could see her moving back and forth in it. In the meantime, the father and the grandfather had also disappeared. The lights had been extinguished downstairs and in another window on the first floor, small glows of light could be seen.

The residents seemed to have gone to sleep. Only Isabella didn't sleep yet, she appeared at the window. Instead of drawing her curtains, she stood motionless in front of it and looked down at him. Somewhat taken aback, he retreated further into the darkness. He narrowed his blue eyes and wondered if she could see him, but then decided that her gaze had only gone in his direction by chance.

When he looked up at her again, she had disappeared at the window and had drawn the curtains. He looked around once again, saw that the lights went out in the other cabins. He, himself, went into the stable.

In the one for the single cowboys, however, the light was still burning and the residents were still in a heated debate.

"Guys, we can't let this happen. The boss must have lost his mind. An Indian on our ranch. He'll sell us out to his people. He'll spy on us and then they're gonna jump us."

"Carl, I think you're exaggerating now. We know he's alone. It's not going to be that bad."

"You say that now because you don't know them. I know these bastards well enough. I know how they act and I tell you, he's the devil in person. We shouldn't let that happen."

"What are you going to do?"

"I don't know yet, but we should not take it so lightly that he's here."

"The boss has been clear about that. The Indian is a guest here. We should accept that. I don't want to lose my job here. It's a good job and it pays well."

"Exactly!" the others joined in.

Only Carl replied, "Yes, you still don't get it. The boss is acting from the wrong motives. The bastard saved his daughter and now he thinks he owes the redskin something. The only thing you owe these red bastards is that they should be hanged from the nearest tree."

"Man Carl, don't let anybody hear that. You're not

planning on getting rid of him, are you?"

Carl noticed that the other cowboys were not man enough to help him in his endeavor and backed off a bit because of it.

"No, of course not. I was just venting my anger a bit. If we're lucky, he won't get in our way, since Malcolm will be dealing with him. It's getting late, I'm going to bed now. Good night guys."

The others seemed to be reassured that Carl had regained his composure, and they went to rest as well. Carl, on the other hand, did not think of abandoning his plan. He would watch the bastard and maybe the opportunity would arise for him to take revenge on him. Accidents happened every day, after all, and only a dead Indian, was a good Indian.

Chapter 11

The sun had not quite risen when Malcolm came into the stable. He was about to wake up Chágha tho when he saw that his bed for the night was empty.

Somewhat puzzled, he looked around, but saw only the Indian's horse standing peacefully in its corner. Where was he? Malcolm went out through the back door and tried to see him somewhere in the twilight. Suddenly he appeared beside him as if from nowhere. Malcolm grabbed his heart and let out a startled sound.

"Boy, you can't scare an old man like that."

Chágha tho grinned with a shrug and went back inside. Malcolm, on the other hand, shook his head and said to himself.

"What have I gotten myself into?"

A little later they were both out with their horses and Malcolm began to show Chágha tho around. They rode along the western boundary and Malcolm stopped from time to time to explain to the Indian how fences were mended and why. First he translated and then he repeated it again in English so that Chágha tho could learn the words. The boy seemed to catch on quickly, because it was not long before he was able to learn the necessary moves on his own, and Malcolm was surprised to see that he had an inquisitive student.

For lunch, they paused at a small river that ran through the ranch grounds. It served as a source of water, not only for the inhabitants, but also for the cattle. Malcolm explained that the river never dried up, even in the driest summer months. It carried enough water to keep both, man and beast alive.

That was a godsend in this area. In the winter it rarely froze, because it had enough flow, and in spring, after the snow melts, it was often not easy to cross. The current could increase intensively. He showed Chágha tho one of the spots where there was a small fork and one could cross the river easily. On the other bank they dismounted and stopped for a rest. Malcolm took from his saddlebag something to eat that Isabella had given him this morning, and handed Chágha tho his half.

He stared at the bread in his hands and was not quite sure whether he should eat it or not. But when Malcolm sat down on the grass taking a courageous bite of his half, he began first to nibble on the bread and then with more and more appetite, he devoured the bread. Malcolm had been quietly watching him. Now he had to smile and said, "Good, isn't it?"

With his mouth full, Chágha tho nodded and continued eating.

"Yes Isabella is a good cook. The man who ever marries her, will have a good time."

"Mmh"

The food was strange to him, but it tasted good. Chágha tho rose, took his water bottle and walked over to the river to fill it. When he returned, he turned to Malcolm with a question that interested him keenly.

"Does Isabella have a husband to protect her?"

Somewhat taken aback by this question, Malcolm replied

"No, she's not married. Her father is protecting her, and someday I'm sure she'll marry a rancher, too."

"Why hasn't her father picked out a husband for her, yet? Is the price too high?"

Malcolm, who had taken a large sip of his water, choked on the question. He had to cough hard. What kind of views did the boy have? But then he remembered that he had heard that Indians approached the subject of relationship and love a little more pragmatically than the Christians did. In his mind he searched for the right answer.

"What does he want? Horses or bison skins? She must have a high price if she is still with her father."

Chágha tho made a thoughtful face and rubbed his chin with his hand. Malcolm, who had overcome his coughing fit, tried to explain that whites did not buy women or exchange them for goods.

"The woman herself can choose her husband. Women and men marry for love.

They make a promise to each other that they will stay together for life, until death separates them. Then they start a new family and live in a house of their own. Before the promise, the man asks the woman's father for permission."

Chágha tho took a seat again and thought about what he had just heard.

"What is love?"

"Boy, you're asking questions. I don't know if I'm the right person to answer them for you."

Malcolm rubbed the back of his neck with some discomfort. He looked into the young man's expectant blue eyes and searched for the appropriate words.

"Well – love, that's a feeling you have when you like someone very much."

The boy's expression brightened.

"Then Chágha tho loves Malcolm."

Joyfully, the boy beamed and nodded at him because he understood, and Malcolm knew he would have to explain the love thing again. What would the others think if they heard that Chágha tho was talking about love when he meant the word "nice".

"That's not quite right. Love is a feeling between a woman and a man. If you say that to a man, you will get into trouble. You can say to me that I am "nice" or "okay." I think that's what you meant. So, we have to move on. We still have a lot to do before we can go home again."

Malcolm got up, relieved to be able to get back to work. He stowed his water bottle on the saddle and a short time later, they both continued on their way. The ranch had to be huge because they had been walking for hours and nothing could be seen except cattle moving peacefully among the bushes and cedars. In the distance, they could see the snow-capped peaks of the great mountains. They rose high into the blue sky while Malcolm and Chágha tho traveled in a terrain of small depressions and hills. Lush greenery mixed with prairie flowers, shrubs and small bushes stretched as far as the eye could see. Occasionally, small herds of black Angus cattle had sought out shady spots.

"Are we still in ranch territory?" Chágha tho wanted to know.

"Yes, we have only seen a small part of it today. After there," Malcolm pointed with his arm in an easterly direction, "it's two days' ride before we reach the border. Another day's ride away is the next ranch. To the north is another area the size of what we saw today, and if you head south from the main house, it'll take you a couple of hours before you reach the border, too."

"Why does the white man need so much land?"

"He has a lot of cattle and they need space, so that they develop well and produce good meat. The boss uses it to feed the people in the town and also the soldiers."

"Why? Don't the people go hunting themselves?"

"Well some do, but not all. You have seen the town. There are a lot of people there and they build houses and stores where they sell their goods. These people don't have time to go hunting themselves. Even the soldiers can't, because their job is to protect us. That's why the boss has these cattle that he sells to people for money. Then he uses the money to get food for us. That's how it works for us."

Shrugging, he rode on, the Indian silently following behind him. Chágha tho had learned a lot today. Even if he didn't understand everything the white man did, he had the feeling that it had been a good idea to come here. The sun had already set behind the mountain peaks and with the dawn came the cold.

In the distance they could see the first outlines of the buildings that belonged to the ranch. Malcolm's bay gelding, knowing he was heading home, tightened his pace a bit and the black horse next to him, started whinnying happily when he realized his owner was not holding him back. The two horses put in a sharp canter and Malcolm wondered why his horse still had the energy after this day. Apparently oats and fresh straw, were motivation enough. By the time they arrived at the stable with the large paddock behind it, the other cowboys had long since finished caring for their horses. The paddock was full and all the horses were eating and drinking. Even the men were no longer to be seen, except for two who were still hauling buckets of oats to the animals.

"Hi Thomas, how far did you get today? " Malcolm turned to one of the two as he dismounted from his horse. The man stopped, handed his bucket to his partner and replied:

" I think two more days, before we have them all together. We were able to bring in a large number today."

"Good, then we are making good progress. We have to go to the east pasture, too, though. We saw quite a few animals there today."

"Okay, maybe we can do it tomorrow. How was it with you today?"

With a movement of his head, he pointed in Chágha tho's direction, who had already started taking care of Malcolm's horse and sending it to the paddock with the others. Now he took his horse, tied it to a wooden peg and was about to disappear into the stable, when he heard a noise. A clang was heard from the main house. Puzzled, he looked at Malcolm, who only replied: "This is the dinner bell. We spend the meals together in the house over there. Hurry up and come over then."

He turned away together with Thomas and headed toward the main house. Chágha tho remained alone.

In the neighboring building the door opened and he watched the rest of the cowboys, laughing and talking, make their way to the house. Soon it was quiet. The men had disappeared into the house and he too made his way to the stable. Surprised, he found out, that in his absence fresh bales of straw had been brought into his box. The bales were draped with white sheets so that it was now an inviting bed for the night.

In addition, someone had placed a wash bowl, towel and soap for him. That must have been Isabella, a clearly female sign, it went through his head. He took the towel and soap and went back out to his horse and galloped away. Tonight he would not eat with the others, his feeling told him that it was too early for that and so he decided to ride to the river to take a long bath and get his dinner there.

Everyone in the house had heard the horse galloping away. Immediately the men had dropped everything and had hurried to the door. In the darkness, they could only make out the outline of the lone rider before he was swallowed in the falling night.

"That was the Indian, for crying out loud. Now I'm sure he's riding off to join his people and we're sitting here clueless at dinner."

Carl cast angry glances at James, who was standing behind him. The porch was crowded with men who were now looking a bit anxiously at their boss and waiting for him to act. Isabella had curiously come outside, too.

James turned to Thomas and said:

"Ride after him. He rode towards the river. Let me know what he's doing, but keep your distance and don't get caught. I don't want him to know we're following him."

"Okay, boss."

Thomas ran over to the paddock, and it wasn't long before he dashed past him. Everyone watched as he disappeared in the same direction as the Indian.

"Well men, let's go inside. Isabella cooked a good meal and we don't want to let that go to waste."

He walked past Carl and the others back into the house. Most of them followed him but Carl and two other men stopped in front of the door, still looking further in the direction where Thomas had disappeared.

"Didn't I tell you. The redskin will bring disaster upon us. If we don't do something, we'll be dead sooner than we'd like."

"Now wait and see, Carl. The boss will do the right thing."

With a snide hand gesture Carl went back into the house and the others followed him. Isabella, who had been standing in the dark corner of the porch, had a worried face. Carl began to stir up the Cowboys against Chágha tho. On the one hand, she could understand the men. What was the Indian up to? Why was he riding away in the dark and where did he go to?

On the other hand, she couldn't, or rather, didn't want to believe that he was up to something evil. If he wanted to, he would have had the opportunity long ago. Still she could not imagine where he was going. She shivered. The nights were still cooling and she had not put on a jacket. She began to freeze in her thin blouse and therefore went back inside.

He knew he was not alone, but there was no danger from the observer. They had sent someone after him because they didn't trust him. It annoyed him a little bit but he could understand the way they were acting. The young man, who was hiding in the bushes, had tried to sneak up on him unnoticed. Chágha tho smiled, the man still had a lot to learn.

Even before he had arrived at the river, he had noticed that he was being followed. The man, who was hiding behind the trees, was Thomas. He had met him outside the stable and he might be about his age. If he wanted to go for it, he could cut the man's throat faster than he would notice. But Chágha tho didn't care and continued to gather a few branches together for a fire. His horse grazed peacefully, while he built a small campfire right on the riverbank.

It didn't take long for the fire to burn well. He quickly took off his moccasins and removed his clothes. Then he balanced on the wet stones along the riverbank until he reached the deep part of the river.

Without waiting he dived into the icy flood. The coldness of the water made his body feel as if it were being covered with a thousand small pinpricks. He drew in a deep breath and began to swim with powerful strokes. The further he swam to the middle of the river, the stronger the current became. But he was a good and powerful swimmer and so a few well-aimed strokes were enough for him to reach the other side of the river.

Over there he remained a little in the water and his body began to get used to the temperature. He was experienced and hardened enough to know how long he could subject his naked body to these temperatures. Honiahake and he had often bathed at night in the lakes and rivers. Even in winter they had taken short baths to build up their strength. There had always been a little competition among them.

Who could ride, hunt or fish better. Or in this case, could swim and dive better. The balance of power had been even between them. Sometimes he had won, sometimes it had been Honiahake. They had both liked these small competitions among themselves. He missed him. In the weeks that he had been traveling alone, he realized more and more how much he longed to be with them again. How much he would like to be with the other warriors, sitting around the campfires and go on the hunt. The cold, which now took possession of him, brought him out of his thoughts back into the present.

He looked across to the other side of the river, where the warming fire was burning and his horse was half standing in the water, drinking. Briefly he dived to clear his head and then swam back. A little later he sat bare-chested by the fire to warm himself up.

On a skewer, which he held in the fire, grilled a fish that he had caught in the river shortly before. While the fish roasted in the fire and he stared into the flames, he had almost forgotten his observer. He was lost in his thoughts again and thought of his father, the great chief, who taught him everything he could and who was now in the eternal hunting grounds. His father had placed great expectations in him and had educated him to be the next wise and strong chief of the tribe. But now it would no longer come.

Since he had given him this amulet on his deathbed, which he now always carried with him and had told him the story about it, nothing was the same as it had been before. His place was no longer in the circle of his tribe and would never be again. Manitou had sent him on a journey, but where this journey should go, he had not been able to see until now. Taking a deep breath, he pushed the gloomy thoughts away from him and turned to the delicious smell of the fried fish.

How hungry he had been, he realized now, when his stomach began to growl. A smile crossed his lips as he pulled the skewer out of the fire and carefully began to eat the hot meat. A little later, he extinguished the fire, put his shirt back on and made his way back to the ranch. As he rode past his observer he had been willing for a second, to call him, but he decided against it and galloped away. At the ranch, the buildings were already in darkness. Only in the main house a window on the first floor was still illuminated.

They were waiting for the return of the scout, thought Chágha tho, as he passed it and rode over to the stable. Once there, he tended to his horse and brought it to the paddock with the others. Once more he looked over to the house and saw his pursuer arriving. Even before he reached the front door, it opened and Thomas was invited in. Was Isabella also still awake, or was she already asleep in her room? He turned away and went into the barn.

Chapter 12

Over the next few days, not much changed in the daily routine. Most of the cowboys were busy all day rounding up the herds. William had joined them. Malcolm had gone on with Chágha tho inspecting and repairing the fences. He had taken to barely speaking to him in the Indian language but for the most part only in English. Malcolm had noticed that the Indian understood quite quickly and seemed to absorb the words just like that. He knew that Chágha tho already understood everything very well, only he could not speak himself yet. At the ranch, Isabella took care of the domestic duties. She cleaned the house, did the laundry and cooked meals with Louisa.

Every morning she gave lessons to her students. In the evenings, when everyone sat down to eat, Chágha tho was still missing and Thomas had also always returned very late in the last few days. That evening, however, he had appeared like the others at the table. In general, everything today was as it had been before.

The cowboys had praised her meal and everyone had eaten with a good appetite. Small conversations about what would happen in the next few days had been held. It had been a harmonious togetherness, and when she was alone with Louisa in the kitchen, still doing the dishes, her thoughts drifted to the Indian. Where might he disappear to and why didn't he come to the dinners?

She knew that Thomas had followed him, but her father had not told her what he had found out. Apparently Thomas didn't have to follow him anymore, since he was at the dinner table tonight.

"Well, I think the plate is dry enough now."

"Excuse me?" Isabella listened up and looked into Louisa's amused looks.

"I said, I think the plate is now dry. Where are you tonight with your thoughts?"

Isabella, a little embarrassed, put the plate down from her hand and picked up the next one.

"Oh, nothing, I must have had a brief dream."

"Mmm, I saw that. Was it nice?"

"Nothing special, actually. I was just wondering where the Indian disappears to every night and why he doesn't come here for dinner."

Louisa continued to wash the dishes and placed them to drain in the second sink, where Isabella was standing and drying.

"Who knows what goes on in the minds of these Redskins . They are and will always be savages."

"But don't you think they could learn to be like us?"

"Frankly, I doubt it. They have different attitudes toward life than we do, different things they believe in. You can teach them to speak our language, try to make them understand our laws, but they will always remain what they are by birth, savages. You will never be able to make them white."

Isabella became thoughtful, was Louisa right? She was torn out of her thoughts when she heard Louisa's voice.

"You are haunted by the Indian in your head, aren't you?"

"Well, I would find it an interesting task to teach him our language."

Louisa was no fool and had known Isabella from a young age.

"I think your interest in him is of a different nature. I must admit, he has a handsome appearance: Young, tall, well built. This striking face with the almost aristocratic looking nose. God knows where he got that from and then these pronounced cheekbones. Fascinating blue eyes and a raven-black head of hair, that really gives him something exotic. If he were a white man, I would think that he would really be something for the ladies, but he's an Indian, and he's gonna stay that way, Isabella. And as such, your father would never accept him."

After this absolutely accurate description of Chágha tho, Isabella could only add one thing in her mind. No matter what his origin was and what she was told about him, her body spoke a completely different language. She was happy when only his name was mentioned, her heart started beating faster when she caught a glimpse of him. At night she had dreams in which they were sitting closely nestled on the horse and his strong arms held her. Could a man be so wrong, if he evoked such feelings in one?

When it had become quiet in the house and only Isabella and Louisa were in the kitchen, cleaning up, James had gone out to the veranda to smoke a cigarette. There he found his father, sitting in the rocking chair and smoking his evening pipe.
"The air is more humid tonight than it has been in the last few days. I think we're going to get rain coming."
"Mmm, may be. I'm going to go back to town with the reverend after his service. There are supplies to be replenished and I need to talk to the commander of the Fort about the coming sales. Think you'll be all right here for a few days?"

James took a drag on his cigarette and blew the smoke out into the night.

"It's not the first time you've been gone. Are you taking Isabella with you?"

Astonished, James looked at his father.

"No! Why do you ask?"

"The girl needs to be around young people. It's no good if she's always here with us old folks on the ranch. How's she ever gonna meet a man?"

"I've been thinking about that, too. I think I'll send her to Boston in the fall."

"To Boston? What would she do there?"

"There she has more chances to meet young men and is introduced to society. In addition, she is a teacher and can teach at a big school. That's what she always wanted."

"James, Isabella is a child of the mountains. She's never been to the big city with the ways of high society."

"I know, but she will learn. Let's be honest. Where is she going to meet someone here who would be a suitable husband for her? In Laramie? Where small shopkeepers make their fortune or one of the soldiers who have only a measly salary? Or perhaps one of the cowboys who moves from ranch to ranch to earn a few dollars? That's not the kind of man I have in mind for my daughter."

James took a seat on the second rocking chair and looked out into the dark night. He knew his father saw this issue differently, but he wanted his daughter to have an easier time than his father had before him.

He wanted a man who had enough money to guarantee her a carefree life and to whom he could later bequeath this ranch with a clear conscience. William looked at his son for a long while, before he now addressed him.

"James, I know you love your daughter above all else

and want only the best for her. But what do you think? She's going to meet some kind of man in Boston? I mean, she's a pretty girl and she'll have no trouble attracting the attention of young men. But is such a man, who from an early age has been used to being in high society, is he the right one? Will she meet someone there who can later take over the ranch? You know this country is unforgiving, the winters are hard and the work on the ranch is a life's work. It never stops. You can't learn, you have to be born to do it. You must experience this country in its beauty and brutality, so that you don't go to ruin. This nature is harsh and Isabella has these characteristics, but I strongly doubt that someone from the east can so easily cope with it."

Having become a little more thoughtful, James replied:" You made it. You came and settled here."

"That's true, my son, but I wasn't born with a golden spoon in my mouth either. My family was ranchers and I've known the hard way since I was a kid, just like you and Isabella. What did she actually say to your proposal?"

"She doesn't know yet. I'll talk to her about it when I get back."

"Well, you're going to have a tough nut to crack, I'm afraid. Well, it's getting late. I'm going to turn in. Good night my son."

William rose.

"Good night, father!"

When William had disappeared into the house, James was still smoking his cigarette. His father was right. Isabella would not take his decision easily, but he thought it was for the best. And then there was something else that was on his mind.

He had met and fell in love with a young widow in Laramie, Marylou Higgins. She owned a small tailor's shop, from which she could just about live.

Two years ago she had lost her husband in a poker game with the wrong people and she was trying to keep her head above water. Marylou had immediately caught James' eye when he had bumped into her at the grocer. He hadn't been paying attention and had almost knocked her over.

For him a quite embarrassing situation, but Marylou had only laughed and her radiance had enchanted him immediately. Her warm brown eyes had made him forget everything. She reached only up to his shoulder and had a slender, shapely figure. Her auburn hair was tied up in a knot and he immediately had the desire to pull his fingers through the shiny hair.

On that day, one year ago, he had felt guilty of developing such feelings for another woman. Isabella's mother had long been dead, but he had a responsibility to his daughter, and he wasn't sure he had the right to fall in love again. For a year they had kept their relationship a secret. Now he wanted to make it public, but he didn't know how to explain it to his father and Isabella.

He toyed with the idea of asking Marylou to marry him, but before he could do that, he wanted to talk to his daughter. When he got back, he wanted to talk to both of them about all this.

Chapter 13

The morning sky was overcast and the temperatures cool. Overnight it had become windy and now the wind was driving the clouds in the sky. Occasionally, the sun fought its way through and its warm rays coaxed nature out of its winter slumber. Something was wrong this morning. Chágha tho sat outside on the wooden fence of the paddock and watched in the distance as three deer's ran across the pasture. The birds were chirping in the trees, and the horses stood still and close together.

The wind blew through the skins of the animals and let their manes and tails dance. Cows called for their calves and in the log cabins the smoke rose from the chimneys in the cold morning air. It was already later than on the other days and still none of the cowboys could be seen. Malcolm had not yet been there. So what was going on today? Because he didn't know how to act, he strolled over to the single paddock, which was a bit off to the side. He had already seen on the day of his arrival that there was a black mustang.

As far as he could observe, the animal had been only given water and one had thrown him hay over the fence. Otherwise, no one had taken care of the animal. This was all more than strange, because all the other animals were well cared for. When he came closer, the horse immediately began to run nervously back and forth in the paddock. It reared up and wedged out backwards. Chágha tho stopped and kept his distance from the fence. Wildly, and with a diabolical look, the horse climbed close to the fence and tossed its head back and forth. Then it ran around in circles, as if possessed.

Chágha tho moved a few yards away from the fence and watched closely what the animal was doing. All at once the horse seemed to become calmer again. It stopped and looked at him. He also stopped and looked the horse directly into the eyes. Then he walked a few steps towards the horse again, without taking his eyes off the animal and immediately it started to run wild again. After he had stepped back again, the animal calmed down again. The horse was completely frightened.

He would ask Malcolm what it was all about. Just as he wanted to approach the animal once again, a bell sounded from the small building with the pointed roof behind him. He turned around and could see, how cowboys, women and children disappeared into the house. Also the inhabitants of the main house went inside. Then the door was closed and shortly after, music sounded to him outside. What was going on there? Curious, he approached the house and looked cautiously through one of the windows.

The music had stopped. He observed a man, whom he had never seen before, as he spoke to the residents of the ranch. They were all sitting with their backs to him and seemed to be listening to his words. When the man suddenly turned and nodded, the music resumed and the people began to sing.

He changed his position a little to be able to see better. Isabella sat in the corner by a box and ran her fingers over white and black wooden keys. She was creating this beautiful music. Devoutly he listened as the lute with the chant to it continued to reach out to him. Then it was quiet again and the man began to talk again.

Something had stirred in him. The sight of those people sitting there and singing together, seemed strange and familiar at the same time. How could this be? He had never heard white people sing before, or had he?

Where else would it come from that he suddenly had the feeling as if he had seen and heard something like this before. Lately, he had often had the feeling that he had seen or experienced certain things before. Did these feelings have something to do with what his father had told him on his deathbed. Unconsciously, he touched the amulet he had hanging around his neck.

The chant started again and tore him out of his thoughts. This time it was a different melody and also the chant was different. The tones seemed to call him. Without thinking, he went to the entrance and opened the door. There he stood in the doorway. The cold wind blew him formally into the house and he suddenly felt out of place. The Reverend looked up, saw him standing in the doorway and froze in his tracks. The congregation, looking at the Reverend, stopped singing and turned in the direction of the reverend's anxious gaze.

When the singing stopped, Isabella looked over her shoulder for the reason. She saw Chágha tho standing as a proud warrior in the doorway and stopped playing the piano. It had become quiet as a mouse.

Everyone was looking at the Indian scrutinizingly. Their gazes pierced him. Some of them were surprised to see him here. Others seemed to feel uncomfortable. One of them, however, gave him looks that could have killed him. But Chágha tho did not notice, because James was the first to overcome his shock and whispered to the reverend:

„Charles, it's all right. I'll explain it to you later."

In disbelief, the reverend looked back and forth between James and Chágha tho. An Indian in his church! James would actually have to explain it to him. He had not experienced anything like this before. But he was a man of God and before God all people were equal and so he gave Chágha tho with a hand gesture to understand that he should take a seat. Without paying any attention to him, he turned to Isabella and said:

"Please be so good and play the song again from the beginning," and addressing to his congregation, he continued, "We will sing the song again from the beginning." The music started and slowly they all turned back to the front and began to sing. Chágha tho did not know what he should do. Should he leave again?

He did not belong here, or did he? Or should he sit down, as the man had signaled to him. Slowly he moved to the right, where he stood in the furthest corner and followed the whole service. The eyes of the reverend rested on him again, but Chágha tho did not move.

After the service, Malcolm approached Chágha tho who was still standing motionless in the corner of the room. He patted him on the shoulder in a friendly manner and grinned.

"Gee, boy! That was a performance. The others soon had their spit stuck in their throats. I should have told you before, we have a service here every two weeks. I'm sorry. Today the field work rests."
"Malcolm are you coming?"
Louisa had appeared in the doorway, looking for her husband.

"On my way, dear. See you later, my boy!" he nodded encouragingly to Chágha tho and turned to his waiting wife. The voices outside the door became quieter. Chágha tho still did not move and watched the only person who was in the room with him. Isabella had begun to pack up her music sheets and collect the hymnals. As she walked through the rows of pews, she felt the Indian's gaze resting on her and immediately a warmth rose in her. Her heart began to beat faster and her hands trembled slightly. She avoided looking at him, because she was afraid he could see what reaction her body had to his nearness. With her back to him, she was standing in front of the teacher's closet, putting the books inside, when she became aware that he was slowly pacing the room and approaching the piano.

Curious, he touched the instrument and let his fingers slide carefully over the keys. But nothing happened, the instrument remained silent. Isabella, who had been watching him curiously, stepped up next to him and pressed a few keys, one after the other, with her right hand. Immediately the individual tones sounded. Then she reached for his right hand, placed it on the row of keys and pressed down his fingers one after the other. Chágha tho's gaze brightened, and Isabella beamed at him. The look in her emerald green eyes touched him so much that his heart warmed up. The touch of her fingers on his hand, he felt it all over his body.

A desire grew in him that he did not know and could only with difficulty conceal. He would have loved to play with his fingers in her soft auburn hair. The flowery scent of her skin that rose to his nose beguiled him. Isabella brought him out of his thoughts when she cleared her throat.

"Do you want me to play anything else?" she asked him and looked at him with a look that he could not really interpret correctly. But he understood the question and nodded to her. Relieved to escape the magical moment that had arisen between them, she sat down at the piano and played her favorite song. The room filled with beautiful sounds and devoutly and admiring at the same time he listened to her. Isabella could hardly concentrate on her playing, because she felt the closeness of the Indian with every fiber of her body. "Isabella!"

James had appeared in the doorway and had been

watching the scene.

"The Reverend and I are about to leave. Would you please put the provisions together?"
Abruptly she stopped playing and turned to her father.
"Yes, Father."

She jumped up and left the room together with her father. James threw Chágha tho a disapproving look.

A few hours later, the wind had increased and dark, threatening clouds hung heavy in the sky. At any moment there could be rain. The two men on the buggy had already turned up the collars of their coats to protect themselves from the cold wind. Their hats were pulled down low on their faces and their neckerchiefs also sat over their mouths and noses. Tirelessly, two horses pulled the wagon across the prairie. The reverend's horse had been tied to the back.

"What weather today. There's bound to be rain," said the reverend, looking up at the sky.

"We could sure use some rain. The wind takes the moisture out of the ground, only wouldn't necessarily have to have it now while we're on the road."
The Reverend nodded approvingly.

"Say, when are you going to tell your family about Mrs. Higgins. You won't be able to keep this from them forever."
"I don't want to, either, but whenever I think it's the right time, I'm at a loss for words."
"James, I didn't know you were such a rabbit's foot."
The Reverend grinned and gave him a nudge in the side.

"Mrs. Higgins is a nice, decent woman, and I think she deserves to be treated as such, and that includes you legalizing your relationship."
"That's what I want. I'd like to ask her to marry me, but I

don't know how Isabella will take it. Maybe I don't have the right."

"Oh, I think you're worrying too much. Isabella will understand. She'll like Marylou, I'm sure of it."

"I hope so, when I get back, I'll talk to her."

"Good! Now tell me how it came about that you took in an Indian. I got a mighty fright just now."

"Well, that's a story. It all started two weeks ago, the last time you were here. Isabella went for a ride and got attacked by a cougar."

"That's terrible. Did something happen to her?"

"Except for a few small wounds, nothing bad. But that's probably thanks to the Indian, because Isabella's horse ran away with her and fell into a ravine. The Indian saved her from falling with her horse. He also brought her home. After that he stayed here for several days and watched us. The whole thing did not please me and we confronted him. He wanted to learn our language from us."

"Mmm, I've never heard that before."

"Yeah, funny, isn't it? Because I found it all strange, I allowed him to stay with us. It seemed to me better to have him on site under supervision than to have him skulking in the woods around our ranch."

"What about his tribe?"

"That's the next weird thing. He says he's out on his own and as a matter of fact, we haven't found any signs of other Indians. Malcolm is taking care of him because he understands his language. He is Cheyenne."

"But this isn't their territory here at all!"

Charles looked incredulously at James.

"Exactly - he's pretty far away from his people."

"I can't wait to hear what you have to tell me in three weeks."

"Why three weeks from now? Is there a shift in something?"

"Yes, I have to go to the countess in a few days. Her foreman's son is getting married, and she asked me to perform the wedding ceremony. So I'll be with her on the ranch next Sunday and after that, it's my turn again in Laramie before I can come to you."

"Well, Elisabeth MacIntyre. She's still holding the reins. After the death of her husband I didn't think she'd keep the ranch going. But she is a remarkable old lady."

"Life had not always been easy for them. When I think of what happened to her only son. I only came to this area later, but you knew him well, didn't you?"

"You mean Robert? Yes, we were good friends. We always imagined back then, that one day we could merge our parents' farms. That would have been a good fit. But unfortunately, everything turned out differently. For fifteen years she has been hoping for a miracle that will not happen. Unfortunately it seems, that she can't let go."

"Well the ways of the Lord are unfathomable. I often think that many things in life are predetermined. Maybe one day we will know more."

Chágha tho had already made himself comfortable on his bed. With a naked upper body he lay on the clean sheets and stared at the dark ceiling. In this weather, there was no thought of him riding to the river tonight. The wind whistled around the stable and whipped the rain against the wooden walls. The first flashes of lightning were already twitching in the sky and thunder could be heard in the distance from the approaching thunderstorm. Tonight everyone was glad to be sitting in the dry.

Suddenly, he heard the barn door open and quickly closed again. Silently he jumped up, grabbed his knife, crept behind a pile of straw and waited for the one who was coming. He relaxed when he saw Isabella approaching his camp with a basket in her hand. He put the knife back on his belt. Isabella paused when she found his camp empty. Where was he in this weather? She was terribly frightened and almost dropped the basket when a hand came up behind her and touched her shoulder.

With a jerk, she turned around and found herself only inches away from him. There he stood. Tall, proud and sublime, with a naked upper body. Involuntarily she had to swallow at the sight. Her eyes wandered from top to bottom. He had broad shoulders, a muscular chest.

His arm muscles were well-developed and the tendons stood out when he strained them. The flat stomach was firm and the muscles formed a V line before disappearing into the waistband of his leggings. Somewhat ashamed of her behavior, she looked up at him. His blue eyes fixed on her and made her strangely nervous. The blood rushed through her veins and, embarrassed, she quickly lowered her head again.

When his hand ran over her cheek and clasped her chin, she recoiled, startled. Isabella was caught with her back to the wall and she could only have escaped forward. Slowly he lifted her face with his hand and forced her to look at him. Irritated, she held her breath and pushed the basket, she had brought with her like a wedge between them. But it did not help.

Slightly amused, Chágha tho pushed the basket aside, clasped her waist with one hand and pulled her closer before he closed her mouth with his lips. At first, his lips touched her mouth only very lightly and she felt a warm wave run through her body. Then his kiss became more insistent and she felt his tongue running over her lips. Isabella felt hot and cold at the same time. She had never been kissed by a man before, but the feeling that he evoked in her was incredibly beautiful.

Without thinking, she dropped the basket to the floor and put her arms around his neck. Inevitably she pulled his head closer to her. Immediately his arm enclosed her tighter and pressed her body against his. Her small, firm breasts pressed against his broad chest and left fire marks on his skin. He felt himself getting hard and was amazed, he had never had such a reaction from a kiss. His body was on fire and he wanted more. Didn't just want that one kiss from her.

His whole body was longing for her, but she was inexperienced. He had noticed that immediately, and if he did not want to scare her, then he had to proceed gently. Chágha tho tried to restrain his passion, but it was increasingly difficult when she moaned with excitement. Her lips parted and immediately his tongue found its way. The kisses became more and more passionate and willingly Isabella nestled against him. She returned each of his kisses with the same passion that took possession of her.

Her hands wandered over his broad back and sent small pleasant shivers through his body. Suddenly, she felt his hand enclosing one of her breasts. This touch made her body tremble, and without her noticing it, little sounds of pleasure escaped from her mouth.

Chágha tho's other hand was placed on her small, well shaped buttocks and pressed her tightly against his body. Isabella felt his hardness against her leg and was startled. Her brain began to send out warning signals, which she seemed to realize, because she pressed both hands against his chest and tried to pull him away.

"No! Stop it!" she shouted, at first somewhat breathlessly, then once more in an energetic tone. Immediately he stopped and breathlessly took a step back from her. Ashamed of herself, she gathered up her skirts and ran out of the barn. She did not stop until she was in her room. My God what had she done? She had behaved lewdly. What if her father were to find out? How had it ever come to this? But was it really such a disgrace, if one got such beautiful feelings from it?

She had never been kissed, but if it was like this every time, then it wasn't right not to do it more often. It was already late and in the house everybody was asleep, and she should be doing the same. But she knew that she would not be able to sleep. Chágha tho still stood at the same place. Breathing heavily, he tried to understand what had just happened.

"Run, Isabella! Run and get yourself to safety from me," he whispered to himself.

He had almost lost control over himself. What was he thinking? But there was some magic from her that had put him under its spell. At their first encounter, he had felt it, and now that he had tasted the forbidden fruit, he wanted more. His desire for her had become greater than ever. He did not understand himself and the best thing he could do was to keep his distance from her and avoid her.

Chapter 14

By the next morning, the storm had passed. The wind had died down and only the cloudy sky showed what kind of storm had raged during the night. Chágha tho had not slept a wink. For hours he had lain awake on his camp and stared holes into the air. Even though the storm outside had long since passed, it raged on inside him. He could not understand that a simple kiss had triggered such a reaction in him.

To bring himself to other thoughts and because he had given up trying to find sleep, he had gotten up in the early hours of the morning. He had lit the kerosene lamp in the barn and had begun to stack the straw better. Then he had cleaned the horses' saddles, which were hanging on the wall in one corner. Even before the day dawned, he had finished all the preparations for today.

The horses were already supplied and he sat outside on the fence of the paddock and waited for the others.

His horse rubbed his head against his leg, nudged him lively and was rewarded by him scratching his neck.

"Hi, Chágha tho. Hey everything is done !"

Thomas was the first to appear.

"Could not sleep," Chágha tho replied in broken English and shrugged his shoulders.

"Yes, was a heavy storm, came down a mighty

lot of water. How good that it has passed."

A short time later, all the cowboys were on their horses and Malcolm divided them into groups.

"You guys know, today we're going to start with the branding. Thomas, Henry and Dave you drive with your groups to bring the cattle to us, so we can start branding them. Chágha tho, you ride in the group of Thomas."

"What? He's coming too?"

Carl sat on his horse and was facing Malcolm.

"You got a problem with that, Carl?" asked Malcolm in a threatening, calm tone.

"You bet I do. The bastard has no business being here and I refuse to work with him in a group together."

A hush had fallen. Everyone noticed the tension that was building.

"I'm only going to say this once. I give the instructions and what I say will be done. You will stay in your group and do your due."

And turning to the others, he said, "And if anyone else has any objections, the same applies to them. Do we understand each other? Then go now!"

The men nodded silently and started to move. Carl led his horse close to that of Chágha tho, who had followed with an expressionless face. In him, however, anger seethed violently. When Carl stood directly in front of him and thus blocked his way, he hissed at him with a face distorted with rage.

"Get out of my way, you son of a bitch!"

And to punctuate his contemptuous words, he spat at the Indian. Then he turned abruptly, put spurs to his horse, and dashed after the others. Chágha tho had been able to evade the saliva, but he had understood. Outwardly he was calm and collected, but his eyes darkened dangerously and his jaw quivered.

The white man could be glad that he was here

among his equals, because for this insult he would have deserved death. His father had always taught him that you had to be smarter than your enemies if you wanted to conquer them. This included, that one should make decisions in a calm frame of mind. He thought he had been quiet for far too long.

This man wanted blood and since the first minute here on this ranch, he had never stopped to insult and threaten him. It was time for him to act like a warrior and not a coward. The next time, and he was sure that the opportunity would come, he would strike back. The others were already quite a distance away when he took up the pursuit with his horse.

The work went on hand in hand. The cowboys, of the three groups, drove the cows and calves before them into the circle that the men of the fourth group, led by Malcolm, had formed. They branded each animal with the hot iron. In the air hung the smell of fire, smoke and burnt fur. It was sweaty work and the men were glad that the sun did not show itself today.

As a supervisor, Malcolm's job was to keep all his men under control. For this reason, he set out with his horse to watch Carl and Chágha tho. It might not have been wise to put them in the same group, but he could not always keep the Indian away from the others. As long as he was on the ranch they had to get along with him. Up to now, he had felt a certain reluctance towards him, but none of them had been violent or verbal against him. Except for Carl.

He did not give the young man a chance. His hatred towards the Indian was plain to see. And Chágha tho? He could not judge him well. Outwardly, he pretended to be calm, but Malcolm was sure that things were boiling inside and that there was a danger that one day there would be an eruption. Secretly, he admired the man for being so in control. At his age, he himself would not have been patient with Carl.

Now, however, he could not detect any of the tension among the men. All of them did what was asked of them and thus the work progressed swiftly. Malcolm could also observe something else. Chágha tho was very skillful in his work. The Indian had his horse well under control. Agile and fast, it dashed after the escaping cattle and seemed to enjoy it. With the lasso over his head, he directed the horse with only his thighs and galloped across the prairie to the next cattle. If the boy wasn't an Indian, he'd be one hell of a cowboy, Malcolm thought to himself as he turned away from the scene and rode back to camp, where the others were doing record work with the branding irons.

A few hours later, it had become late afternoon, everyone had gathered in the camp. Together they sat around the fire, ate, drank coffee and talked. It was a relaxed atmosphere. The men joked with each other. For the first time Chágha tho joined them in the circle. At first, some looked up in surprise, but they accepted him in their midst, for nothing was said and they continued to talk. But this peace did not last long. When Carl rode into the camp and joined the circle, he went straight to Chágha tho. Without warning he kicked him in the side with his boot, causing Chágha tho to fall sideways to the ground. He was shouting at him: "You dirty Indian, get out of here!"

The Indian sprang up, pulled Carl to the ground and threw himself on top of him. With one hand he tied the man's breath with his own shirt collar, while his other hand pulled the knife from his belt and held it to Carl's throat. When Carl had overcome the moment of shock, he tried to fight back and reach for his revolver with his hand, but Chágha tho held him in check with his weight and pressed his knee to the ground.

With the knife at his throat, he was in a hopeless position. and Carl gradually became frightened. Chágha tho shouted, in pure English: "You -don't you ever call me a dirty Indian!"

He just pulled Carl's face closer to him and set the blade to the cut, when he heard the cocking of a revolver's trigger behind him.

"Let him go, or I'll put a bullet in your back."

Malcolm was the first to realize what was suddenly happening. He had jumped up and was aiming his revolver at the Indian's back. But the Indian made no move to let go of Carl. The situation was extremely dangerous. At any moment Chágha tho could slit Carl's throat with the sharp blade. He had to prevent it. In an unmistakably sharp tone, he repeated himself.

"You shall let him go, now!"

Chágha tho shook with rage. His body was tense like a bow and his carotid artery throbbed wildly. The man deserved to die. But the rat was not worthy to go to the eternal hunting grounds. With a massive blow, he rammed his knife up to the hilt into the ground next to him. Malcolm inwardly breathed a sigh of relief, but continued to aim his weapon at the Indian.

Chágha tho, on the other hand, rose from the ground, pulling Carl to his feet with him. Without removing his hands from Carl's shirt, both men stood close together, glaring at each other. Again Malcolm's voice sounded behind him.

"Release him and step away."

Slowly, the grip on his shirt loosened and he could breathe again. The boy, was not man enough to go through with it, Carl thought to himself and slowly twisted the corners of his mouth into a sardonic grin. When Chágha tho saw this, he didn't care if he was about to feel a bullet in his back. He lashed out and landed a powerful strike to Carl's temple who immediately sank unconscious to the ground. Chágha tho reached for his knife without turning, put it back in his belt, and swung onto his horse. He galloped out of the camp in a fast canter. Malcolm's gaze and those of the rest of the stunned men followed him.

"Shall we follow him?"

Thomas had stepped up next to Malcolm, who put his revolver back in its holster.

"No, it's better he lets off his steam somewhere else other than here. Take care of Carl."

Malcolm turned away and looked for a quiet spot while the men tended to the unconscious Carl. That idiot! He had started a private vendetta and now he had to see how he could stop it. He was glad that the Indian had left the camp for now. He would take care of him later. Now he had to first try to teach this brainless idiot some sense again. What was he thinking? He would have liked to try to beat some sense into Carl's brain with his fists, but that would lead to nothing.

"Where is the son of a bitch, let go of me! I'm gonna kill that bastard!"

Malcolm turned around and saw the angry Carl coming toward him. Two of his men had tried to grab him by the arms, but Carl had fought them off.

"Shut up, Carl. You've done enough already. You're lucky to be alive."

"Where'd he go? He'll pay for this."

Carl was about to start toward his horse when he was rudely prevented from doing so by Malcolm.

"Gee, Carl! Have you taken leave of your senses? How dare you attack him like that. He could have killed you and it would have been his right. Give it a rest. And I'll give you some good advice, and if there's any brains left up there, you'd better take it, too. Stay away from Chágha tho. You should not underestimate him. He's fast and strong, and before you know it, you'll have his knife between your ribs and there may be no one around to help you."

Malcolm threatened Carl with his finger.

"As long as that Indian is on the ranch, you stay away from him. Do you understand me?"

"Pah!"

With a snide motion Carl turned on his heel and disappeared from Malcolm's sight. Malcolm shook his head and fervently hoped that Carl would heed the advice. Carl, on the other hand, was thinking about how he could get one over on the Indian. Chágha tho would not get away with humiliating him in front of the others today. He had underestimated the man, that would not happen to him again. Who could have expected that he could get to his feet so quickly and pull out his knife. Next time he would be better prepared. He would think of something. The son of a bitch would not get away again, he swore to himself.

It was already deep in the night when Chágha tho returned to the ranch. When he left the camp in the afternoon, he had ridden aimlessly through the area, until he had stopped somewhere. His first thought had been that he would not return to the ranch, but that would have been cowardly. And he was not a coward. So far he had faced every fight and he would do the same this time. The old man had declared war on him and Chágha tho had accepted it. This time he had been lucky, but next time, Chágha tho swore to himself, he would die. He would show no more mercy.

When the outlines of the buildings appeared in front of him everything laid in darkness. The residents had long been asleep. Quietly he got off his horse and brought it to the paddock with the other animals, then he opened the door of the barn and went inside. A small glow of light emanating from the kerosene lamp made him see the outline better in the darkness.

Wasn't it a bit reckless to leave the lamp burning here, Chágha tho wondered as he made his way to his camp. When he made out a movement to the left in front of him, immediately he reached for his knife.

"Put the knife down, I've got the revolver pointing at you. You're late, thought you might not come at all. Come out of the shadows over to the light, so I can see what you're doing. And no funny business, or I'll pull the trigger."

Chágha tho took his hand off the knife and walked over to the lamp as instructed. He turned the light on more and illuminated the room with it. When he turned, he looked directly into the face of his visitor. His gaze tried to find signs in the other person to understand this situation. Was he in danger? He decided to stay calm for the time being and wait. His nocturnal visitor slowly approached. Always mindful to point the revolver ready to fire at Chágha tho.

"Who are you? And what was that back there?"

"I don't know what you mean!"

"That, for instance. Why did you lie when you told us that you didn't speak our language?"

"I wasn't lying. At the time. I didn't know it."

"Don't take me for a fool. No human being can learn a foreign language so quickly and then suddenly speak it without an accent. So, who are you and you better tell the truth, because my finger on the trigger is starting to get nervous."

Chágha tho leaned against one of the wooden beams, closed his eyes for a moment and began to speak.

"I did not lie. When I came to you, I did not

understand a word, nor did I speak it. In the course of my time here I have often had the feeling that the foreign sounds became more and more familiar to me and it became easier to understand you. That day when you were sitting over there in that house," he made a movement with his hand in the direction of the church, and sang, I already knew all these songs. I must have heard them before. Where that could have been, I don't know. From then on, I could understand you perfectly. But only today I was able to form the words the way it sounded. And now Malcolm? Is that my crime, that I am able to have a conversation with you here. That we face each other on the same level?"

Chágha tho paused and watched as Malcolm put his revolver back in its holster and continued to walk toward him.

"Who are you?"

"I am Chágha tho. Son of Chief Kitchi Honovi, which in your language means, brave stag, who has gone to Manitou. At least I was, until a few months ago. Until the day when the chief called me to him and told me on his deathbed that I was not his biological son. Hon Avonaco, his wife, could not have children and so he had bought me from the Sioux a very long time ago. I must have been four or five when I was taken in by him and raised as his son. I only know this name, although it is probably not my real name. Who I really am, I can't answer you, I don't know myself."

Malcolm was silent for quite a while. He first had to understand what he had heard.

"Have you been cast out by your tribe?"

"No, after I realized that I could not take on the task for which I had been trained to do all my life, which was to continue the tribe as the new chief, I decided to leave. Since then I ride through the countryside alone. If you want me to go now, I'll be gone in the morning."

"No, you don't have to go because of me. I'll have to tell the boss when he gets back. Then he can decide. In the meantime, you can stay here. Only one thing should be clear. Such an action like this afternoon will not happen again."

Immediately Chágha tho wanted to say something about it, when Malcolm raised his hand and continued speaking.

"I'm going to tell you the same thing that I told Carl. You get out of his way, as long as you are here, there will be no attacks on the other guy. Are we clear on that!"

Chágha tho nodded. He for his part would not launch an attack, but he would defend himself to the blood if he had to.

"Tomorrow you stay at the ranch. The Boss will be back soon and then we'll see further."

Malcolm was about to leave when Chágha tho held him back by the sleeve.

"What's the deal with that black mustang standing out there alone in the paddock?"

"The boss caught him a few weeks ago. He wanted him for himself, but the animal is a beast. Lets no one touch him, rises and strikes wildly. None of the men has yet managed to approach the animal, let alone get into the paddock. That would be outright suicide. When he gets back, he will have to decide what to do with the animal. We can't leave it in there forever. I'll see you tomorrow."

Without adding anything else, Malcolm left the hayloft, leaving Chágha tho alone.

Chapter 15

The next morning the world seemed to be normal again. The Cowboys had left the ranch shortly after sunrise and would not be back until dinner. Louisa and the rest of the wives had arranged to have laundry day today and had all gone to the river with a wagon and their laundry. The sun was shining hotly from the sky and so the clean laundry would later be able to dry well in the air. Isabella had given lessons to the children.

It was already after noon and school was over for the day, when she stepped out of the school building. She heard the regular beat of an axe, followed by the splintering of wood. Chágha tho was apparently still busy chopping firewood. Shortly after the men had left the ranch, he had begun. He must be totally exhausted from the work. Curious, she went in his direction.

He stood with his back to her on the log, grabbed a large piece of wood and laid it out for himself on the block. Then he lifted the axe above his head and let it down with a crash. The edge of the axe bored into the center of the piece of wood.

Then he lifted the axe up again, together with the heavy piece of wood, and let both crash onto the block. The piece of wood burst into three pieces and the axe was free again. Isabella was spellbound by the sight.

Chágha tho stood in front of her with his naked upper body. His buffalo hide shirt lying in the grass next to a wooden trough with water in it. It was incredibly hot for a spring day and a light film of sweat had formed on his skin that shone in the sun. The muscles on his shoulders and arms jumped out strongly with the effort.

For a few seconds he paused, reached sideways into the trough next to him and took out a ladle of water to quench his thirst. As he drank, his larynx rose and fell and some water trickled down his chin. Isabella couldn't help but swallow. This sight was absolutely not befitting a woman, but she also could not stop following him with her gaze. She thought again of his kiss and how good his skin felt under her fingers. A shiver of desire ran through her and she became quite hot.

"Isabella! We're back!"

At the call of her name, Chágha tho turned abruptly and their eyes met. He seemed surprised to see her standing near him. The sight of him, on the other hand, captivated her so much that she simply could not take her eyes off that magnificent body.

Unabashedly, she let her emerald green eyes travel along his body, then their eyes met again. Ashamed of the fact that he had been watching her the whole time, she noticed how she blushed, while Chágha tho, on the other hand, had become more than hot.

Her looks literally undressed him and his body began to react. An irrepressible desire for her grew in him. He wanted to hold her in his arms again. Kiss her, feel her, sense her, pull his fingers through her soft hair and soak up the scent of her skin. Involuntarily he had to swallow. His imagination suddenly sprang up with images of what he would like to do with her, and if she stood there like that for much longer, he wouldn't be able to hold back. Isabella must have sensed this, too, because without a word to him she turned around abruptly, gathered up her skirts and walked quickly over to the house.

Chágha tho breathed a sigh of relief. Isabella seemed to have no idea how hard it was for a man to hold back when he was being looked at like that.

The looks had been unambiguous, and under different circumstances he would have been happy to show her where that would have led. But it was better for him to stay away from her, and so he would have to chop wood for a bit longer to get his mind back on other things. At least he hoped so. And even before Isabella had closed the front door behind her, she could hear the regular beat of the axe again.

A little bit later he gave up trying to distract himself by chopping wood. Isabella continued to haunt his mind. He had to admit to himself that her charm, her grace and her looks drove him out of his mind. One look from her and he was lost. One touch from her and he was on fire.

But she was taboo for him, there he did not have to pretend anything. Even if he had the feeling that it was the same for her, they would have no future together. As an Indian, he would never be recognized among the whites.

And she was not cut out for a life with his tribe. They came from two different worlds and therefore, it was better to nip any feelings that might arise in the bud. But that was easier said, than done.

All day long he had been thinking whether it would be better to leave the ranch and move on, but somehow he could not make up his mind. He had wondered if there was any point in looking any further. In recent weeks, he had ridden across the country looking for clues, but had found nothing.

Maybe it was all useless and he was just pointlessly wasting his time. Perhaps the time had come for him to settle down somewhere again.

But where should that be? With these thoughts he strolled back to the hayloft. It was late afternoon and the men would soon return home. The sun was already low in the sky and the adjacent mountains cast long shadows over the pastures. The women were busy hanging the laundry on the lines to dry. He could see Louisa hanging up Malcolm's pants at home.

Arriving at the ranch, he was about to open the barn door when his eyes fell on the black mustang pacing restlessly back and forth in the paddock. Maybe he should take another look at the animal.

He was quite good with horses. Maybe he could figure out what the problem was. Slowly he approached the run. When the animal saw him, it snorted and whinnied wildly. With its hooves pawing and ears tightly folded, it watched Chágha tho very closely.

Quite slowly Chágha tho approached and spoke to the animal with soft Indian sounds. At first the stallion nervously walked back and forth, stood and wedged out backwards. Then it ran around in circles as if being mad. Chágha tho did not stop speaking softly reassuring words. When he had arrived directly at the fence and continued to talk reassuringly to the horse, it stopped abruptly on the opposite side.

White foam had formed between the hind legs. The mane stuck to the sweat-soaked neck of the horse. The animal was totally distraught.

"What a beautiful animal you are!", Chágha tho fluted to the horse in Indian.

"You don't like it here, I can understand that. Maybe we can change that. Come on, I won't hurt you!"

Patiently he waited for a reaction, looked directly in the animal's eyes and continued to speak calmly. The mustang apparently let itself be lulled by the sounds of words and finally it seemed as if he would become calmer. The ears of the animal straightened and turned in Chágha tho's direction.

"Come on, I dare you. In a way we are very similar. You don't belong in here as much as I do. Yes, that's good. Come to me, I won't hurt you."
The animal seemed to have understood, for it came slowly, step by step toward him. But when the stallion was only a few inches away from him, he suddenly rose and tried to hit the fence with his hooves.

Chágha tho jumped back to avoid being hit but immediately approached the fence again, when the mustang had run into the middle of the square. There he stood with his face turned toward the Indian and waited. Chágha tho was not intimidated and continued to speak to the animal in the same low voice as before.

"You won't get rid of me so quickly, so come on, try again. Such a beautiful animal as you are, don't be afraid. Come here to me."
Once again, the animal slowly approached him and this time, it stopped right in front of the Indian. Chágha tho blew lightly into its nostrils. The mustang snorted and shook his head.

"Yes, that's it. That's a good boy. Allow me to touch you now? It won't hurt. You see, I just very lightly put my hand on your nose and I take it away again. That wasn't so bad, was it? And everyone likes it, if he gets a few strokes. Yes, you see, you like it too."
Chágha tho gently stroked the head of the animal and the mustang seemed to take a liking to it. He came even closer and put his head on Chágha tho's shoulder. Chágha tho took the opportunity and stroked the head and neck of the horse. Its fur was dull and dirty from the dust. He would have to be groomed, so that his coat would shine again, but this was not the time.

He considered it a great success that he had managed in a short time to touch the animal. Now he had to try to build up trust with it. He would start on this tomorrow. It would soon be dark and he still wanted to go to the river. After work today, a bath in the river was the reward of the day.

So he rubbed and stroked the mustang for quite a while, until the animal had apparently had enough and slowly turned away from him. He let the animal go and went to his own horse. He swung onto it and galloped off in the direction of the river.

"Malcolm! Malcolm! The Indian's got the mustang out of the paddock."

Thomas came riding excitedly to the pasture. Today some of the men had been busy counting cows in the pasture behind the main house.

"What, I don't believe it."

"Yes, he does, he got him out of the paddock and now he's sitting in the grass in the middle of the pasture and the Mustang is romping around him like crazy. He must have gone mad. I certainly won't catch the devil again. The boss will be raving when he gets home."

"You've got to be kidding me. Henry! Take over here, I'll be right back."

"Okay!"

When Malcolm and Thomas had arrived at the pasture, William was already standing there with several other residents watching the spectacle. Isabella and Louisa were also watching and when Louisa saw her husband coming, she said to him:

"Malcolm, the boy must be insane. The animal will trample him. You must shoot the mustang."

Malcolm looked from his wife to Chágha tho and his heart seemed to stop. The horse rose dangerously close to the Indian, but it did not seem to frighten the boy.

He sat in the grass with his back to them at some distance and seemed to be calm. They could hear a soft, indian chant. The horse galloped around the Indian at a murderous pace, until it abruptly stopped in a distance.
It lowered its head and suddenly began to graze. Chágha tho's chanting had stopped but he remained sitting there quietly watching the grazing animal.

"Malcolm, I think the boy knows what he's doing. Leave him alone, I want to see what happens next. So far, none of us have managed to even get close to the animal. The Indian seems to have nerves of steel."
"If you say so, Mr. Hunt. I don't feel good about the whole thing, though."

Both leaned against the fence and continued to stare at the two in the pasture. Hours later, the crowd at the fence had increased. In the meantime, word had spread what Chágha tho was doing and everyone did not want to miss the spectacle. But the Indian had been sitting for hours in the same spot in the grass, not moving a bit, and the wild mustang grazed peacefully nearby. So far he had come only a little closer to Chágha tho. Suddenly he seemed to have had enough of grazing, for he raised his head, looked once in Chágha tho's direction, as if to make sure he was still there, took three steps in his direction, and put his head back into the grass. The horse repeated this procedure until he was only a few steps away from the young man.

The spectators whispered nervously, at any moment the mustang could wedge out or climb again and then fatally injure Chágha tho. A murmur went through the crowd as they watched the animal slowly raising its head when Chágha tho rose very slowly. Both stood only a few inches apart.

The Indian seemed to be saying something to the animal, because as if it had understood, it nodded and continued to stand still. Chágha tho started to turn away, caught sight of the crowd at the fence, but pretended that it was not there, for his concentration was completely on the horse at his back. Slowly he started to walk away from the mustang. The horse followed him at a constant distance. Chágha tho went to the right and the horse followed him. He turned to the left and the horse continued to follow.

When he went again in the opposite direction, the mustang followed him curiously like a dog. When he stopped and turned to the horse, it came trotting slowly toward him and laid his head on his shoulder. Chágha tho stroked the horse's strong neck with both arms, caressed the animal's head and spoke soft Indian words into its ear. The spectators on the sidelines could not believe their eyes. They had never seen anything like this before. Suddenly, a horse-drawn cart stopped beside them.

"What's going on here? Why isn't anyone working?"

"James! You're back!"

"Father, come see this. Chágha tho has let the mustang out to pasture. Look, he can touch it."

Not believing what his daughter was telling him, James had climbed down from the coach box. He past his cowboys and saw with his own eyes how Chágha tho had the horse's head resting on his shoulders. His father stepped up beside him.

"We've been watching him for quite a while. At first it looked as if Chágha tho's last hour had come. But then, I don't know how he did it, but the horse followed him every step of the way. Incredibly, I have never seen anything like this."

James himself could not believe what he saw. Actually, he himself was good with horses but he had failed with the mustang. He had not managed to get even close to the animal. He knew that there were people who had a gift for being able to deal with animals particularly well. These people could create a connection to the animal which remained denied to the most. He had only known one person in his life who have had this gift, but that had been a long time ago. Chágha tho seemed to be such a person.

"Henry! Charles! Would you take the cart over to the house and unload it."

"Will do boss." Both of them swung onto it and drove off.

"I'm sure everybody else has something else to do. Isabella, I think it's almost time for supper."

"Yes, Father."

She glanced once more toward the willow. Saw Chágha tho still standing there with the horse and went over to the house. Now that the crowd of spectators had dispersed and gone to their work, Malcolm and William were the only ones left standing with James.

"What's going on here, anyway? I'm gone three days and the ranch is upside down."

"There was an incident at the branding two days ago and I told Chágha tho that he should stay here. He asked me about the Mustang and I told him what it was about him. Little did I know that he was planning to take the horse out of the paddock."

"Well, he seems to have found the right way to handle the animal. But what kind of incident has there been?"

William spoke up:" Carl and the Indian went at each other. Malcolm was just able to prevent the worst. We waited for you to return so you could solve the problem."

James took off his hat, ran it through his hair and put his hat back on.

"Bloody hell. Then the Indian will have to go."

"I warned you, didn't I? I told you the Indian was going to be trouble. I'll get him here, then you can talk to him. The sooner he goes, the sooner peace will be restored here."

William was about to leave, when Malcolm spoke up.

"With respect sir, it was not Chágha tho's fault. Carl attacked him for no apparent reason and he was only defending himself. Since he has been here, he has been subjected to Carl's hostility. He insults him and spits on him. Assaults him physically. So far, the boy has had self-control, but the incident two days ago was the straw that broke the camel's back. I know you both disagree, but I know Chágha tho quite well and know that he is not a hothead. I have always wanted children. Unfortunately, I did not have them, but if I had had a son, I would have wanted him to be like him. So it would only be fair to take Carl to task too. Oh, and there is one more thing. Chágha tho speaks our language."

"Then he lied to us from the beginning?"

"No, the matter is different. He told me that....."

Malcolm told William and James exactly what had happened that afternoon two days ago and how he had confronted Chágha tho in the barn that evening. He repeated the explanation that the Indian had mentioned . When he had finished his report William and James looked at each other irresolutely.

"Well."

James rubbed his chin and looked to the willow, where Chágha tho was approaching with the horse.

"I don't know what to make of all this. What do you think, father?"

"Honestly, until a few minutes ago. I was of the opinion that we should chase him out of the yard. Now I must confess that I have become curious to know what the story is behind it, and there is no doubt that he has a talent for dealing with horses, as we could see.

Maybe you'll let him have another work out with the animal. It would be interesting to see how far he will go with the horse and we might have a chance to find out his secret. The only problem is Carl."

"Let me worry about him, Father. I'll talk to him after dinner and trim his horns. Malcolm, send Chágha tho to my office in half an hour. I want to talk to him, but first I want to freshen up."

"Will do, boss."

Malcolm disappeared in the direction of the Indian and father and son headed for the house.

Half an hour later Chágha tho was on his way to the main house. Isabella's father wanted to talk to him. About what, he could well imagine. Malcolm had certainly told him about the fight with Carl and now the sword would be broken over his head. But he would not justify himself for what he had done. Carl had attacked him and he had defended himself. With long strides he climbed the steps to the porch and knocked on the door. James Hunt opened the door for him himself, let him in, and proceeded to his office. Chágha tho was amazed.

He had never been in a white man's house before. The room he was in was large and on the far wall was a large open fireplace. Quite a few pieces of wood were piled up against the wall to the side of it. A long table with wooden benches dominated the room. Here, the men took their meals. On the other side of the room was a door, which was now closed, but behind it one could hear voices and the clatter of cooking pots.

There the meals seemed to be prepared, for a delicious aroma drifted out to him. His stomach immediately began to make itself known. In front of him a staircase led to the upper floor. James was standing behind the staircase, calling his name and had wondered why Chágha tho had not followed him.

When he followed him in the office James closed the door behind him and went to his desk which was piled with a number of papers. Chágha tho was astonished here too. Apart from the desk and the two armchairs, there were a few wooden shelves filled with books and an open cupboard in which six rifles hung. The floor was covered with a huge colorful carpet. The curtains on the windows had the same dark green as in the main room.

Chágha tho wondered, why did the white man need so much space? There were only three people living in this house. In a teepee often lived the whole family and the space they had was no comparison to this room. However, the tepee was mainly used for sleeping, since life took place in front of the tent. James had taken the seat at his desk and observed his guest. The Indian was an imposing figure. With his stature, he was taller than the Indians he had seen so far. His upper body was in an embroidered buffalo-skin shirt, but it gave a hint of the hard muscles underneath. The black hair was braided into two pigtails hanging to the right and left of his head. At the back of his head was a single eagle feather in a leather headband. His leggings were sewn from the same leather as the shirt and fringes decorated the sides of the legs. A snakeskin belt held both together.

His feet were barefoot in moccasins. But James also knew that he still owned suede boots, because when he had joined them on the ranch a couple of weeks ago, he had been wearing them. The only weapon he carried was a hunting knife, in a leather embroidered sheath hanging from his belt. The unusual blue eyes rested on James, waiting for him to finish the inspection and to address him.

"Why don't you sit down?"

James pointed to the chair in front of his desk, but Chágha tho did not stir.

"I'd rather stand."

"Okay."

James stood up again, circled his table and leaned his back against it. He casually crossed his arms in front of his body and his feet.

"Malcolm told me that you speak our language, as I can hear for myself, it's true. He also told me that you don't know where you learned it. Is that right?"

"Yes."

Proudly and with his head held high he stood before him. His feet firmly on the ground, his legs slightly apart and his arms folded crossed in front of his body. James continued.

"Well, you have to admit, this all sounds very strange, but I suppose you don't want to give me any other explanation."

"No."

"I saw you with the Mustang earlier. I liked that, even though no one allowed you to let him out of the paddock. What do you think - could you get him under the saddle?"

"I don't know, yet"

The conversation was proving difficult. James got only monosyllabic answers and didn't know quite how to draw the Indian out of his reserve and was surprised by the following question.

"Why does the white man want to ride the mustang?"

"Well he is a beautiful, powerful animal. I saw him and wanted him. But no one has been able to get to him and I've thought about releasing him."

"You can't do that anymore."

"Why?"

"The mustang was the leader of his herd, wasn't he?"

"Yes, how do you know?"

"If you let him loose, he'll go to pieces. His old herd no longer accepts him as the leader, the position has long since been taken over. A new herd would not let him get close to them, because he has the scent of the humans and alone, he is a welcome meal for the mountain lions."

"Mmmh, I hadn't thought of that. So what do you suggest? You seem to know a lot about horses."

"Chágha tho can try to see if he can ride it. But that takes time. He is distraught and has no confidence in people."

"Then that will be your job from now on."

"You don´t want me to go?"

"No, unless such a thing happens again what happened to Carl. And I wouldn't care whose fault it was. Are we understood?"

James looked urgently at Chágha tho. The Indian's eyes narrowed and for a moment he seemed tempted to say something in return, but then he refrained and just nodded.

In the evening after dinner, James asked Carl to a conversation. When the other men had gone to rest and it had become quiet in the house, he and Carl went out to the porch, where they both lit a cigarette.

It was a warm night for spring, and the first crickets could be heard chirping. Somewhere a horse was puffing. Dusk had set in and the moon would soon be shining. James took one more pleasurable drag on his cigarette, before he addressed his word to Carl.

"I have decided that Chágha tho will stay with us for a while and take care of the mustang. Do you have a problem with that?"

"I make no secret of the fact that I don't like him. But it's your decision. I don't have to approve of it."

"Exactly. It is my will that he stays here and you have to accept it. Part of that is, that there is no friction between us. If that happens again, you can pack your bags, Carl. Have I made myself clear enough?"

"There is no misunderstanding. Does that count for the Indian, too?"

"It applies to everyone here on the ranch. I don't tolerate any arguments here. Not from anybody! I appreciate your many years of work for us Carl and have understanding for a lot of things, but don't push it too far."

"Is that all?"

"That's all. I'll see you tomorrow."

Without another word, Carl walked over to the cabin, where he had his room. James looked after him thoughtfully. He hoped Carl had really understood and would now give it a rest.

And how he had understood. The son of a bitch, as it seemed, had everyone under his spell. The Hunts - both father and son - were on his side and yet Malcolm had become an Indian friend.

Did no one but he see the danger that came from the red devil? He was clever, he had to give him that. First, he made himself indispensable, so that everyone trusted him and then he would steal the cattle and burn the ranch. Isabella would be raped and murdered. As Carl thought of her, he realized how aroused he was getting. He had been here so long, he had seen her every day. Had watched her grow up. She had grown from a cute child to a beautiful woman, who was completely to his liking. Her tall, slender figure with well formed breasts would feel good in his hands.

She was always friendly to everyone, but when she smiled at him, he realized that there was more. He would be the perfect husband for her. Because of her youth she could still bear him enough children and he would make her a submissive wife. When her father died, he would be the powerful cattle baron here. He had already planned to ask James for his daughter's hand, but now after the unfortunate incident, his standing with him had sunk a bit. If he did not want to enrage James even more, he had to plan his next actions better. He would take Isabella as a wife, no question about it, and after that anything could happen - even an accident. But first he had to get rid of the Indian.

Chapter 16

The fire crackled in the mild spring night. Chágha tho had just added some wood and was now staring at the blazing flame. The warmth of the fire dried his wet skin. He would have liked to have something edible grilled, but tonight he had not yet had any hunting luck.

Neither a small hare or a fish had come in front of his spear. His stomach was empty and it looked as if he would stay that way tonight. He reached down beside him, took the spear in his hand and rose to make one last attempt when he heard sounds in the distance. Immediately he scurried into the darkness of the forest, hid behind a tree and waited for what was coming.

He didn´t have to wait long, until he saw who was coming on her horse through the night. He put the spear away, crept around the person and suddenly appeared beside her.
"What are you doing here?"

Isabella cringed in horror and nearly fell from her horse when Chágha tho suddenly stood beside her and took the reins of her horse.
"My God, you scared me. Why are you hiding?"
"You never know who's coming. Why are you here?"
"I was curious where you always went at night."

Isabella made an effort to get off the horse, but Chágha tho grabbed her waist and lifted her down.

Slowly, much too slowly, he let her slide down his body until her feet were on the ground. Her pulse accelerated and all at once she felt hot all over. It seemed to her that they stood close together for an eternity and his blue eyes seemed to hypnotize her.

His hands, still resting on her waist, pulled her closer. Automatically she rested her hands on his bare chest and could feel his heart beating faster. His head tilted down a bit and it seemed to her that he was about to kiss her. Waiting for his lips to touch hers, she closed her eyes. But instead of her lips, he only kissed her forehead and then released her. Somewhat confused, she opened her eyes and saw him walking over to the fire. Why had he done that? Didn't he want to kiss her? Embarrassed that she had misunderstood the situation, she turned to her horse, reached into her saddle bag and pulled out a small sack. With the bag in her hand, she went over to join him by the fire.

"I wasn't sure if you had eaten anything, so I packed some food. Here."

She handed him the bag and took a seat by the fire. Chágha tho accepted it, sat down as well and reached inside. He took out a tin can, which was still warm, a spoon and some bread. When he opened the tin, a delicious aroma rose to his nose. He dipped the spoon and put a portion in his mouth. Isabella watched as he greedily devoured the stew with the bread.

"Does it taste good?" asked Isabella, somewhat miffed.

Puzzled, Chágha tho paused. "Yes," he answered with his mouth full and continued to eat with relish.

Somewhat annoyed that for him it was apparently the most normal thing in the world to have a woman cook his food and bring it to him afterwards, she turned up the corners of her mouth.

"What is it?"

He had almost finished eating and it had really felt good

to get something in his stomach, but something didn't seem to be going right for her. He could tell that from the expression on her face and her posture. Had he done something wrong?

"I don't know how it is with you, but here we say thank you. I don't have to do that. If you don't come to dinner, it's usually your own fault, but I thought maybe you're hungry."

He did not understand exactly what she wanted from him. He had finished up everything. Wasn't that a sign enough for a woman that the man had enjoyed the meal? Apparently he had hurt her feelings, by whatever means, and that was the last thing he wanted, so he replied, "It was very good, thank you."

Before she could reply he rose, walked over to the river and washed the can and the spoon. Then he handed the bag of clean dishes and sat back down by the fire again. Isabella had followed his every movements. His damp hair which he wore open tonight reached slightly above his shoulders.
His hair shone in the light of the fire, like velvet.

He had probably taken a bath, because his shirt and the headband with his feather was lying next to the campfire. But something else was there. Something small and made out of silver. Curious, she bent forward to see what it was and recognized a chain with a pendant. But this one did not fit an Indian at all and she wondered where he had gotten it. When he returned to the fire she could no longer hold back her curiosity.
"Who are you and why do you speak our language all of a sudden?"

He had heard the question several times in the last two days, but the right answer to it he did not know himself. He gazed fixedly into the flames and searched for the right words. But somehow he could not think of them.

"I don't know. I bear the name Chágha tho, but I am no longer sure if it is my real name."

"I heard the conversation with my father earlier, so I know what you said to him."

"You were eavesdropping?"

Chágha tho shook his head in disbelief. Such a woman as Isabella had not yet occurred to him.

"Will you tell me more about yourself?"

"Why do you want to know?"

"I'm just interested, and I'm curious about your story. And now that we can communicate, we can learn more about each other."

She threw him an enchanting smile and Chágha tho would have liked to take her in his arms. This ravishing creature sat so close to him that he only had to reach out to her to take her in his arms. To hold her , feel her, kiss her and ...

His eyes were buzzing with images. His inside was longing for her and she was sitting next to him looking at him with her big, green eyes innocently. Apparently, she had no idea what her presence was doing to him. He exhaled deeply and tried to concentrate on the question she had asked him.

"I bear the name Chágha tho. I don't know any other name, but it is probably not my real name. Where I come from I do not know. When I was a little boy I came from the Sioux to the Cheyenne, where the chief took me in as his son. Until his death a few moons ago, I believed that he was my father. Since that day I have been searching for answers, he didn´t know."

"Is that why you're traveling alone?"

"Yes."

"How do you know our language? You didn't speak it when you came to us."

"It was just there all of a sudden. I know how it sounds, but it's the truth. Since I've been here, I've been feeling more and more like I've seen things before or experienced something similar. The day you sang, I suddenly knew those songs. And finally one day I could understand everything that was being said."

"It must have everything to do with your past. What is that necklace there?"

Chágha tho reached for it and held out the amulet to her. Carefully, she took it in her hand and looked at it more closely.

"You can open the amulet. There are two marks on the back."

Isabella turned the amulet over and saw clearly the letters engraved on it.

"Those are the letters M and F. You can't read, can you?" Chágha tho shook his head.

"I'm sure they stand for a name. Maybe your name? Unfortunately, you can't see the two pictures but it seems that one picture shows a man and the other a woman. Where did you get that? This is not an Indian necklace."

"My father, I mean the chief, gave it to me and said that I wore the necklace around my neck when I came to him."

"Then maybe the picture shows your parents!"

"It's hard to tell, the photographs are barely recognizable and for the last few weeks I've been trying to find clues to my origins. But I have not been successful. It's just been too long ago."

Isabella flipped the amulet closed again. This necklace had been finely crafted and was made of pure silver. She suspected that it had once belonged to whites. Whether this chain really had something to do with the origin of him or whether the Sioux or Cheyenne had brought it from one of their raids, could not be said. The photos of the two people were almost destroyed and no one could tell which skin color they had once. But maybe something could be gotten through the chain.

She gave him the amulet back. He put it around his neck and was just about to reach for his shirt, when she put her hand on his arm and said:

"Let me help you, and if you want, I can teach you to read."

This light touch of hers, together with the encouraging look she brought to him, was too much for his reticence. He turned to her, took her face in both hands and said," Galilahi Leotie."

"What....what does that mean?"

His touch and his closeness to her made her shiver pleasantly.

"It means that you are beautiful. Like a Prairie Flower."

"Oh."

She didn't get to say more, for he had closed her mouth with his. Her pulse began to race, and unconsciously she clung tightly to him. The touch of her clothes on his skin drove him out of his mind. He felt her firm breasts through the fabric. Her lips opened slightly and immediately his tongue explored her mouth. Isabella moaned out. Her body trembled with passion.

It was like the other night when she had fled from the rising feelings. This time she wanted more. She enjoyed his passion. Chágha tho shifted his weight slightly and gently pushed her down to the ground. When he paused for a moment and looked at her, he could see her eyes had darkened with desire.

She put her arms around his neck and pulled him down to her. Immediately their mouths found each other and her hands slowly ran down his back. This touch drove him crazy. He wandered with his mouth along her neck and elicited more small pleasurable sounds.

At the same time his hands tried to open the small buttons of her top. After what seemed to him a never-ending eternity, her top gaped open to the sides, revealing a corsage that encircled her white breasts. The beginnings of them pressed plumply against the fabric. Isabella sharply drew in air, which made him pause briefly. Never before had a man seen her like this.

Her brain told her to stop him, but her body demanded more. She wanted to feel his hands on her skin, the way she felt his. Wanted him to keep kissing her. Their eyes met and fervently he hoped that he would see in them the permission to continue, because he no longer knew whether he still had the strength to stop.

His loins ached and he had not had a woman for a long time. He could, without regard for her, get his satisfaction, but somehow he wanted her to give him permission. Inwardly, he shook his head. What was it about this woman that he cared what she thought of him? That he wanted to be considerate. He was a man and men had their needs and here was this woman lying quivering beneath him.

What was to stop him from finishing it? But when he had seen her shocked look, when he had opened her top, caused him to change his behavior. She trusted him and he strangely didn't want to lose that trust and so he paused. Instinctively, Isabella had noticed his hesitation. She took his head in her hands, pulled him down to her and kissed him. Chágha tho immediately returned her kisses and let his right hand pass over her naked shoulder until he got hold of a small ribbon. Slowly he undid the bow on the corsage, pulled the ribbon out of the small hooks and thus exposed her breasts free. Cold air enclosed her chest and she moaned with pleasure when his head lowered and his lips enclosed her buds.

His touches made her shiver, her body trembled and craved for more. She noticed how hard his breathing was and knew that he was feeling the same. Her hands slid along his back deeper and deeper until she felt the fabric of his leggings. Boldly, she slid fingers slowly under the material and realized what kind of power she had over him, and then he quietly called her name. When she felt his hand on her naked thigh and pushing up her skirt, it was all over her.

Her body trembled and demanded him. His hand touched her most intimate place and Isabella gasped out. Her body twitched and moved passionately under him. She noticed how he slid between them, and for a brief moment she was surprised that he was suddenly completely naked.

When had he gotten rid of his clothes? The passion had her firmly in its grasp. She didn´t care. She did not want to think now, she only wanted to feel. Never before had she experienced something so beautiful and somehow she knew it was not over yet. He kissed and caressed her and let her body dance under his, until she suddenly felt him inside her. For a moment he lay still and gave her body time to absorb him. Then, before she could say anything, he penetrated her deeper.

A pain ran through her and she cried out. Chágha tho paused, kissing her until the pain had passed and she returned his kisses again, then he began to move slowly inside her. Her body adapted to his rhythm and in the rush of feelings the passion carried her further and further up. No longer master of his senses, he penetrated deeper and deeper. Isabella reared up and screamed his name out into the night when she had climbed to the peak of pleasure. Chágha tho, however, withdrew from her shortly before he himself found fulfillment, so that his seed would not pour into her.

Later she lay contentedly and exhaustedly against his chest, gliding her fingers over his chest. She was still quite intoxicated by the feelings that she had just experienced and followed the steady rise and fall of his chest. She suspected that he had fallen asleep.

Becoming courageous, she lifted her head a little bit and looked at his body at length.

He was a handsome man. Tall with muscular, long legs and a narrow waist. His upper body was free of hair, his belly was hard and his muscles firm. When her eyes fell on his best piece, she noticed how she blushed.

She had no idea what wonderful feelings a man could give a woman. Quickly she averted her eyes only to find out that a pair of sky-blue eyes had quietly observed her.

"Oh, I thought you were asleep."

Embarrassed, she tried to hold the front of her corsage together with her hands and smoothed out her skirt again.

"If you keep looking at me like that we're going to end up right back where we left off."

Was that possible? Was it possible to repeat that? Her gaze fell directly on his middle and she could see how he reacted to it. Quickly she turned her flushed head, but she had not counted on Chágha tho. He turned his arms around her, and pressed her down to the ground again. A small gasp of shock escaped her mouth, but it was immediately smothered by a kiss from him. The passion between them was rekindled anew and so they loved each other in this night a second time.

How long they had lain there that night, no one knew exactly. The fire had already gone out and only a small ember was still glowing. Chágha tho was the first to wake up, and he was surprised to find that he enjoyed holding Isabella in his arms.

She was a beautiful passionate woman. But she had been inexperienced, as he had suspected, and he had taken her virginity. According to Indian law, he had made her his wife tonight, since she had freely shared his camp with him. It was supposed to make him happy. But he was not yet ready for a wife. Who was he and what could he offer her? He had no place where he could live with her. She belonged here on the ranch that would one day be hers. She needed a man by her side who lived in her world, who could run the ranch, and who people would accept. All things he could never offer her.

It was better if he left. She would forget him in time and be free for the man at her side. If he had not given his word to her father that he would take care of the mustang, he would probably still be on the road today. But he was a man who did not break his word and so he had to finish his job first. But until then he would try to avoid her as much as possible, because he no longer trusted himself. Carefully, he peeled himself out from under her, grabbed his clothes and got dressed. Then he leaned down and gently woke her.

"Oh, was I asleep?"

"Yes, come. We should ride home before everyone wakes up."

Isabella looked up in horror.

"Yes, you're right. My father must not find out about this under no circumstances. Not now, anyway, or there will be big trouble."

No one would find out from him, and he was relieved to see that she seemed to share the same opinion as he. Isabella quickly got dressed, took her horse and was lifted by him into the saddle. Then he also swung himself onto the back of his horse and rode ahead through the forest.

Chapter 17

Everything was still dark outside, but the new day was not far away, when Isabella gave up trying to find sleep. She therefore got dressed and quietly slipped down to the kitchen. Instead of staring at the ceiling or counting the stars in the night sky, as she had been doing for the last few hours, she might as well preheat the oven and prepare the dough for the daily bread. She needed a distraction, she had all night, thinking only of him.

But no matter how hard she tried to bring herself to other thoughts, she kept reviewing the memories of the last few hours. They had ridden silently side by side until they had arrived at the back door of the house. Isabella had hoped that he would kiss her again, but he had done nothing of the kind. She had not let her disappointment show when she had gotten off her horse. However, he had waited, until she had disappeared in the house, and then had taken her horse with him over to the barn. Thereupon she had tried for hours to find sleep, but the memory of the beautiful hours with him had not let her come to rest. What she had done was so wonderful and at the same time so reprehensible.

She had given herself to a man in a way that was reserved only for a husband. Shamelessly she had thrown all misgivings overboard and had paid a high price for it by forfeiting her innocence. But he would surely ask her to marry him and then everything would be all right and no one would need to know what she had done. But before she had even finished the sentence in her mind, doubts grew inside her.

Her father would never accept an Indian as her husband. And even if a miracle happened and he would do so, there would still be many others who would not. They would face hostility. Could they be so strong and fight against it? And what about herself? Could she imagine herself becoming the squaw of an Indian? Would Chágha tho be able to go native on a cattle ranch? Perhaps if her father got to know him better, he would like him after all.

"Good morning, Isabella. You are busy already." Louisa had stepped into the kitchen and jolted Isabella from her thoughts.

"Good morning, Louisa. I didn't sleep well and started early."

A little bit later after the breakfast, James announced:

"Father. Before you go out, I'd like to talk to you for a moment. Isabella? Please come with me over to the office too."

Isabella and William exchanged glances over the breakfast table, shrugged their shoulders and went together into the office, where James was already sitting at his desk, waiting for them.

"Please close the door behind you. I would like to tell you both something."

"Well, you're making it exciting. What is so important?"

"Please sit down."

William and Isabella complied with the request and looked eagerly at him. Her father seemed suddenly nervous, because it did not hold him in his chair. He walked over to the window and looked out as if the words he was about to say would be standing there. Isabella and her grandfather looked at each other anxiously. What could there be of such importance that he had called in a family council. At last he seemed to have found courage, because he turned around resolutely and announced, "What would you say if I told you that I had met a woman?"

"Well, I would be happy for you, my son."

"Me too, father. It's been so long since Mom died and I think you are still young enough to meet someone else. Who is it and what is her name?"

"Where and when did you meet her?"

"Her name is Marylou Higgins and she's been a widow for two years. I met her in Laramie about a year or so ago. She is a dressmaker there and has her own little store."

James paused so the other two could process what he had told them.

"Well, now, I'm not surprised that you always wanted to go alone the last few times. You are a real rascal, my son. You've an affair with her for a year and you don't tell anyone about it."

"Honestly, it's not a fling. Marylou and I, we love each other and I've asked her to marry me."

He looked expectantly into the two pairs of astonished eyes that looked at him.

"You want to get married again, Father? I thought I could take care of you. When....when were you planning to do so, and why didn't you tell us about her before?" Isabella was honestly surprised.

"Yes, this really is a surprise!"

James nervously ran his hand through his hair, then circled his desk and took a seat in his chair.

"I confess that I've always put it off, because I didn't know how to explain it to you. Marylou is a warm-hearted person and I have become fond of her during my visits over the past year. I am sure that you will like her too. I never thought that I would be lucky again to find a woman who loves me.

And I hope you can understand that. I would like to marry her as soon as possible, so she can come here and you can meet her."

"It's all a bit much at once, that I have to understand at my age, but you have my blessing, son." William stood up and held out his hand across the table. James also rose and came around the desk toward Isabella. When he stood in front of her and she looked up at him, he could see sadness in her eyes.

"Isabella, you're going to like her, and when she's with me, it will give you the freedom to take your future into your own hands. I was going to tell you later, when Marylou is here, but I can tell you right away, because I already got the answer I've been waiting for in Laramie. I will send you to Boston to friends. They have written to me that they're happy to accommodate you and also introduce you to society. You will have the opportunity to teach at a large Girls' School."

Isabella jumped in horror.

"You want me to go to Boston?"

"Yes, are you pleased?

"Father, you are sending me away? Why? Why should I go so far away from home? My place is here."

"But I always thought you wanted to teach at a huge school. In Boston you'd have the best opportunities to do so and you would attend big balls and maybe meet your husband."

"I'm not going to Boston. If I cannot stay here, I will go to Laramie and help the Reverend with his school."

"But Isabella, you are young, you should be attend glittering balls and have the opportunity to meet a young man who can one day take over this ranch. It will be yours one day, and even marriage will not change this. I have already discussed this with Marylou and you need the right man by your side."

"And I'm supposed to meet him in Boston? Some posh

dandy? No!"

Gradually, James lost patience with his daughter. How could she rebel against his will. He only wanted the best for her and would not allow her to go to Laramie to work for the Reverend. Laramie was still not the place for young single women. Even though the law had taken hold in Laramie and the new sheriff had everything pretty well under control, there were still occasional saloon brawls and shootings occurred.

"You will go to Boston, my lady, and this is my last word on the matter."

"I will not."

Enraged Isabella rushed out of the room. James angrily wanted to go after her, but his father held him back.

"Let her be. She'll calm down again."

"How dare she confront me like that? She will go to Boston whether she likes it or not."

"I told you right away that she would not take the decision so easily and honestly, I don't know if it's such a good idea either. Maybe you'll think it over again. In any case, I would let the topic to rest for a while. It's still a while until fall and you should first introduce us to your future wife."

When William left the room and James was alone, he had to admit to himself that the conversation had not gone well. He felt overwhelmed with the situation. His daughter was developing the same strong personality as her mother had and he wished she were here now to tell him what to do. He had always wanted Isabella to become a strong, self-confident woman, yet she was not allowed to rebel against him like that. He was her father and he knew what was good for her. She would go to Boston, whether she wanted to or not.

She certainly wouldn't go to Boston. What was she going to do in the big city. Here was her place. Here she wanted to stay. She loved the mountains, the open spaces, the country. Here she was free. The anger against her father had driven her out of the house.

She ran over to the pasture. Maybe she should grab one of the horses and go for a ride. So far, a ride had always helped when she had problems. When at full gallop, the wind whistled around her ears and her cheeks were rosy with cold, then she felt free. Annoyed, she trudged on, wiping a tear from her eyes with the right sleeve of her blouse which was not ladylike at all.

Why did he have the right to demand such a thing from her. Just because he was her father? What about her opinion and her feelings? Why did the men always decide what was good. Were women never allowed to have their own opinions and represent them?

"Whoops, young lady."

"Oh, Malcolm. Sorry, I didn't see you ."

"I noticed. What's got you so riled up?"

"Oh nothing, I just needed to get out of the house. Maybe I'll go for a ride."

"Yeah, you do that. That always helps me, too. But don't ride too far."

"I'll be careful."

Malcolm looked after her, still shaking his head, as she disappeared further toward the pasture.

She grabbed the first mare that was standing near the fence, saddled her up, mounted her and rode off at a wild gallop. Chágha tho, who was working at a distance with the black mustang, turned around at the sound of loud hooves. He could tell that Isabella seemed angry at something, because she was driving her horse violently. Whatever had her so upset, he hoped that their nocturnal get-together had nothing to do with it. Forward faster and faster she rode across the prairie.

The wind ruffled her hair. She breathed deeply in and out and noticed how gradually the anger disappeared. This was freedom. This was her world. The mountains, the vast prairie, the rides, the ranch.

She loved this life and couldn't imagine living in a big city. How did her father get the absurd idea to send her so far away from home? Everything she needed to learn, she could learn here. She didn't need one of those posh gentlemen who aren't used to working on a cattle ranch. By now she was old enough that she had definite ideas about how she wanted to live and since last night, she also knew which man she wanted to marry.

She would fight for both. There were still quite a few months until fall came and she hoped that she would be able to change her father's opinion.

When horse and rider had exhausted themselves, she reined in her mare and drove her up a small hill, where she stopped and dismounted. She let the horse graze and sat down on a small rock, from where she had a breathtaking view of the rugged mountains in the distance. The mountain peaks were still covered with snow and shone brightly against the blue spring sky.

In the valley in front of it, the cattle of her father grazed. Her heart opened at the sight and suddenly her sorrow and worries seemed to evaporate. This massive mountain world, made one feel so small and the land around it, rough and unforgiving. All of this was her life. Why couldn't her father understand that. He, himself, had been here all his life and she wanted the same.

Her decision was made. She would rebel against his decision if he still demanded her to go, but for now she would keep quiet. He wanted to marry again and she was curious about the new wife. She also didn't want to deprive herself of the anticipation of an upcoming wedding. There would be much to prepare for that beautiful day.

Isabella was just about to get up and be on her way home, when Carl emerged from the bushes behind her.

"Hi, Isabella. I saw you riding by and it looked like you might need some help."

Carl dismounted and came up to her.

"Hi, Carl. Thanks, but everything's fine. I was just heading back home."

She was about to mount her horse when Carl got in the way and grabbed her arm. Astonished, she looked first at his hand on her arm and then at him. Carl must have followed her gaze, because he immediately let go of her arm.

"It's a good thing that I'm meeting you here alone, because I wanted to discuss something with you."

"With me? What did you want to discuss with me?"

"Sit down."

He pointed to the rock where she had been sitting a moment ago. But something in Carl's voice she didn't like.

"Thank you, but I think I have to go home now. I've been gone way too long."

She made an effort to walk past him, when she was grabbed roughly and pushed back to the rock.

"I told you to sit down."

Horrified by his rudeness she settled down on the rock. What on earth had gotten into him. She had known Carl all her life, and he had always been a nice kindly worker, first to her grandfather and now to her father. But lately he seemed to have changed.

Isabella had heard the curses from him toward Chágha tho, and had heard about the story at the branding. So what did he want from her? In a now friendly tone he said to her:

" I'm sorry. I didn't mean to be rude, but I really need to talk to you."

He turned to her, took her hands in his and spoke:

"Isabella you have become a beautiful young woman and it is too dangerous for you to be out here alone. Something can happen too quickly, as you have experienced it yourself. You need someone to protect you, a man to watch over you."

Isabella was surprised. Was Carl proposing to her?

"Is this a marriage proposal?"

"Well, yes. You're of marriageable age and you need a man who can run the ranch one day. I know I'm not the youngest anymore, but I'm still man enough to give you children and make you happy."

Isabella was shocked by the frank words and did not know how to act. How did he come up with the absurd idea that she would want to marry him? The mere thought of her sharing a bed with Carl made her sick.

He looked quite passable for his age, and his tall, broad-shouldered figure was still toned and muscular. But his brown hair was already graying at the sides, and she knew that he was a few years older than her father. Under no circumstances would she ever become Carl's wife, but how was she to tell him this?

"Carl, I'm flattered that you're proposing to me, but I must confess that I can't answer that right now."

Carl took hope, squeezed her hands and replied, "oh, yes, of course I understand. Take some time to think about it and then we'll talk again."

"Yes."

Relieved to be able to escape the situation, she stood up and was about to turn to her horse when Carl jumped up with her and held her once again.

"Please Carl, let go of me. I have to go."

"Not until you have given me a kiss. Now that we're practically engaged, I'm entitled to one."

Angered by this insolence, she replied:

"We're not engaged, Carl. I haven't said yes, and that's why there's no kiss."

But Carl seemed to see it differently. He grabed Isabella with his arms and wanted to steal a kiss from her. Isabella, on the other hand, panicked and began to fight back. She tried to free herself from the embrace, but she was not strong enough against Carl's strong arms. Isabella tried to put both of her hands against his chest to keep him at a distance and turned her head to the side so that he could not kiss her.

"Carl, please don't, stop it."

"Now don't be so coy. Once we're married, you'll see what pleasures I can give you."

"No, stop it," Isabella shouted in his face, but Carl did not let go of her.

"The lady has said no, and I would let go of her if I were you."

The calm, yet deadly voice emerged from behind. Carl stopped abruptly and spun around. Over there, sitting on his horse, was Chágha tho aiming a rifle directly at Carl. Isabella breathed a sigh of relief. She freed herself from Carl's clutches and hurried over to her horse. Gratefully she gave Chágha tho a relieved look, but the Indian did not take his eyes off Carl.

Carl was carrying a revolver, and Chágha tho was certain that he would use the gun immediately if he got the chance.

"Get on your horse, Isabella, and ride home."

Without turning around, she lovingly did what Chágha tho ordered her to do and rode away. Carl was raging inside. Once again this bastard had won. How dare he interfere in his affairs.

"Mount your horse, ride in front of me and make no mistake. I'm not only good with a knife."

Gritting his teeth, Carl mounted his horse and rode ahead of Chágha tho back to the ranch. Right now it was not wise to defend himself against the Indian. He had all the trump cards in his hand, but his time for revenge would come and then God have mercy on him. He would send this red devil to the eternal hunting grounds.

Chapter 18

He had been there at the right moment. She did not want to know what would have happened if Chágha tho had not appeared. Maybe she should tell her father about the incident, he would surely confront Carl, but then she would also show her father that she was not yet adult enough to take her life into her own hands. But that was exactly what she did not want to do under any circumstances after this morning's confrontation. Isabella decided to keep the incident to herself and later to thank Chágha tho for his help. At the front gate of the ranch, Chágha tho let Carl run. He himself rode back to the ranch and went back to his own work. The black stallion was out in the pasture and raised his head when the Indian approached him. Chágha tho stopped and let the animal come toward him. The horse seemed to build more and more trust in him, so he waited until the animal put its head on his shoulder and was rewarded with a head massage from him.

The scene between Carl and Isabella was still on his mind. He had to keep a close eye on Carl. This man was capable of anything.

When the Indian had let Carl free at the gate, he too had returned to his workplace.

Carl was a little worried about whether Isabella would

tell her father about their conversation.

If she did, then he might get into trouble. He had to take the risk. If you didn't dare, you couldn't win, and after all, the ranch was at stake. Did the Indian have to show up, too? The next days would have to bring clarity about this and he also wanted to have an answer from Isabella.

A week had passed and everything had remained quiet. After the initial warm spring weather, May had shown a cold and wet face. The last days it had poured down and softened the earth. A cold front had brought additional hail and snow. The temperatures had fallen drastically close to zero and one hoped, that it was the last rebellion of winter. Humans, like animals, wanted to finally say good bye to winter.

The ranch residents had moved their work indoors and were back out in the pastures just this morning. While Chágha tho was getting back to work with the mustang and getting him used to a halter over the past week, Carl was out with the other cowboys to finish the branding. He thought about the matter of a week ago and was certain Isabella hadn't talked to her father about what happened. For whatever reason, for him it meant that he could plan further. But still he did not know quite how he could get rid of the Indian without running the risk of being punished himself.

To simply shoot him, as he would have preferred to do, would raise too many questions. He had to come up with something better. He was the obstacle that had to be overcome. Beyond it lay the path free to wealth and power, and he was sure that the solution was within reach.

The rider, with his collar turned up and his hat pulled down low on his face, approached the ranch. He was glad to be able to warm up a bit right away.

These cold days had it in itself. Normally he would be sitting at home with a warm fire, but he had come from the neighboring ranch and had a message to share. Just as he stopped in front of the main house, the door opened and the man he had come to speak stepped out.

"Charles, this is quite a surprise. To what do we owe the honor in this atrocious weather?"

"Hi, James. I came straight from the MacIntyres. You remember them, don't you? I did the wedding for the foreman over there."

„Yeah, how was it, but come on in and warm up first. I've got some good whiskey in the house, I'm sure your throat will be dry from that long ride."

"Oh, the lord will allow me a glass," he pointed upward with his finger, "and a cozy fire for the stiff limbs, I won't say no to that."

He dismounted and went with James into the house. James led him into the warm office, retrieved two glasses and a whiskey bottle from a small cupboard and poured them both. He handed a glass to the Reverend and indicated him to sit down. Charles took off his coat, threw it over the back of the chair and took a seat.

"So, tell me, what's the latest news?"

Charles took a sip, let the whiskey run down his throat, accepting the pleasant warmth that the alcohol spread through his body and set the glass down on James's desk.

"Really a good brand. Well, the wedding was nice. I don't know if you remember the foreman. His name is John Kendall, he is the youngest son of the blacksmith in Laramie. His wife Felicitas is a housemaid with the MacIntyres."

"How is the old lady?"

"Oh, she still has a firm grip on all the reins. She's having her summer party again this year and that's why I'm here. I'm supposed to present you with her invitation, and here it comes ..... the invitation is not only for your father, Isabella and for you, but you should also bring the Indian as well."

James almost choked on his whiskey, he was drinking.

"We're supposed to what?"

"She wants to see the Indian!"

"What makes her think that, and how does she even know about him? Oh, yes, you told her, of course."

"Yes, I told her the story, and she said that there has been nothing more exciting recently, that's why she wants to meet him. She asked me to make sure that you bring him along."

"How do you envision that Charles? We can't bring a savage to the feast."

"Well, you still have a little time, maybe you can make him a little more presentable before then. Besides, Lady Macintyre is no fool. After all, she knows he's an Indian."

"And has she ever seen any real Indians? I doubt it. Why, Charles, that's insane!"

"Well, that's the way she is."

Charles shrugged and took another sip from his glass.

"Whatever happened to you and Marylou now?"

"I'm glad you brought that up. At the next service you can marry us, and since you're already here, I can also give you a letter for her, so she can prepare herself."

"That's great. I'm happy for you. Are you sure she'll be able to prepare everything in less than two weeks? Women need a little longer than we do."

"She knows that it should happen as soon as possible and she is just waiting for my letter. The last time I was there, we already arranged everything else.

She will sell her finished dresses through Henry, the general storekeeper. Marylou plans to work from here on orders. So she will bring her fabrics and sewing machine with her. Her small carriage will stow everything she wants to bring. So the next time you come up to us, you will travel in nice company. Hopefully in better weather."

"Yes hopefully. Winter is holding off quite long this year."

"Stay for dinner. The women have cooked a hearty stew. Just a good meal in this weather."

Isabella stood at her window and looked out into the clear, cold night sky. A small crescent moon was visible, surrounded of thousands of small celestial bodies.

It would have been a breathtaking picture, if she had an eye for it tonight. But she was with her thoughts completely elsewhere. For over a week she had not seen him. The bad weather had forced her to spend almost all her time indoors. On school days, she had run between house and school so she wouldn't get wet.

The rest of the days she had cooked and sewed and had helped her father in the office.The subject of Boston had not been discussed between them since that day. It seems to her that both of them tried to leave the delicate subject alone. In all the days that followed, she had not seen Chágha tho again. She had not had the opportunity to thank him and that did not let her rest. With every day she became more and more restless.

At first she had convinced herself that the reason for it was the anticipation of the existing wedding of her father. Or was it the weather, what tugged at her nerves? Her gaze lay on the haystack, which was only an outline in the darkness. She could lie to herself as much as she wanted, but the real reason for her restlessness lay down there in the hay. Since the night at the river a desire grew in her, which became stronger every day. She dreamed at nights, that he was holding her in his arms again. That he would kiss her and do the things with her that made her body quiver. Just the thought of it made her feel warm all over. They were so close and yet so far away.

She wondered if he felt the same way. Was he also lying there now and thinking of her? If the weather hadn't thrown a wrench in her plans, then he would have been back at the river and she could have snuck away from here. She could just go over to him, but that was a bit too risky for her. With a heavy heart, she detached herself from the window and went to bed.

Chágha tho had been standing in the shade of the barn and let the cold wind blow around his nose. He missed his daily bath in the river, which had already become a ritual of his. But even more he missed Isabella. Since he had met her together with Carl at the hill, he had not seen her again. He had been busy with the Mustang, which had made great progress. The animal had allowed him to take him by the halter and he had managed to groom and brush him.

After initial displeasure, the mustang had quickly noticed that the brush strokes did him good. Now the black fur shone like velvet and showed the whole beauty of the animal. Anyone who now saw the mustang would not have thought that this was the same horse, which a week before had stood neglected in the paddock. From now on, the successes would come in larger steps, he was sure.

The mustang trusted him. During the day, the work with the animal helped him not to think about Isabella, but in the lonely nights he often lay awake. The hours at the river did not let him go.
Even now he knew how her skin felt under his fingers.

How soft her hair had been draped on the ground around her when he had made love to her. How she had trembled with arousal. The very idea of it made his desire for her immeasurable. He looked over to the house and directed his gaze to her room. His heart beat faster. There she stood. How beautiful she was.

He wished that he could once again turn back the clock to the night at the riverbank. Chágha tho wondered if he should make himself known to her. Just as he was about to step out of the shadows, she turned and disappeared. Disappointed, he pushed his breath out into the cool night and tried to get his troubled emotions back under control.

Chapter 19

The ranch was bustling with activity. After the weather of the last few days had improved considerably, the sun had come out and dried the ground out. The final preparations for the wedding of James and Marylou were at full speed. Tomorrow should be the big day and nervousness spread, because still not everything was ready. All residents had been busy for days to get the last work done. James had decided that the ranch should be presented in perfect condition to his new wife, and so the men had been given the task of tackling small repairs to the house and stables that had been long overdue.

The women were still plucking the weeds from the vegetable garden, arranging tables into a long buffet and selecting tablecloths and dishes. James had planned a barbecue for tomorrow and everyone was invited. After the temperatures had become pleasantly warm again, he had planned to set up the table behind the house on the lawn where everyone should find a place. For the physical well-being, Isabella would serve steaks, beans, potatoes, bread and quite a few casseroles.

After the meal, perhaps a few of the cowboys would play for the dance. He knew, that at least one of his people played a fiddle and two had a guitar. James was nervous. Soon his wife would be arriving and he hoped that everything would be perfect by then. He didn't know exactly why it was so important to him, but he wanted to create a beautiful home for her. Just then, for the second time, he went out to the veranda to see if his future wife was ready to be discovered when Isabella was about to sweep the veranda.

She had done everything the last few days to make the house shine. His daughter had washed windows and curtains, scrubbed floors. She had delegated and supervised the women's work and had worked out the list of dishes with Louisa. He was so proud of his beautiful daughter. She had developed into a perfect housewife and would make a good match in Boston. When Isabella saw her father, she stopped sweeping and smiled at him.

"Father she is not yet to be seen."

"Where do they stay. They should have been here by now."

"She'll come all right. It's not dark yet."

"Is everything ready so far?"

"We're in the final stages, but we'll definitely make it today. You can relax. It's going to be a beautiful day."

James walked up to his daughter, lovingly put his arm around her and kissed her forehead.

"And I have to thank you for that. You worked so hard this past week. I thank you for that."

"I want you to be happy. Don't worry, she will be here in time. But now I have to move on or I won't make it."

"Okay. Got it. I'm in the way."

Smirking, he went back inside. He still wanted to look through some of his business papers. A while later, Isabella caught sight of a carriage and a rider in the distance. Here they come. The Reverend and her new stepmother. She was nervous, for she hoped so much that they would get along. Oh, it would certainly be fine. She threw her doubts overboard and opened the front door. Then she called inside: "They're coming!"

James immediately hurried out of the house past Isabella. From upstairs her grandfather came down the stairs.

"Well, let's have a look at the new lady of the house, won't we Isabella?"

Her grandfather hooked himself under her arm and led her outside with him.

"Well, it won't be that bad."

He sensed the tension in his granddaughter and squeezed her hand reassuringly.

"No grandfather, I think so too,"

And so they both stepped out on the porch laughing and watching the carriage drive up. Immediately James rushed up to Marylou, lifted her from the carriage and kissed her passionately.

"Hey, we're not there yet. You have to be patient until tomorrow."

"Just look away, Charles."

But Marylou, who was embarrassed to have been kissed in front of the crowd, gave him a little peck in the side and mentioned, laughing:

" James Hunt you are incorrigible."

She smoothed out her light blue traveling suit, quickly adjusted the small hat, which matched the outfit and looked at James expectantly. He seemed to have eyes only for his bride and had forgotten the rest of the family members behind him. With a small clearing of his throat, William drew his attention to himself. Marylou walked around James, shook William's hand and introduced herself.

"Mr. Hunt I presume. I'm Marylou Higgins, and I'm very pleased to finally meet you."

William gallantly bowed his head and indicated a kiss on the hand.

"The pleasure is all mine, Mrs. Higgins. Now we know

why my son could not wait to marry you. If I were a few years younger, I'd be competing with him."

Marylou laughed out. "You're a real charmer, Mr. Hunt, and your son has already warned me about you, but please call me Marylou."

"So he did? Interesting, but please call me William. Anything else makes me terribly old."

"So now is the end of the banter. Marylou, may I introduce you to my daughter Isabella?"

James had meanwhile stepped next to his future wife and resumed his duties.

"Welcome, Mrs. Higgins."

Isabella extended a friendly hand to her future stepmother. Somehow she had imagined Marylou differently. Perhaps more like her mother looked, but this woman was the opposite of that. Her mother had been tall and had had dark blond hair. Marylou was a small petite woman with auburn hair, as she could see under her hat, and her brown eyes radiated a warmth that she found made her instantly sympathetic.

"I think we'll leave that right there. I am Marylou and it's a pleasure to meet you. I hope you can help me from tomorrow on to find my way around here. I haven't lived on a ranch before and I don't know my way around that well."

"I'll be glad to do that. But right now we should go inside and have some refreshments. I'll take care of the luggage in a minute."

The small group went into the house and Isabella called Thomas , who was riding past the house.

"Thomas, our guests have arrived. Would you please get someone to help and bring the luggage in the house?"

"Yes, will do in a moment. Miss Isabella."

"Thank you."

Inside the house, everyone had already made themselves comfortable and James had provided them with drinks. Isabella brought from the kitchen some baked cookies as the front door opened and Thomas came in with Chágha tho.

Both were laden with suitcases, cloth and other items that Marylou had brought with her. James ordered to put the things in the office first. As Chágha tho walked close to Isabella, their eyes met. But he said nothing and followed Thomas. Her heart began to beat and she feared that the others might notice her reaction. Quickly she looked around, but no one seemed to have noticed her. She handed the plate with the cookies around and was glad that she had turned her back on the two men behind her, when she heard Thomas voice:

"It's all in the office now, Boss."

"Okay, thanks."

When the two had left, Marylou commented:

"I didn't know you had an Indian here. Isn't that dangerous?"

"No, you can rest easy. Chágha tho is only with us for a while. He will not stay forever."

"I see."

Isabella's heart clenched at her father's words. She knew he was right, but the thought of it, that one day Chágha tho would leave, she felt quite sad. She did not want to lose him. Just the mere sight of him made her blood boil. When he had just passed her, she had immediately felt it again. This magical attraction, that seemed to exist between them. She had to try to see him again alone.

Chapter 20

Isabella did Marylou's hair. She looked beautiful in her beige muslin dress. It was sewn according to the latest cut of the Parisian fashion and it suited her perfectly. White lace lined the long sleeves and the high neck of the dress. Isabella had artfully pinned her chestnut hair up and had left a few small corkscrew curls at the sides. She paused and looked at her work.

"You look stunning. I have never seen such a pretty dress. It looks amazing. Father will have only eyes for you."

„Thank you Isabella."

She turned around and gave Isabella a radiant smile.

"If you ever get married, I'll make you a dress out of the most beautiful fabric we can find."

"You'd do that for me?"

"Why not ? Certainly I would. I think every woman should feel like a princess on such a special day and that definitely includes a pretty dress."

Isabella started to dream. Yes, that's how she wanted to get married one day. A beautiful dress, a church wedding, a glittering party and the man of her dreams.

"Come on, I don't think we should make the others wait any longer."

The day had been beautiful so far. The Reverend had performed a nice ceremony and the weather had cooperated. It was warm and sunny and a few small clouds in the sky had provided the necessary shade from time to time. The wedding guests had enjoyed a delicious meal and had a good time. They had joked, laughed and the newlyweds had taken congratulations from everybody. Everything had been perfect.

"Almost perfect," Isabella added in her mind.

For the man who would have made it the most beautiful day for her was missing. At the wedding ceremony she had seen him standing a little apart and had noticed that he had observed everything with interest. Later Malcolm had brought him to dinner.

Far away from her, he had sat at the lower end of the table and had felt noticeably uncomfortable. In the few moments when their eyes had crossed, she had seen a sadness in his eyes. She did not know why, but she suspected that this was the reason why he had disappeared as soon as he had an opportunity.

Isabella had wanted to talk to him, but so far she had been busy in the course of the day and had not yet had the opportunity to do so. Now that it was beginning to slow down and the cowboys were playing for the dance, would find the time. The party would not last long and then she could go to him. She had to take the chance today. Isabella searched the surroundings with her eyes, but no matter where she let her eyes roam, she could not see him anywhere.

Chágha tho had retired. He had observed the ceremony with curiosity and was surprised that the customs and manners of the whites were not so different from those of the Cheyenne. The whites exchanged, as a symbol of togetherness, rings. In the case of the Indians, the shaman tied the couple's hands with a richly embroidered leather band. The whites, as well as the Indians, ate together and danced around the fire.

And despite the common ground, it had become

clear to him today that he would never belong. He was and remained always the Indian, which one tolerated. But not more. His decision to leave the ranch had been made today at dinner. They had been nice to him, there was nothing else to say. Nevertheless, they kept him at a distance. They still didn't trust him, even though he had not given them any reason to the contrary.

Manitou was his witness that he had tried to fit in. He had learned their language, had done their work, had avoided trouble as best he could. And yet, they did not give him the trust he deserved. For this reason, he would leave and move on. His search was not over yet. While in thought, he had made his way to the black mustang, which he had named Black Storm. Now he sat on the wooden boards of the fence and organized his thoughts. When the mustang recognized him, he joyfully approached, but stopped inches in front of him, as if noticing the gloomy mood of his friend.

As if to cheer him up, he came closer and gently laid his head on Chágha tho's shoulder. The young man nestled his head against the warm neck of the horse, put his hands on the shiny coat and began a vigorous neck and head massage.

"You are like me. We both do not belong here, but you can change it. You have it in your own hands. I can help you, but I also need your help. Let me ride you and they will treat you well. They will love you and take good care for you."

When Malcolm came along the way, he had been able to observe the scene. Actually, he had wanted to talk to Chágha tho to encourage the young man to join the others. He had noticed that the Indian had something on his mind. Something was gnawing at him.

But when he saw the young warrior in intimate togetherness standing there with the horse, he did not want to destroy the moment.

This sight spoke volumes. In this moment, the Indian was one with the animal and the sadness of the young man spoke out of it.

So, this is where the guy hid almost every night. If he had found out earlier he could have put a bullet in him long ago. But today he sat together with Thomas at dinner and he mentioned that the Indian rode down to the river nearly every evening for a bath. Carl had to grin inwardly. The Indian could bathe as often as he wanted, he would always remain a dirty redskin. It had not at all suited him when Malcolm brought him to dinner. This man had become a real Indian friend and Carl felt he was betraying the people of the ranch.

If one day he owned the ranch, Malcolm would be the first to be fired. He needed people around him that he trusted. Or maybe he wouldn't have to wait so long. The plan he had come up with could still be changed and with that he could kill two birds at once. Carl almost slapped his thighs with glee when he realized just in time that although he was sitting in the bushes some distance from the Indian's campfire, the Indian could still hear him if he wasn't quiet enough.

Just as he wanted to sneak away, he heard someone coming. He ducked into the bushes and saw Isabella coming. She was riding past him not two feet away. What was she doing here, at this time?
Soon she would meet the Indian. Maybe he should sneak a little closer to see what was going on here.

"Isabella!" Chágha tho jumped up when he saw her coming. She heard his voice and her heart began to beat up to her throat with excitement. With long strides he came toward her, as she steered her horse toward the campfire. She had been so sure of coming here today, had been so anxious to see him alone, but now that she saw him and he was close to her, she was suddenly not so sure anymore. On the contrary, nervousness spread. He grabbed the reins of her horse and held it, then he turned his gaze on her. Something in his unbelievable blue eyes made her hesitate to dismount.

"I didn't think I'd see you here today," he said.

"It's been so long since we were last alone. I just wanted to come here today.."

She did make an effort to dismount, but Chágha tho put his hand on her thigh and stopped her. Irritated she gave him a questioning look. Did he not want her here, or why was he dismissive of her today?

"Isabella, I..."

"Don't you want me here?" she interrupted him. Chágha tho heard the disappointment in her voice and suddenly did not know how he should tell her that he was leaving.

"I wanted to...you don't understand."

"What don't I understand? I thought after our last meeting here, you might be happy to see me. Apparently I was wrong."

She stiffened in the saddle and was about to yank the reins, when she felt two strong hands at her waist, lifting her out of the saddle. Actually, she should have been annoyed, because just a moment ago he had given her the understanding that he did not want her here and now he was pulling her off the horse. Slowly, he let her feet slide to the ground, her back rubbing along his body. This touch was enough to send pleasant shivers through her body. When her feet touched the ground, she remained motionless. He enclosed her body with his arms and kissed her neck.

Isabella closed her eyes and let the feelings go, she put her head back on his shoulder so that he could have better access.

While he tenderly kissed her neck, his hand slid up and cupped her breast. Isabella drew in sharply, for all at once she felt hot. She felt his breath on her skin and could feel his growing arousal. His kisses became more passionate. Chágha tho inhaled the scent of her hair and caressed the sensitive spot on her earlobe. Isabella had the feeling of going insane. Her body began to tremble, she wanted to feel him, but not yet did he allow her to participate in this game.

On the contrary, he increased the intensity of his touch by bringing his other hand downwards and let it slide into her lap. Isabella moaned with pleasure and her desire for his touch grew. For a second he released her and that was enough for her to turn around and throw herself against his chest. She wrapped her arms around his neck and their mouths found each other.

The vehemence with which the passion between them broke through, surprised them both. Isabella forgot her shyness and restraint and pressed her body against his. She slipped her hands under his shirt and touched the warm skin. Chágha tho moaned a sigh of relief.

More courageous by his reaction, she lifted the shirt with both hands and pulled it over his head. For a moment, she stepped back to take in the sight of his muscular body. Then she tilted her head forward and touched his chest with her lips. His heart began to race as if it were about to burst. By Manitou, this woman was driving him crazy. What magic did she possess that one touch of her was enough to drive him mad so that he forgot everything.

She attracted him like light attracts a moth. He had intended to avoid her, not to let her magic touch him, but it had been pointless. For the last few weeks, he had wanted nothing more than to hold her in his arms, kiss her and love her. Now that she was here he couldn't wait to feel her. His hands fiddled with her blouse and uncovered her corsage. With a few movements he had pushed the blouse and corsage off her shoulders. At the sight of her firm breasts he had to swallow. She was so beautiful. Isabella had held her breath as he uncovered them, but now she pulled him back to her and kissed him passionately. Chágha tho lifted her up in his arms and carried her over to the fire where he placed her on the blanket where he had been sitting before.

Isabella could not wait. She unbuttoned her skirt with trembling hands and let it slide to the floor, then she laid down on the blanket and invited Chágha tho to join her. He quickly stripped his leggins off before he covered her body with kisses. In a frenzy of passion, their bodies moved.

Their hands touched the most sensitive places and gave each of them wonderful moments. Here and then the world around them could have collapsed, they would not have noticed it. They had eyes only for themselves and did not notice, that a pair of eyes was following their lovemaking.

Carl could not believe his eyes and thought what a lucky twist of fate it was that he had come here tonight. He was witnessing this secret meeting. At the sight of the two naked bodies, who gave each other love, his own excitement rose immeasurably.

His body reacted to the erotic images he was watching and realized how he became hard. He imagined how he would lie there with Isabella, and how she would give him relief. It has been a hell of a long time since he had one of the saloon girls in Laramie.

What a lying little whore Isabella had been. She had denied him a kiss with her virginal chastity and for this bastard she spread her legs. Carl's arousal rose in rage and vindictiveness. He drew his revolver and pointed it directly at Chágha tho's head. His trigger finger twitched. All he had to do was pull the trigger and the son of a bitch would be in the afterlife. But then he would never know who had put him there, and Carl didn't want that. He wanted the Indian to suffer immeasurable agony and that he knew exactly who he had to thank for his death.

And after that, he would take care of Isabella. He would show her that a white man was a better lover. But first she would have to learn obedience to him. Carl put his revolver back in his holster with a satisfied grin. His plan had been incomplete until tonight, but now the redskin had supplied him with the missing part himself. There was nothing more in the way. Tonight the bastard had once again escaped with his life, nor would he know how close he had been to death.

But it was only a postponement. His days were numbered. Carl was already looking forward to the day when soon Isabella would share his bed. Cautiously, Carl tried to move away. No noise was allowed to reach the ears of the two, otherwise they would be warned. However, he doubted whether they would hear a buffalo herd at the moment. They were much too busy with themselves. Isabella quivered with desire.

Chágha tho gave indescribable pleasures to her, and so she climbed the peak of pleasure. She reared up. Her body jerked under him as she cried out his name and found her fulfillment. Before Chágha tho surrendered to the climax, he withdrew from her at the last moment to prevent his semen to pour into her. Happy and exhausted they remained lying closely embraced.
Dreamily Isabella let her hands glide over his chest.

She was happy. Here she lay with the man she loved. Had she really said love? Yes, she loved him, she never wanted to be without him again. For her, everything felt so good, so absolutely right. But she would not reveal her feelings to him.
Isabella wanted to know first if he felt the same way.

But that still had time. Here and now she did not want to think about it, she just wanted to feel this incredible magic and so she realized how the desire for him was still far from being sated. Once again, the power took over her body and she was ashamed that she couldn't seem to get enough of him. Chágha tho propped himself up sideways and looked lovingly into her eyes.

For this look from him she would do anything. Tenderly he caressed her face, kissed her mouth passionately and pulled her on top of him. She felt his hard body underneath her and saw the rising desire for her in his eyes.

"Sit on top of me, take me inside you and ride me."

Shocked by this idea, she began to move tentatively. But when she enclosed him tightly and started moving she felt the intensity in her own body. The growing ecstasy drove her forward. She moved faster and faster until the feelings in her seemed to explode. At the climax, she called his name and felt his muscles tense up, his arms held her tightly and he too called her name. Satisfied and fulfilled she lay on top of him. Chágha tho wrapped the blanket around both of them to keep them warm. Their hearts were still racing at a wild pace, until they finally calmed down and fell asleep exhausted.

When Isabella awoke, she no longer lay on top of him. Chágha tho held her tightly in his arms. The fire was still burning and gave them a warmth in the cool night. It was a wonderful feeling of security. Isabella took a look at him. He had closed his eyes and his facial features were relaxed. How good he looked.

"Are you asleep?"

"Mmh."

"I wanted to tell you something else, which was actually the reason I came."

Chágha tho opened his eyes and was nowhere near as sleepy as he had probably pretended to be. With watchful eyes he looked at her.

"Actually, I wanted to thank you for rescuing me from Carl the other day. I don't know what would have happened if you hadn't shown up. Why were you there, anyway?"

Now he sat up, pulled Isabella close to his side and spread the blanket around her again for protection.

"I had seen how angrily you rode off and I was worried that maybe I was the reason for it. When I saw you sitting on the rock I knew that you wanted to be alone and I was about to leave when I saw Carl coming. That's when I stayed."

"Thank you." She grabbed his hand and squeezed it tightly. For a while they sat in silence together.

"Isabella."

He had to tell her now, but somehow it was incredibly difficult for him to say the words.

"Yes?"

He took both her hands in his and held them tightly. How could he possibly tell her?

"What is it? What's wrong?"

"Watch out for Carl. I don't trust him and I won't be there next time."

"What do you mean?"

She looked up at him and fear spread. The love and the warmth of a moment ago had disappeared in his eyes and made way for something new. She could feel that sadness again that she had already seen in him in the afternoon.

"Chágha tho, what do you mean?"

"I will go."

"No!" horrified, she snatched her hands from him and drew back.

"Why do you want to go? I thought you and I..."

"I know what you were thinking, but it can't be."

"Why not? I don't understand. This here, doesn't mean anything to you?"

"Yes, it does, and precisely because it does, I'm leaving." He turned to her.

"I made a big mistake, when I came here. I thought that if I tried hard to fit in, that I would be able to. But it is not so."

"I don't understand what you are trying to tell me."

There are no problems after all. Isabella got up and dressed. She did not understand what he wanted to tell her. Had she done something wrong? She had to try to change his mind. When she had finished and turned around, Chágha tho had also dressed. He stood a few steps away from her and looked lost. She walked toward him, took his face in her hands and said, "We can overcome all problems together."

He took her hands from his face, backed away to keep the necessary distance he needed now.

"We can't, Isabella. That is a misconception. Before I came here, I thought that too, but it's not true. I've been trying to become one of you. I have learned the language, I have cooperated, I have allowed myself to be insulted and attacked. All this hasn't helped, because they still don't trust me."

"That's not true. They like you."

"No! - They tolerate me. But only because they know I won't stay forever. Because they know that I'm a guest and your father told them to be nice to me. If they had the courage, they'd scream their disapproval in my face the way Carl does."

"That's not true. I never treated you badly, and neither did Malcolm."

"That's right. You two are the only people who have been good to me from the beginning, but that's not enough. Don't you understand Isabella. I can do what I want. They'll never see me for the man I am, but only the Indian that I am by birth, and I can't change that. I realized that this afternoon and that's why it's better if I move on."

"We could go together. Somewhere where nobody knows us."

"And what good would that do? There would be hostility there, too. People would despise you for being with a savage. You belong here. This is your life here. The ranch, your family. I could never give you the life you have here. That which I have, I wear on my body. But one day you will own this ranch and for that you need a man who can help you and who is accepted by the others. Something I can't give you."

Isabella fled into his arms.

"Then let's go to your people. I don't need this ranch. I need you, please."

Tenderly, he stroked her hair with his hands.

"Oh, Isabella. I wish I were one of you, but I'm not. I can't take you with me to my people. Life there is so much different than what you're used to. It is hard and full of deprivation. The women are different. You would go to ruin and I would never want to do that to you. Believe me, I wish I could change something."

Isabella felt her eyes begin to burn. She tried to hold back the tears, but she couldn't. She did not succeed.

"Don't cry. Even though you may not understand, one day you will be grateful that I left. You will have a husband you love and a family and you'll forget all about me."

"No! No. I will never forget you. Chágha tho, please don't do this to me."

The tears in her eyes tore at his heart, but he knew that if he did not stand firm for them both now, he would lose the courage to leave.

"My mind is made up, Isabella."

Desparate for what more she could do, she heard herself ask, "When?"

"As soon as I ride the mustang. I told your father that I would try to ride him, and I'm a man of my word."

"Are you going to say goodbye to me? Or will your seat be empty one day?"

"You'll know when I leave. That I promise."

"Thank you."

Without another word, she walked with drooping shoulders to her horse.

"Wait I'll take you home."

"No! I'll ride alone."

She would not have been able to bear ride back beside him now. She wanted to get back as fast as she could and crawl into her room. He let her and when she left the camp, her tears flowed in streams.

Chágha tho, however, remained sitting for a while by the fire. He had told her that she should forget him, that she should be with another man. He knew that he had done the right thing, but why did he feel like he had betrayed himself? He loved this woman, and because he loved her, he set her free. He knew that he would never forget her.

Chapter 21

Isabella spent the rest of the night crying in her room. Now her head ached and her eyes were burning. With cold water she had tried to remove the marks on her face but she had not succeeded properly. Louisa had looked at her worriedly when she had come into the kitchen that morning. Isabella had used the excuse that she wasn't feeling well and was probably getting a cold.

She had gone back to the kitchen right after breakfast. It was necessary to somehow pull herself together, but it seemed to be too much for her today. When her father and Marylou had appeared for dinner, she would have liked to flee immediately.

Today she could not stand to see both of them beaming happily and in love together. It reminded her too much that this happiness would be denied to her and that made her heart so heavy. And something else had been different this morning. Carl had looked at her so strangely that she had become afraid. Chágha tho had warned her against him and probably he was right. Something in Carl's look made her shiver.

The weather had adapted to their mood. The day after had started overcast, the sky had turned black around noon and its floodgates opened . Masses of water fell from the sky and drenched the ground. Chágha tho cursed inwardly. He could not use this weather now. For his plans he needed dry ground. It would be much too dangerous to ride the mustang if the ground was wet and slippery. So he was inevitably doomed to stay a little longer on the ranch, although he couldn't stand it any longer at the moment. Since his decision to leave was made yesterday, he did not want to stay a minute longer than necessary. He did not trust himself and his feelings towards Isabella.

The longer he would stay here, the more danger there was that his decision could waver and he wanted to prevent that. He did not want to make it harder than it already was. He looked up to the sky. Today he would not be able to do anything.

Two days later, the time had finally come. The sun had been merciful to him and dried the ground to such an extent that he could dare to ride. He was just on his way to Black Storm when Malcolm came along.

"It's a good thing I see you. I need your help."

"What is it, Chágha tho?"

"I want to ride the mustang out at a gallop. For that I need someone to open the gate at the right moment.

"Do you think he is ready?"

"I'm not sure, but it's time to find out."

Malcolm looked down at the things Chágha tho held in his hands, and pointed.

"Are you going to break him in like that?"

"Yes. I have a better feeling when I sit on him without a saddle."

"Boy, are you tired of living? The satan's brat will throw you off and you'll break your neck."

"We'll see about that in a minute. I know it is a risk, but it has to happen sometime, why not today?"

Chágha tho opened the gate, walked through, and then closed it again.

"When I call "Now", you open the gate as fast and as far as you can to let me through."

"Okay, but I don't think that's a good idea."
"Just do it."

Malcolm watched, shaking his head, as Chágha tho laid the blanket he had brought with him on the ground, holding the halter in one hand and then walked slowly toward the mustang. The animal came peacefully toward him. He addressed it softly, rubbed his neck and head and slowly put the halter over his neck and ears. Malcolm still couldn't believe it.

The mustang let everything happen to him calmly. The Indian had actually been able to build up trust with the horse in the last few weeks, something that no one had ever been able to do before. Just as Chágha tho was about to pick up the blanket, James came along.
"Hi Malcolm, what's he up to?"
James pointed with his head in the direction of the Indian.
"He wants to ride him and wants me to open the gate for him."

"That's way too risky, if he's out there with the animal instead of here in the pen something else can happen."
"Don't bother, I've already tried to talk him out of it. He's determined."

Both men were standing by the fence and watched the Indian's handiwork. The latter carefully put the blanket on the horse's back. He had been teaching the animal for days. Then he took the reins of the riding halter loosely in the hand and reached into the mane of the horse. With a nimble and powerful movement he swung on the back of the animal, which immediately began to buck wildly under the weight of the rider. Chágha tho squeezed his thighs together and tried to sit out the first humps easily.

The mustang made wild capers and the two men on the other side were frightened but Chágha tho held his ground well. Malcolm prepared himself to open the gate at any moment. "Now," Chágha tho shouted. Malcolm pulled the gate open with a powerful jerk. Chágha tho heeled his heels into the mustang's belly, loosened the reins and gave him the opportunity to gallop forward. At a furious pace the animal shot past the men with the Indian on top and dashed away across the prairie.

"I wouldn't have given that boy a minute on that horse. That's incredible."

"Let's hope he holds out. The mustang is powerful, and it's a matter of finding the stronger of the two."

Isabella had witnessed the scene by chance from the porch of the house and at that moment had painfully known that Chágha tho was right. She had realized that the horse and the rider formed a unity as she had never seen before with another rider.

For not a second had she doubted that Chágha tho would have any difficulty riding the animal. He had a gift to deal with these creatures, that was clearly out of the norm. When she saw him on the horse with hair blowing, determined and with a highly concentrated face, she knew it. This man needed his freedom, like others need air to breathe. He had given the mustang a part of his freedom again, in which he let him now run. It would give freedom to Chágha tho by letting him go, as difficult as this will be for her.

At that moment, she had seen more of the Indian in him than he was even aware of. Despite this realization, her heart was heavy. That he rode the mustang today meant that he would leave tomorrow. Tonight he would be here on the ranch for the last time. She wished so much that the morning would never come.

His thighs were on fire. The animal had an enormous endurance. At murderous speed it shot across the prairie, covered mile after mile and showed no signs of fatigue. Concentrated muscle power propelled it forward and Chágha tho tried to keep himself on his back. Gradually he felt his strength begin to wane, but he could not afford to be weak here and now.

The Mustang would immediately exploit it. Slowly, he tried to shorten the reins. The first attempt the animal still acknowledged with a wild jerk of the neck, but the more often he tried, the more the resistance of the animal finally weakened and it slowed down the pace. He reined it in, let it leisurely trot and could finally bring it to a walk. As a reward he patted the animal on the neck and whispered soothing Indian words in his ear. It was a magnificent horse. Powerful, persevering and supple were the attributes that distinguished the animal. The silky black coat shone now wet from the exertion, yet the animal was still attentive and listened to his words. After man and animal had caught their breath and came to rest, Chágha tho turned and steered the mustang back towards the ranch.

"This was truly a master stroke. We were about to send a search party after you to collect your bones. I never thought you could do it."

James and Malcolm slapped the young Indian's shoulders appreciatively, then they left him alone.

Chágha tho, however, took care of the animal, sat on the fence and watched the beautiful stallion drink. He had made it and that meant his stay here was over. Tomorrow he would leave the ranch and get back to his own mission. He had neglected his own task for far too long.

Chapter 22

He didn't need to turn around to know who was coming, he knew it was Isabella. He recognized her by how she moved and how she had opened the barn door. Without turning around, he continued to groom his horse that he wanted to have near him tonight, since he wanted to leave at dawn.

Isabella approached him without a word. He felt her closeness at once, for his heart began to beat wildly. She nestled against his back and put her arms around him. Immediately he stopped his work.

"I just had to see you again. I couldn't help it."

He was silent for a while, took a deep breath and released her hands from his body.

"You're not making this any easier."

"I know, but in the last few days it's been driving me out of my mind knowing you were so close to me and yet so far away. You're leaving tomorrow, aren't you?"

"Yes, and it would have been better if you had not come, because the longer you stay, the less I have the strength to leave."

"Then stay, please! No one is sending you away," she begged him, taking his face in her hands.

"Isabella, it would only be a delay. I know it and so do you. Let's not make it any harder."

"Kiss me one last time. Give me something to think

about, please."

By Manitou, how could he resist that look, that desperation in her eyes? His mind said he should send her away, but his heart spoke a very different language. He knew that if he kissed her now, he would want more from her and it would be even harder for him to turn his back on this place tomorrow.

Nevertheless, he ignored the warnings in his head, pulled her to him and kissed her passionately. She clung to him like a drowning woman, sucked in the scent of his skin and returned his kisses with full devotion. When he took her in his arms and carried her to the straw, they made love for the last hours they had left.

At some point during the night, Chágha tho woke up. Something had caught his attention.

He sat up and listened into the darkness. His horse was snorting excitedly. The animal had also heard it, but what had it been? Now everything was quiet. He carefully touched Isabella, who was lying asleep in the straw.

"Isabella, wake up."

"What is it? Is it morning already?" she asked sleepily.

"No, but something is wrong. Listen! There is a crackling sound."

Isabella heard it too and sat up abruptly.

"I'll take a look, and you'd better get dressed, who knows what's going on."

He pulled the leggings on and reached for his shirt when he was almost at the door and opened it.

It was quite clear now. The crackling sound became louder and he smelled the smoke.

"Isabella, there's a fire! Malcolm's cabin is on fire! Run and wake the others!"

With these words he had already run out of the barn and rushed over to the burning block house. Isabella grabbed her blouse and ran over to the main building.

173

"Fire! Fire! Quick we have to put it out! Help! Fire!"

She had just reached the main house when the door was ripped open and her father appeared, dressed only in pants. His gaze immediately fell on the burning hut, then he ran and called to her.

"Get the buckets!"

From everywhere the startled residents came running from their cabins. Armed with buckets, they immediately formed two lines, fetching water from the well to extinguish the fire. James backed away.

The heat was enormous. The fire was already out of control only the entrance and the left rear side were from the outside not yet affected. The flames were shooting high through the roof and he reckoned that the whole structure could collapse at any moment. Just at that moment, Chágha tho came out of the burning house with the lifeless body of Malcolm on his arm. James came to his aid and together they carried him away from the house. Isabella, Marylou, and William came running and examined him.

"I think he's just unconscious," said Marylou to the others.

"What about Louisa? Where is Louisa?" cried Isabella excitedly. Nowhere could she find Malcolm's wife.

"Father, have you seen Louisa? Has she come out?"

"No, I haven't."

"My God, she's probably still in there. We have to save her."

Isabella was about to run toward the burning house when her father held her back.

"You can't go in there now. It's all about to collapse. I'm sorry."

"Noooo! Father we must save them all."

Chágha tho, looking over at the house, took off his shirt, ran over to the water trough and dipped it into the water.

Then he took the soaking wet shirt, threw it over

his head and shoulders, and stormed over to the house.

"Chágha tho, don't. It's too dangerous," he heard someone shouting behind him, but he took little notice of it. He ran around the house found a window at the back, which he broke with a stone lying on the ground.

He climbed through the window into the house. Inside there was a murderous heat that cut off his air. The smoke was thick and he could hardly see anything through the flames.

Where could she be? This was the only room where the flames had not yet reached, but they ate closer and closer. He had to hurry, he would not be able to stand the heat and the smoke for long.

Chágha tho noticed how the shirt on his back began to get hot. Suddenly he bumped his leg on a wooden post, in the middle of the room. With his hands he felt his way and realized that it was a bed that he had bumped into. He quickly searched the surface with his hands and breathed a sigh of relief when he found a lifeless body on the bed. He quickly tore his shirt from his back, which was about to sink into his skin and reached for Louisa. He shouldered her with an ease and crawled out of the window into the night.

When the others caught sight of him, they came running and took the burden from him.

"She's still alive! Thank God."

"Get them both inside and take care of them,," James shouted to a couple of his men who followed William and Marylou into the house. Isabella rushed to Chágha tho, who was sitting on the floor coughing. His body and the rest of his clothes were blackened by soot.

"You saved her, thank you." She put her hand on his arm and looked deep into his eyes.

" Are you all right?"

He nodded, unable to answer because of a coughing fit. While the cowboys continued to try to put out the fire,

James approached them. His daughter rose and James reached out to the Indian a hand for the first time.

He grabbed it and was pulled to his feet by Isabella's father.

"Thank you. Without you, they probably wouldn't have gotten out in time. That was very brave."

"Don't be so hasty, boss. Maybe we should ask him why he was first on the scene of the fire."

Carl came out of the darkness toward the three of them and held something hidden behind his back.

"What do you mean Carl?"

"Well, it is quite strange that the hut is on fire at all. There was no thunderstorm, so it stands to reason that it was helped along."

Chágha tho's eyes narrowed. The alarm bells were ringing in his head. Carl was up to something. The guy was just too sure of himself.

"Carl, if you have something to say, say it and don't talk in riddles."

"I mean to say that he," he pointed his finger at Chágha tho," was only here so quickly, because he set fire to the hut himself and was therefore already on the spot."

Angry and horrified, Isabella glared at Carl. But before she could say anything in reply, she heard her father say:" That is a heavy accusation. Do you have any proof of that?"

"Yes. Here."

He took out from behind his back two almost burnt arrows. The color drained from Isabella's face, how could Carl spread such a lie? James looked the Indian in the face and asked him reproachfully, "Are these your arrows?"

"Yes," answered Chágha tho truthfully. "But I didn't do it."

Carl stormed forward. "You rotten liar. Here is the evidence that you set the cabin on fire. Hey guys, seize him! He tried to kill Malcolm!"

Immediately, a couple of the cowboys came running and arrested Chágha tho, who tried to defend himself but could do nothing against the growing number of men.

"Father this is a lie. He didn't do it."

"You stay out of it, this is men's business."

James replied angrily and turned to Chágha tho whom four men were now holding down and had pulled his arms behind his back. Carl tried to stir up the atmosphere a bit more by confronting James and said:"I warned you right away. I told you on the first day that you can't trust these red dogs . They are murderers and this one is no exception. We can only hope that it was not too late for Malcolm and his wife."

"And why should Chágha tho set fire to the hut himself, if he saved them? That doesn't make any sense, does it? Do you have an answer to that, Carl? You seem to have the best overview anyway."

Isabella was raging with anger. Why did Carl tell such a lie. Her father stopped her and turned to the Indian, whose eyes looked at him belligerently.

"Have you anything to say in your defense?"

"I didn't do it."

"But these are your arrows. Confess."

"I can't confess to something I haven't done."

"Open your mouth, you pig."

Carl drew his revolver and pointed it at Chágha tho. Horrified, Isabella stood protectively in front of him.

"Father, he didn't do it. I know it."

"Go into the house Isabella and leave us here alone."

"No, I know he couldn't have done it because..."

"Don't, Isabella. Don't do it."

She turned to Chágha tho, who shook his head and whispered, "Don't."

"Yes, I will tell him."

"What's the game here, Isabella?"

She walked toward her father. What she had to say was not going to be easy.

"Father, it couldn't have been him, because...I was with him."

James thought he had misheard.

"What did you say?" he repeated in a dangerously calm tone.

"I said I was with him. All night and that's why he couldn't have done it."

James was stunned by what he had heard and his anger was mounting. Furious, he punched his daughter so hard in the face that she went down. Chágha tho wanted to lunge at James and tried to break away, but he was held in check by the four men. Slowly Isabella got up again. She put her hand to her aching cheek and no longer recognized her father.

Never in her life had he hit her. Horrified by what had just happened, she stood in front of her father and let the harsh words come over her.

"You behaved like a whore. How could you do this to me."

"Father please. You can be angry with me, but he didn't do it.

"Get out of my sight."

He turned to face the prisoner. Seething with rage, he shouted at him.

"You will pay for this. Tie him to the stake over there and bring me a whip."

"Father, no! You can't do that. He is innocent."

Isabella had thrown herself at her father's feet and pleaded with him.

"Get out of my sight!"

He called for a few women who had been watching the scene from a distance.

"Get her out of my sight. Lock her in her room."

"No, you can't do that to me."

"You'll see what I can do to you. Take her away before I forget myself."

One of the women helped Isabella to her feet.

"Come along, it's better this way for now."

Three women pulled the weeping Isabella away and brought her into the house. The four men, one of whom was Carl, had Chágha tho tied to a pole in such a way that his back was exposed. His hands had been lashed above his head, so that he could no longer move.

While the three others stepped back from the prisoner and one of them fetched the whip, Carl stood close to Chágha tho and spat the words at him in such a way that only he could hear them.

"Finally I have you where you belong. It was so easy. All I had to do was just place a few arrows in the right place and you'll get what you deserve. When the boss is done with you, the sheriff will take care of you and then you will dangle. Dangle from the gallows. Ha, you dirty Injun. You'll finally be sent to the eternal hunting grounds and I will spit on you when the time comes. The agony you will have to suffer and I do not need to get my hands dirty. But the best thing is that I will take care of Isabella. It will be my hands that will soon glide over her breast and then she will spread her legs for me."

Chágha tho seethed with anger. He jerked his hands to get them free, but the shackles only cut deeper into his skin and slit it open. Blood gushed out. He could have strangled Carl with his bare hands or brake his neck.

"I'll kill you, I swear!" he hissed. "I'll rip your heart out alive! If you so much as touch a hair on her head, my revenge will be terrible."

Grinning maliciously, Carl laughed in his face.

"Ha, ha. That's what I'm afraid of now. You seem to misjudge your situation. It's not me that's getting clobbered, it's you."

"Carl step back!" yelled James, who was holding the whip in his hand. Chágha tho inwardly braced himself for the pain that was about to come. He tensed his muscles, closed his eyes, clenched his teeth and waited for the first blow.

It came immediately and hit him with full force. His body jerked from the pain that flowed through his body, but a sound did not pass his lips. James cracked the whip over and over again on the Indian's back. With all his might, he cracked the leather whip and watched as it left one bloody welt after another on the Indian's back. Chágha tho heard the crack of the whip, felt the leather rod strike him and tear his back to shreds.

His blood ran warmly down his back. The pain was immense, but still no sound came from his lips. He had the feeling that he was going black before his eyes. James however, was in a blood frenzy. The blows became firmer and firmer but the red dog did not scream in pain. Carl watched the scene with great pleasure. Yes, the boss would beat him to death. The agony had to be great for the son of a bitch and it would be interesting to see when the dog finally started to whine.

When the three women brought the upset and crying Isabella into the house, she saw Marylou and her grandfather taking care of Malcolm and Louisa. Both were lying on the long dining table and had not yet regained consciousness.

"What's going on?" asked William of the women as they were walking past him with his distraught granddaughter.

"Mr. Hunt, your son has ordered us, to lock up Isabella in her room."

"He did what? For what?" William and Marylou looked at each other and could hardly wait for the answer.

"We don't know the reason exactly."

"Isabella, what's wrong?" William addressed the words to her. But she did not seem to have realized that she was facing her grandfather. He shook her lightly by the shoulders.

"Isabella? What's wrong?"

"Oh grandfather, please you have to save him. He beats him to death."

"Who is beating who to death?"

"Father is beating Chágha tho to death because I spent the night with him. Please tell him to stop, please."

"Take her upstairs. I'll take care of it."

Marylou was just as horrified as the other women, at what she had heard. William hurried out and saw the ghostly scene before him. His son stood surrounded by cowboys, who were lighting the place with torches, and he was thundering at the Indian. When he came closer and was able to grasp the situation accurately, he first looked over to the prisoner, whose skin on his back was barely visible from the blood, and then to his son, who was swinging the whip like a madman.

"Stop it James!", he shouted energetically at his son but he did not respond to the words.

"I said stop it right now." He grabbed his son's arm just as he was about to lash out again and lunged and snatched the whip from him.

"Give it to me. I'm not done with him."

"I think you are. You're beating him to death. Untie him and take him to his camp. Tie him up there so he can't escape. And you come with me to the house and calm down."

"You want me to calm down? The bastard has taken advantage of Isabella and he deserves to die. And he took the risk that two people would die there. For that he will dangle."

"If he's guilty of that, the sheriff will sort it out. You've had enough for tonight."

He pushed his son in front of him. Before they could enter the house, one of their men approached them.

"Boss, we've got the fire out."

James looked over at Malcolm's house and saw the last of the smoke rising. It was beginning to dawn outside and soon the sun would rise. What kind of night.

"Oh Parker?"

"Yeah boss."

"Grab Ed and ride on down to Laramie as fast as you can and bring the sheriff here, and you'd better bring the Reverend along with you too. Who knows if we're not going to need him as well."

"Will do. We'll be on our way."

"What's the reverend doing here? Nobody's died yet!"

"That may change in time. You excuse me, Father, I have another conversation to have."

"Maybe you should calm down before you talk to your daughter."

"I don't want to calm down, though. She's going to have to live with the consequences of her actions."

"What are you going to do? You're not going to do violence to her. I'm not going to let you do that. I don't recognize my own son."

"You can calm down, I will not do violence to her."

With these words he left his father and hurried into the house. He took a quick look at his wife and the two unconscious bodies in his living room and stamped up the stairs.

Isabella was desperate. What could she do? She tried to get the door open, but it was locked from the outside. Just as her father had ordered. She was the prisoner of her own room. What had she done? With her confession she had wanted to save him and had only made it worse. Somehow she had to get out of this room and try to save what there was left to save. Just as she went to the window to see if she could dare climb out of there, she heard angry footsteps coming up the stairs from below. She turned around at the moment the door was pulled open and her father entered.

"I wouldn't try that if you don't want to break your neck. Besides, I'll post one of the men downstairs, so you don't get the wrong idea. You will remain in this room until I figure out the punishment for you. How could you do this to me? My own daughter is whoring around. How many of my men sit at my dinner table every day and laugh in my face because I have no idea that my daughter is ready to share camp with them? I wanted to send you to Boston to the best families in the country. None of them will take you now."

"Father, you don't understand. I..."

"Silence! I've heard enough from you today. I'll think about what to do with you and until then you'll stay in here, because I can't bear the sight of you right now."

James turned away and left the room. Before Isabella could react, she heard the key turned in the lock and the footsteps move away. She was horrified at what her father had said to her. He thought she was an easy girl. How could he think that of her? Hadn't he always told her that she was his sunshine? What was wrong with being together with the man you loved? Chágha tho - She didn't even know how he was doing now. After her father still had such a rage against her, she feared that his revenge against him was terrible. She absolutely had to find out something about his whereabouts.

But how should she do that? She was trapped here. She went to the window and looked down. Her father had kept his word. Under her window was already one of his cowboys. Despairing of her situation, she sank to the floor and buried her head between her knees.

The tears that she held back until now flowed in streams. Her father would punish her, but whatever her punishment would be, she had to find a way to help Chágha tho escape. Once the sheriff arrived, it was too late. And once again she had to realize that Chágha tho had been right when he said Carl was not to be trusted. He had rescued Malcolm and his wife from the flames. Had risked his own life and it had only taken Carl and his lie to make her father believe the worst.

Innocent, they would bring him to the gallows if he could not escape and she had to prevent that somehow. Isabella sighed and tried to wipe away her tears with her hand. Her cheek was still hot from the blow. Tonight she had met a side of her father that she had never seen before. This rough, brutal and unyielding way frightened her. But no matter how awful her punishment would be, she would endure it, if she knew that Chágha tho had his freedom. Yesterday her world had been fine, but now it was in shambles.

Chapter 23

The sun was already high and shone on the dramatic scene of the previous night. Malcolm's house was only a ruin. The fire had destroyed almost the entire cabin. Only the back part with the room in which Louisa had been lain and the fireplace in the middle of the house were still standing.

Three outer walls still held the skeleton, the roof had collapsed and had been completely destroyed. Also the whole right side lay in rubble and ash. Over the whole area lay still the smell of burning wood. There would not be much for the Sheriff to see. Carl knocked on his boss's office door and awaited his answer. He really needed to talk to him.

"Boss, I'd like to talk to you."

"This is not a good time Carl. I'm not in a very good mood today."

"Maybe that will change if you listen to me."

Without waiting for an invitation, he took a seat in the chair across from James' desk. If the latter was surprised at Carl's audacity, he did not let on, but only fixed him with his eyes.

"What could there be that is so important that would make this situation seem more pleasant?"

"What would you say if I asked for your daughter's hand?"

"Then I would ask you seriously, why?"

"Well I proposed to her a few weeks ago. She hasn't given me an answer yet and we both know now why."
"You proposed, she never told me about it."
James was honestly surprised.

"Well, yes. The situation has changed now, but I'm still willing to take Isabella to be my wife. This would calm the situation and you would not be exposed to the gossip of the people. I would get a young wife who could give me children and you an heir. I think that would be a reasonable solution for all. Besides, I think Isabella needs a strong hand and forgive me for saying so, you have been too lax in that regard."

"Well, you may have a point there. She clearly had too much freedom. But that's over now, and I would leave it to her husband how he would deal with her in that regard."
James, who seemed to like the idea of marriage more and more, continued.

"If I were to actually give her to you as a wife, you'd have to take her away from here for a few months so there wouldn't be too much talk. I can't allow myself, as a businessman, to have people talking shit about us. In exchange, I'd cede you some of the eastern pasture and you could build a house there. Besides, the succession would stay and future grandchildren included."

"That's a fair offer. Make it and I'll marry your daughter as soon as the reverend gets here and then we could be on our way in two days."
Carl had stood up and held out his hand to James. He shook it and sealed the agreement.

While the men in the office were having their conversation Marylou crept up the stairs and stopped at Isabella's door.

"Isabella are you all right?" she whispered through the doorway.

"Marylou? Is that you?"

Isabella settled on the other side of the door.

"Yes, what's going on? Your father has forbidden me to open the door and is beside himself. Right now he's talking to Carl, so I took the opportunity to check on you."

"Carl is in the house?"

What did Carl want with her father. That liar.

"Marylou, do you know what he wants and how is Chágha tho? What did they do to him?"

"Your father whipped him. More I don't know. I haven't been out of the house yet, because Malcolm and Louisa still haven't regained consciousness. Kid, what were you thinking?"

"I love him, Marylou. I know he's a good man, but Father doesn't want to see that. Marylou, you have to help me. Run over to him and help him escape. By the time the sheriff gets here, it'll be too late."

"I can't. I can't go behind your father's back. Carl's evidence is overwhelming. Maybe you're wrong about him. When you're in love, it's easy to be."

"No! I know it wasn't him and Carl, I don't trust him. He has tried from the very first day to make Chágha tho look bad. I, on the other hand, owe him my life and now his life is in danger. Please Marylou. Do it for me. I know we haven't known each other long, but I know I can trust him."

There was a long silence on the other side of the door and Isabella already had the fear that Marylou had simply left. But then she replied, "Well, I'll try to see him to see what I can do. But I can't promise you anything."

"Thanks Marylou. He has a bag of herbs with his belongings. Put them on his wounds, if you can.

They helped me a lot once."
"I must go now. If your father sees me up here, he will
be angry. I'll let you know."
"Thank you."
Isabella listened to the footsteps moving away again and
hoped fervently that Marylou would find a way to be in
time to help Chágha tho.

A few hours later, Marylou finally had the
opportunity to get out of the house. James had gone back
into his office and William had agreed to look after the
two injured people. They were beginning to get worried,
since neither had awakened yet. She had spoken to
William and urged him to look at the wounds of the
Indian. Now she was armed with a bowl of fresh water
and bandages on her way to the hayloft. The two men
who were standing guard stopped her.
"I'm supposed to look at the wounds on the Indian."
"He don't need you no more, he'll be dangling soon
anyway."
"Maybe, but in the meantime, I'm going to take a look at
him anyway."
Shaking their heads, they opened the gate and
brought her to Chágha tho. After they had checked his
bonds and found that he could not do anything to her,
they left Marylou alone with him. The Indian lay on his
stomach. The arms stretched out in front of him and tied
to a post. His feet were also tied to another post.
He was dressed only in his leggings. Marylou
had never seen a man before, who had been whipped.
Horrified, she saw that his back was covered with long,
deep welts that had torn open his skin. Dried and fresh
blood covered his entire back. Her heart clenched shut.
No matter what this man had done, it was not right that

he had to suffer such agony. She looked around and discovered his horse, standing not far from him. She put down the things she had brought with her and went over to the animal. She found the described bag and took it with her. Then she sat down carefully next to him.

The two men outside had assured her that he could not fight back, but she still wanted to be careful. She dipped a sponge into the lukewarm water and very carefully began to clean the blood from his back. His eyes were closed and yet she knew that he sensed her. His chest rose and fell.

"Are you in a lot of pain? I'm trying to be as careful as possible."

Marylou didn't get an answer, and was already thinking that she was mistaken and that perhaps he was unconscious, but then she heard him exhale deeply.

"How is Isabella?"

Marylou was surprised by the question. There he lay in his own blood, suffering great pain and his thoughts were with Isabella?

"She is better off than you are. Her father has locked her in her room."

"What will happen to her?"

"I don't know. You shouldn't talk so much. It only exhausts you. Did you set fire to the hut?"

"No."

"Did you sleep with Isabella?"

"Yes."

The honest answer shocked her a little, but she let the subject drop. From a female point of view, she could understand that he had impressed her stepdaughter. Carefully she cleaned the back further of his blood.

"The sheriff will be here tomorrow to take you away with him, do you know what that means?"

"They've all told me often enough, and they've all

gloated over it as if it were the nicest thing that could happen. I don't understand the white man. Why is it that he is more likely to believe a liar, just because of the color of his skin than a stranger who saved the lives of three people? I am to be killed for something I didn't do, and the real culprit gets away with it."

Chágha tho spoke quite calmly, did not seem to be upset, as others would have been in his situation. She paid him respect. The man was quite interesting. Marylou had cleaned his back in the meantime and now saw the full extent of his punishment. Doubts came over her as to whether her husband was doing the right thing. She took the herbs from his bag and was about to put them on the the wounds, when he spoke again.

"Isabella told you about the bag," he said.

"Yes. She said that it helped her get well."

"They work better if they are made moist or if you chew them first."

"Oh. I'd like to bandage you up. Do you think you can sit down so I can put the bandage around you?"

Chágha tho made a move to sit up, and she helped him to do so. Then she put the wet herbs on his wounds and began to bandage his back.

"If you were to be free, could you find evidence of your innocence?"

"I don't know."

Marylou made a decision and hoped that she would not regret it.

"I will not free you, because I do not want to lie to my husband if he should ask me. But I will loosen your shackles before I go. Everything else will be up to you. I hope that you are worthy of the trust Isabella has placed in you."

"Why do you do this?"

"Because an injustice is done quickly, and in this case it would cost you your life. I am not sure my husband is doing right. So it would be good for you if you leave here and don't come back. But I have one condition. You must promise me that no one will be harmed."

"I will do my utmost to prevent that from happening."

"Good."

Marylou finished her work. Then loosened his hands and feet, so that he could free himself with a few grips and left. A few minutes later one of the cowboys came in, saw Chágha tho lying on his bed again and checked the shackles. Satisfied that the Indian was still well tied up, he left the barn again. Chágha tho had been able to use a trick to lead the man into believing that the shackles were still tight. He waited until it was dark outside and the guard had looked in on him a second time. Then he loosened the shackles on his hands with a few twists and freed himself.

Quickly he untied the shackles. He scurried to his horse, found his knife, which was lying with his other belongings and quietly climbed onto the second floor. There he would hide until dawn. His plan was to sneak over to the fire site and take another look. To see if he could find anything that would exonerate him. The plan was risky. If he did not manage to get there undiscovered, it would mean his death.

An escape right now in the dark he had also considered, but immediately dropped it again. He had to put a stop to this bastard Carl, and he had sworn revenge, and this time he would get it. With any luck, the cowboys would assume in the morning when they discovered he was gone, that he had escaped from the ranch and send out a search party. That would give him enough time to investigate the remains of Malcolm's cabin.

Chapter 24

That night everything remained quiet, only in the main house was there finally something pleasant. Malcolm and Louisa had regained consciousness. Except a headache and thirst, both were well again. Marylou had cooked them a broth to strengthen them, which they ate gratefully. Since they no longer had a place to stay, they had agreed that they would spend tonight in the living room and that a solution would be sought until the hut was rebuilt. While Louisa and Malcolm ate their meal, James joined them.

"I'm glad you're all feeling better again. We were seriously worried."

"Well, old weeds don't go away that quickly. Do we know why the cabin started to burn?"

"It was arson. Chágha tho set them with incendiary arrows."

"Chágha tho?" Malcolm looked at James aghast. Louisa had also stopped eating and was now listening tensely to the conversation.

"I can't believe that, James. Why would that boy set fire to our house?"

"We haven't figured out the reason yet. Anyway, Carl found his arrows at the cottage, and that's proof. Tomorrow afternoon I expect the sheriff and then he'll be tried for attempted murder in Laramie."

Malcolm heard what James told him, but he could not

believe it. Carl, of all people had found the evidence. It stank to high heaven. He simply could not imagine that Chágha tho could have done it.

"Where is he now?"

"He's tied up in the hayloft. Very uncomfortable for him at the moment."

Something about James's voice made Malcolm suspect. Had he done violence to the Indian?

"What do you mean. What did you do to him?"

"He got a taste of the whip."

"Because of the fire, or is there something more to tell?"

James rose. "The rest is of no consequence and is my business. Get some sleep and then we'll see tomorrow, good night Louisa, Malcolm."

"Yes, thank you. Good night."

When James reached the upper floor, he was still listening at Isabella's door. But it was all silent and so he went to join his wife. Malcolm, on the other hand, was mulling things over. Something was wrong, his gut told him so. In the meantime, Louisa had carried the dirty dishes into the kitchen and was preparing a makeshift night's lodging.

"Something's on your mind, Malcolm!"

"I don't know what to make about this. James is so sure that Chágha tho did it. Why should the boy do it? He has no reason to."

Louisa put her hand on her husband's arm and looked at him tenderly.

"I know you like him, but he is and always will be a savage, and you never know what they're capable of. Come to sleep . Tomorrow you can always rack your brain over it."

"Yeah, you're right. Besides, my head is almost bursting. I hope tomorrow will be better."

What time it was exactly, Chágha tho did not know, but it was still dark outside. The night had remained quiet. No more guards had appeared and so far he was safe from the cowboys. He crept out of his hiding place down to his horse.

With the shackles and and a scrap of cloth he had torn from his bed sheet, he wrapped the horse's hooves. Now there would be no hoof noise and he dared to disappear into the darkness with his black stallion. Quietly he whispered something into the horse's ear, whereupon the animal ears stood alertly. Without a sound he opened the back gate, peeked out to see that there was not a guard there, and led his horse out.

The cowboys were apparently very sure that he could not escape, because, except for the two men outside the door, no others were to be seen. He swung himself on his horse, made it go forward at a walk, and led it in a wide curve away from the barn and toward the back of the burned hut. At a safe distance from the cabin, he dismounted and gave his horse a pat on the butt.

This one knew what it had to do and trotted silently off into the night away. They would catch it for him again, he was sure. He, however, would sneak the last part on foot. It took a while until he arrived, but the effort was worth it. No one had seen him, and as he peeked around the corner, he could make out the two shadows of his guards.

He crept on to the broken window, from which he had rescued Louisa and sought a hiding place in the the only room that was still intact, where he could wait until it was light. In the darkness, he would not be able to find any evidence.

A few hours later, a flurry of activity broke out. Chágha tho listened to the sounds. It was better to stay in his hiding place for a while, even though he saw that it had become light. Apparently they had noticed that he had fled, for he could hear hoof beats and riders circling the hut. Now it came down to them believing that he was no longer on the premises, but had fled into the distance. Would they send a search party after him, as he hoped they would?

James was informed by his father that the Indian had escaped and that he wanted to know what his instructions were. Hastily he ran down the stairs and ordered his men to pour out and recapture him.

Armed with rifles and revolvers, the cowboys dashed away. Left behind were only Carl, William, James and Malcolm, who, although was getting better, still felt too weak to mount a horse. Carl couldn't believe it. How had the dog escaped and did he have to be afraid now? He thought of the words the Indian had prophesied to him that night at the stake. Would he really be so stupid and attack him here on the ranch?

Well one could never be sure. It certainly wouldn't be wrong to stay nice and close to the Hunts until they had caught the guy again.

"How did that son of a bitch escape? I don't understand and nobody heard anything. How did he get off the ranch on his horse without a sound?"
"I have no idea. The guard checked twice and said his ties were tight."

"I hope they find him. The sheriff should arrive today, and I want him to have someone to take with him. As a precaution, we'll have our rifles ready to fire. You never know."
Carl, William, and James went back into the house.
"Are you coming inside, Malcolm, or is there something else?"

James had stopped at the doorframe and saw his foreman standing further on the porch.

"I think I'll take another look at our cabin. See if there's anything I can salvage. Maybe there are a few items still intact. Louisa would be happy if the fire hadn't destroyed everything. I'll catch up with you in a bit."

"Okay."

With that, the men separated. William and Carl had taken the rifles from the gun cabinet with ammunition and were loading the weapons in the office. James, on the other hand, climbed up the stairs. He opened his daughter's room without knocking and found her sitting on her bed.

"The Indian escaped last night. Apparently he didn't care much for you or he would have tried to take you with him."

Hope sprouted in Isabella. Marylou had indeed helped him and he was free. James watched his daughter closely and saw for a second a hint of joy on her face. Immediately the anger about her rose up in him again.

"You need not be pleased. My men are already on his heels, and if they find him, then God have mercy on him. The sheriff will arrive today and with him the reverend. Then you'll marry Carl today, and you'll leave the ranch tonight."

Her father was about to leave the room again when Isabella came storming up to him in a rage and grabbed him by the sleeve.

"You want me to marry Carl? I'll never do that. How can you think such a thing?"

"I don't need to think. I command you! Carl has agreed to marry you and that will put an end to this miserable story. I can't afford to have people talk about you. You are going to marry him tonight and I don't care whether you like it or not."

"Father, no. You can't do that to me. I don't love him."

"You're lucky your punishment isn't worse. You will obey and take him as your husband and be an obedient wife to him. Do we understand each other?"
"Never!"
"We'll see about that."

Angrily her father tore himself away from her, slammed the door in her face and turned the key in the lock again. That was it - Isabella was feverishly trying to find a solution. Her father seemed to have lost his mind. He wanted to force her to marry and to Carl of all people? And why did Carl want to marry her so badly? She had considered everything.

That her father would give her more housework, or that she would no longer be allowed to teach the children. She had even expected that he would send her to Boston much sooner, but never...never had she thought that he would marry her off to the first man who came along. With Carl, she would live an existence that was filled with disgust, hatred and brutality.

She had to think of the scene at the rock. Where he wanted to force a kiss from her with violence. What would happen when he was her husband according to the law? She felt sick at the thought. Only the fact that Chágha tho was out of danger made her bear her fate better.

Malcolm saw the full extent of the fire in front of him. There was not much left of his home. The right side of the cabin was burned down. Only the fireplace, which had stood in the middle, loomed as a memorial. Their bedroom, where he had heard noises before the fire in the night, was the only room that remained standing. As Malcolm drew closer, he tried to remember that night. He had been roused from his sleep because of something he had heard. Louisa had gone back to sleep, but he had gotten up and listened in the living room. Then when he had heard another noise, he had stepped out. But in the darkness he had seen nothing suspicious and so he had gone back inside. But then something hit him on the head and he had fallen to the ground.

He felt the back of his head and felt a big bump. Someone had struck him down. Had it been Chágha tho? Malcolm tried to remember further. Had he seen the attacker, or could he still tell how tall he had been? Chágha tho was a very tall man and he was not necessarily short himself. How could it be that the bump was sitting so far down? Completely in thought, he shuffled through the charred room. Nothing had been left by the fire. In the cooking area the remains of the dishes and the cooking utensils could be seen.

His two rifles, which had been standing on the wall in a shelf, now laid deformed in the ashes on the floor. His favorite rocking chair had collapsed. The door to the bedroom was open and he saw that the window was broken. It was already strange. Behind him the fire had raged and left nothing and here he was in his bedroom, which looked as if nothing had happened.

A few ashes were the only traces of the night. In the corner stood her armoire. It seemed to be in order and so at least her clothes survived the fire. Malcolm looked around the room, not really knowing what he was looking for. When he stood with his back to the armoire, it opened silently and Chágha tho jumped out.

Before Malcolm realized the danger he was in, he had the Indian's knife at his throat and his hands twisted behind his back.
"Not a sound or you're dead!" hissed Chágha tho in Malcolm's ear. The latter made no effort to defend himself and waited to see what the Indian intended to do. "You should not have come here. I can't let you go now."

Malcolm tried to say something, but with the knife at his throat and his posture dislocated, it was not easy for him. "Why did you come back? It's too dangerous."

"I haven't been away at all."

"Then why are you here? I don't understand."

"I'm trying to find evidence. It was Carl, not me."

"Carl? Are you sure about that?"

"He confessed it to me when he was sure, that I was going to die, but no one would believe me and he knows it. That's why I need evidence and I was just about to look for it when you showed up. That's a problem now. I don't want to hurt you, Malcolm, but I can't afford to let you go either."

"I'm going to help you. I just found out about all this last night, and I had my doubts that it was you. I'll be honest with you, though. If we don't find anything that connects Carl to this, then we're not going to be able to prove your innocence."

Chágha tho thought for a moment, then he let go of Malcolm's arms and took the knife from his throat.

"Thank you. I heard that you pulled us out of the fire. Me and my wife, I want to thank you on behalf of my wife. For that reason alone, I will help you. Where did you find me?"

"You were lying behind the door. I almost tripped over you in the night, because I didn't expect you to be at the door."

"That figures. I think someone knocked me down. I have a bump on the back of my head. I was outside that night, because I had heard noises."

"And you think too it could have been Carl?"

"At least he has a motive to try to frame you. But why does he want to burn down our cabin and didn't try to finish you off directly, I don't understand, but that doesn't matter anymore."

"Have you been able to find anything yet?"

"I haven't had a chance to look yet."

"We'll have to hurry. We don't have much time. The others are on their way looking for you. I'll check out the front entrance again. Maybe you can look behind the house."

Chágha tho nodded and disappeared through the window. Malcolm set out to search. He pushed the ashes away with his shoe. However, no matter where he did it, there was nothing conspicuous to be seen. Just as he stepped outside the door, his eye caught a glimpse of something, that shone silvery. Only a very tiny piece seemed to be in the ground. He knelt down and wiped the ashes aside with his hand. Under some wood and ash residue, he pulled out a silver boot cap and his face got a broad grin. Quickly he walked around the house and indicated to Chágha tho to go back into it. When they were back in the bedroom, he showed what he had found.

"What is this?"

"This is your proof you need. It's a boot cap and I know it's Carl's. He's mighty proud of his caps because they were once a gift from his late wife. And now he should be missing it. He must have lost it when he knocked me down, because it was in the entrance area, or was Carl involved in the rescue?"

"No, he didn't come until I pulled you both out of the house."

"Then we got him. Listen. I'm giving you the cap. I'm going to go over and get James here. It's better if he comes here alone, than you coming into the house with me."

Malcolm put his hand on the Indian's shoulder.

"Trust me. I'll just bring James with me and then you can talk to him."

"I'm going to have to trust you. I have no other choice."

With that, Malcolm left the cabin and walked over to the main House.

When Malcolm entered, he was relieved to find that James was alone in his office.
"Malcolm come in."
"I need to talk to you."
"What is it?"
"Not here. I want you to come over to the cabin, I have something to show you."
"What is it?"
"You'll see in a minute if you come with me."
"You're making it exciting, okay. I'm coming."
A short time later, Malcolm went ahead to his old bedchamber.
"What are you going to show me now...what is he doing here?"

James immediately drew his revolver and pointed it at Chágha tho. Malcolm grabbed James's arm and pressed the revolver down . Angrily, he glared at his foreman.

"Are you making common cause with him? I never thought you'd betray me and now step aside so I can arrest him again."

"Now stop it already. I'm not in cahoots with anyone, but I've been thinking about this thing. I heard noises that night that woke me up. When I went to check, someone knocked me down and it was not Chágha tho. The one must have been smaller.

When I came here earlier, he was there and had the same feeling about it. Namely to look for more evidence. You should have done that long ago. Chágha tho, give him what we have found."
Chágha tho handed James the boot cap.

"You know as well as I do who this cap belongs to, don't you? He also told you the story about it.
It was in the entrance under ashes and wood. That means it was there before the fire."
Chágha tho looked at James waitingly. He saw that he was not convinced.
"That alone is not sufficient proof."

"But a few arrows presented to you by Carl is proof enough? Give yourself a break, James. You know that Carl has a problem with Chágha tho...And that he's been against him from the beginning. So it's been easy for him to try to frame him for something. If you were to look at the whole thing neutrally, then you would have to admit that I'm right."
James ran his hand through his hair. He was undecided, but had to admit to himself, that the boot cap was a powerful piece of evidence.

"Ok, we will ask him how his cap got here. And you come with me," with that he pointed to Chágha tho. "I won't let you out of my sight for a second. Come here and lead the way."
Chágha tho left the room without a word, followed by James, who now had his gun pointed again at the Indian's back, and Malcolm, who was beginning not to understand James.
"Where did you pick that one up again? I could have sworn he was long gone."
William looked up from his coffee as the group came into the house.
"Do you know where Carl is?"

"Carl? No, he left the house shortly after Malcolm. He said something about going to take care of the horses, and he hasn't come back here since. Maybe he's over in his room."
"You know this one?"
James handed the boot cap to his father. The latter

twisted and turned it before saying:

"Mmm, I've seen these before. It definitely belongs to one of our boys. Wait a minute I think Carl wears caps like that on his boots. Why do you ask?"

"Malcolm and Chágha tho found these in the burned-out shack."

"Jesus, if that's true, then we should ask Carl how that thing got there."

"That's exactly what I intend to do, but first I'm going to tie up Chágha tho here in the office and you watch him while Malcolm and I go look for Carl."

Chágha tho flashed angrily and would have liked to have his knife to lunge at James, but James' revolver was still pointed at him.

"Don't even try it. Go over to the office!

"James, why don't you let him go. You know that he didn't do it."

"I want to talk to Carl first and then I'll decide, and to make sure he's still here when I get back, he'll be tied up. His innocence has not been proven one hundred percent."

He pushed the Indian over to an armchair and tied his hands and feet to the backs of the chair, as well as the chair legs. Then he left his father to supervise.

Malcolm and James split up. But no matter where they looked, there was no sign of Carl.

"He's nowhere to be found."

"His belongings are gone and so is his horse too. I think he's made a run for it. That should be enough for a confession. So what do we do now?"

"The sheriff should be here soon. Let him go out and look for Carl."

Suddenly, they heard the sound of many hooves coming toward them.

"The men are coming back. Look, they have Chágha tho's horse."

While the other cowboys went straight to the paddock and took the Indian's horse with them, the leader rode up to his boss.

"We're sorry, but we haven't found the slightest trace of the fellow. Oddly enough, we found his horse grazing not far from here."

"It's all right Henry. We found the Indian at the cabin. He's tied up again by now. Did you happen to run into Carl?"

"Carl? No."

"All right, get those animals taken care of."

"Ok, boss."

When the young cowboy had gone, Malcolm addressed James.

"Do you still want to turn Chágha tho over to the sheriff?"

"No. I have other plans for him in the meantime. The sheriff can go in search of Carl, because we certainly don't want to let him get away with it."

"What are your plans with Chágha tho?"

"Wait and see."

With these words he left Malcolm behind and went back to the house to present the news to his father.

Chapter 25

Damn, how could this mishap have happened to him? He hadn't even noticed that the cap on one of his boots was missing. Oh well. It couldn't be helped now. What luck, that he had followed Malcolm and had heard what Malcolm and the cursed Indian had come up with.

Once again this red devil had thwarted his plan, but he did not want to give up yet, not for a long time. There just had to be a change of plans. He had to make sure that the sheriff didn't find him, because he was sure that James would set the sheriff on him.

How much of a head start did he have left? Would the cowboys ride after him when they realized that the Indian had led them all around by the nose? He, too, had thought that the son of a bitch had escaped. Who could have guessed that the dog was still hiding out on the ranch and took the risk of being discovered.

If only William had not come in the night. His son would have beaten the Indian to death. Carl was sure of that. He had seen the mad rage in James' eyes. But unfortunately, William had appeared, and so the son of a bitch had escaped with his life and could now spit in his soup again. But he would not enjoy his life for long.

As soon as the coast was clear again, he would get his Isabella and put the bastard to rest once and for all.

Isabella was desperate. The whole day no one had come to see her. Neither had Marylou talked to her through the keyhole, nor had she heard her father's boots on the stairs. Under her window stood the guard still. Something was going on in the house, however, and it almost drove her crazy that she didn't know what it was. She had heard voices and footsteps from downstairs. Doors that were opened and closed again.

There was a lot of movement in the house, but no one seemed interested in her up here and that worried her. It must have been afternoon, because the sun had moved to the west. Her stomach growled. It had been a long time since the last meal. Her father seems to have forbidden everyone from bringing her something to eat. His anger did not seem to be yet subsided.

Horsemen seemed to be coming. She heard the horses clearly and ran over to the window. Maybe she could see who was coming. It was not the cowboys, for they had already returned this morning. Without Chágha tho. That meant he had made it and was out of danger. She thanked God for that. But who came then?

She could count five riders, but she could not recognize them from her position. She hurried to the door and put her ear to the keyhole. Perhaps this would tell her who it was.

"Sheriff, Charles , good to have you here."

"Mr. Hunt, what's so urgent. Did you have a fire?" The sheriff pointed toward the burned cabin.

"Yes. But first, come on in, you and your men. A refreshment will do you good and I can explain everything to you. Charles, you too, please."

James did not wait for the men to get off their exhausted animals, but went ahead into the house.

"Louisa? Bring our visitors something to eat and drink. Come on in, gentlemen and take a seat at the table."

The five horsemen gratefully took their seats and were immediately served a cup of coffee, which Marylou brought them.

"Sheriff, I'd like you to meet my wife. Marylou, this is Sheriff Dawson. I'm not sure you two met in Laramie before."

"Yes, the sheriff and I have met many times. Good to see you again. How's your wife and kids?"

"Thanks for asking. Heather is pregnant with our third child and we are looking forward to that very much."

"Oh, that is wonderful. You and your men must be hungry. I'll have something brought in right away. But for now I'll leave you with my husband. I think he has important things to discuss with you."

At that moment, Louisa brought in bread and soup and put everything on the table for the men. Malcolm and William also joined them at the table. The ladies fed the eight men and then retired to the kitchen.

After dining better than they had in a long time and quenching their thirst with good coffee, the sheriff returned to the reason for the visit.

"Now let's have it, James. What happened that we had to drop everything to get out here?"

"That burned down shack out there was Malcolm's house. He lived there with his wife Louisa. That cabin burned down two days ago. As we discovered, not without external influence. My foreman was knocked down and then the hut was set on fire."

The five men looked at each other. There had not been arson in the area for a long time.

"Did they get a look at the perpetrator, Malcolm?"

"I'm not sure. I was awakened by noises that night and went to see what it was. When I opened the door, I thought I saw a shadow, but I could have been mistaken. Anyway, I could not see or hear anything suspicious and went back into the house. As I was just through the door, something hit me from behind and knocked me out. From then on I know nothing more, until I woke up the next evening. They pulled me and my wife out of the flames. Just in time I want to say. However, I went over this morning to see if any of our stuff was salvageable, and I found something that didn't belong to us."

"I see, what is it?"

"This," James held out the silver boot cap.

The sheriff took the piece of evidence in his hand.

"And this cap doesn't belong to you, Malcolm?"

"No, it belongs to one of our cowboys. Carl Webster."

"Carl?" astonished, the reverend looked at Malcolm. He had been quietly, but intently, listening to the conversation.

"Well, that's hard to believe. The man has been here on the ranch for so long. Are you sure about that?"

"Yes, Charles. And when we tried to call him on it, he was gone. His belongings and his horse are gone too."

"I don't believe it."

"Sheriff, when we sent for you, we only knew about the fire and that it wasn't legal. But now that we know it was Carl, you know who you're looking for."

"That makes our job a lot easier. Do you know if there's any place he could have gone to? He might have gone into hiding? A wife or any other relatives?"

"No, I'm afraid not. As far as I know, he has no relatives. I'm sorry, but I can't help you in that regard."

"Okay. Then we'll be on our way. Tell your wife thank you for the fine meal."

"Sheriff, your horses are tired. Exchange them for fresh ones from us, we'll take care of your animals. Malcolm, would you take care of that, please."

"Yeah, come on, I'll lead them over."

"Thank you Mr. Hunt. And don't worry, we'll get the

guy."

"Thank you."

When the sheriff left with Malcolm and only William, James and the Reverend were sitting at the table, the latter now addressed James.

"And what did you have me come here for, if I'm not supposed to give anyone their final absolution or a funeral in the offing?"

"It's simple, you're supposed to perform a wedding ceremony."

William looked at his son as astonished as the reverend.

"And who am I supposed to marry? A few days ago, when I married you here, there had not been any mention of another wedding. So who is it?"

"I'll show you in a minute, as soon as the sheriff is on his way and Malcolm is back here."

"James, what are you up to? You're not going to..."

"Father, this is my business and I'd appreciate it if you'd stay out of it," James interrupted his father.

Chapter 26

Isabella had just been able to observe that four of the horsemen had left the ranch when she heard her father's energetic footsteps on the stairs. A short time later the door was pulled open and her father stood in the doorway.

"It's time. Your groom is waiting downstairs for you."

"I will never marry Carl, Father."

She glared angrily at him. But he did not say a word back, but came toward her with angry steps. He grabbed her arm and pulled her behind him. Isabella tried desperately to escape her father's grip, but he was stronger.

"Father, please. Don't do this to me. Let go of me. You're hurting me."

But all the clamoring did not help. James pushed her down the stairs in front of him and then pulled her towards the office. When he pushed the door open with his shoulder and shoved her in, she instantly fell silent at the sight that met her eyes. Standing in the room in the left corner, Marylou and Louisa, who were now looking at her pityingly. William and Malcolm were standing on the other side, and did not look very happy either. Directly in her field of vision was the Reverend, who was standing in front of a person who was sitting with his back to her.

He was covering this person so that she could

not see exactly who it was. She felt as if she were being led to her own execution. Her stomach began to rebel and she had to swallow to stop the rising nausea.

Now she would become Carl's wife and before she could think about it, her father opened the floor.

"So, we are all here. You can start Charles. Isabella, go to the reverend."

With that, he let her go, closed the door behind her, and went after her. Slowly and with heavy steps she walked towards the reverend, who now stepped a little to the side and walked around the chair he had covered. Isabella could not believe her eyes.

It was not Carl sitting there in the chair, but Chágha tho, who was tied to the chair. Instead of his suede shirt, he was wearing an old shirt of her father's. That was probably the reason why she did not recognize him right away. His shirt had been left in the house during the fire. But what was happening?

James walked over without an explanation to Chágha tho, untied him and ordered him to stand up.

"Come here Isabella and stand next to your future husband so Charles can get started."

"I don't understand, I thought you wanted me to marry Carl?"

"He's no longer available," her father replied sarcastically.

"Get the hell over here," he called to her gruffly and caught her arm to pull her closer. The jerk caused her to stumble and she almost fell, but she was just able to prevent a fall. Anger and rage rose up in her and she glared angrily at her father.

"You two are going to say yes in the right place," he said and to Chágha tho he mentioned, "If you don't do what I say, I will blow a bullet into your skull, are we clear on that?"

Horrified by what her father said, she looked first at him

and then at Chágha tho. Isabella saw it in her father's eyes and knew that no one could stop him.

He would go through with this here and now. In Chágha tho's face she could see no emotion. He stared straight ahead and had avoided looking at her until now. But his tense posture and the twitching of his chin told her that he was trembling with anger.

"James, I've got to ask. Surely I can't help make a forced marriage."

"You'll do as I tell you. Get on with it so we can get it over with."

Completely unsettled, the reverend picked up his Bible, looked around once again at this unusual wedding party and then began to speak.

"We have gathered here today to honor this man and the..."

"Charles!" James interrupted the reverend's word. Irritated, the latter stopped talking.

"Yes?"

"We only need the bare essentials. So save yourself the procedure and get to the important part."

Isabella found herself in a trance. She didn't really know the words that were being spoken. One after the other, she looked around and into the eyes of her grandfather and Malcolm, Louisa and Marylou. All of them followed what was happening with fixed gazes.

What thoughts they were having, Isabella could not tell. She tried to catch a glimpse of Chágha tho, but he too, was staring with empty eyes, in front of him. He was doing all this only because at his head was pointed her father's revolver. Why was he here? They had said that he had fled. Had her father's men captured him again? The reverend's words brought her from her thoughts.

"Chágha tho, do you wish to make the present Isabella Hunt, your lawful wife and to love and honor her until death do you part? Answer yes."

Tensely, the reverend held his breath to see what was happening now. If the Indian did not answer, James would shoot him, he was sure. Inwardly, he begged the young man to be aware of the danger he was in, and not do anything unwise. Nothing happened for a while and he could see in the Indian's narrowed eyes that he was struggling with his temper. He sent another push prayer to heaven.

"Will you answer the question finally? The reverend asked you a question and you better give the right answer."

James pulled the safety off the revolver and the sound made everyone else in the room startled in horror.

"Yes, I do," Chágha tho gritted out.

James relaxed a little and signaled the reverend to continue. Deeply taking a breath, he immediately turned to Isabella with the same question, and again there was a pause. This was now her wedding. Ever since she was a little girl, she had precise ideas about how she wanted to get married. She had always seen herself in a beautiful dress and on the arm of her father, she had been led down the aisle in a beautiful church.

In the end, in each of her dreams, there had been a young handsome man who had looked at her lovingly and promised her heaven on earth. Each time it had been a love marriage. And what did she actually get?

She stood here in an old dress, still dirty from the night of the fire, because they had not brought her water to wash in her prison. The man who was supposed to take her as his wife, was forced at gunpoint, and the people who had loved her so far looked glum. What a beautiful wedding that had taken place here a few days ago. Was it really only a few days ago? She had the feeling an eternity had passed.

"Isabella we need your answer."

The reverend's quiet words brought her back to reality. If her father was doing this to her, she wanted to take it in stride. She felt like crying, but she did not want to show this nakedness to her father and so she answered defiantly, "Yes, I do."

Relieved to have gotten that part done, Charles quickly concluded, "Then, by the power vested in me. I pronounce you husband and wife. You may kiss the bride now, Chágha tho."

Smiling shyly, he had addressed these words to the young man, but instead of the latter turning to his bride, James replied.

"We don't need that, they've both had that already."

Completely exhausted, the reverend now sat down on the chair. Such a wedding had never happened to him in all his years. James, on the other hand, now addressed the two married individuals in a calm but very dangerous voice.

"Now that you are no longer under my care, but under his," he pointed disparagingly at the Indian,

" I give you one hour to pack your belongings and leave the ranch. As of today, I have no daughter and you will never set foot on this ranch again. That goes for both of you."

"James, you can't do that, she is and always will be your daughter and my granddaughter,"

William exclaimed in horror. All the others now surrounded him and talked to him. Everybody tried to change his mind, to withdraw the harsh sentence he had passed on the couple. Only Isabella knew better. Horrified, she had recoiled when he had thrown the harsh words at her. She had realized by now that her father would never forgive her and so she heard her father's next words.

"She has brought shame on this house and received her punishment. No one will change my mind. I have the right to do so. You have an hour, Isabella, use it. You can take with you, what fits on a horse, everything else stays here. Go and pack, your time is running out. Malcolm, you get the two horses and bring them to the house. In an hour, I don't want to see either one of them."

With that, he walked out of the room, leaving everyone distraught.

"Isabella, I'm so sorry, I'm going to talk to your father. Maybe I can change his mind."

"Thank you, Marylou, but you've already done enough for me. I don't want you to jeopardize your marriage to him. I know my father and so I know he will not change anything. I'm sorry that I've caused you all this trouble. I mean it for all of you. That was not my intention. Grandfather? I'm sorry."

Isabella wanted to throw herself into her grandfather's arms, but she felt the tears coming, and she ran out of the office and up to her room. Marylou and Louisa followed her. The girl did not have time to pack, so they wanted to help her. Left behind were a horrified reverend, William and Malcolm, who didn't know what to say and a silent Chágha tho, who all the time still stood rooted to the spot. For quite a while none of the four men spoke a word until William turned to Malcolm.

"I think you had better get the horses and take Chágha tho with you. Charles, we both can use a good brandy."

Malcolm merely nodded, patted Chágha tho on the shoulder and left the office with him.

William and Charles filled their glasses with brandy and took their seats exhausted.

"William, what just happened here, if I had known about it before, I wouldn't have come. James must be out of his mind. He's making a grave mistake."

"Oh, Charles. I hope he realizes that. My granddaughter has made mistakes, too, but this here would not have been necessary. I'm afraid that he's leading her to ruin, and he doesn't seem to care. I don't know how to help him anymore. Talk to him."

One floor up, Isabella was crying her eyes out. Her father banished her from the ranch and from his life. She couldn't think straight at the moment and so she was glad that Marylou had taken her in her arms to comfort her. Louisa, on the other hand, dug out a large bag from Isabella's closet and approached the two of them.

"Isabella, you need to pack. Your father has not given you much time, and I don't know what he will do if you are still here when it has elapsed. Come, for the moment it is better to submit. One day he will realize what a mistake he has made today."

"Yes, you're right." She rose listlessly and packed up a few things. The beautiful riding dress she left in the closet, as well as the Sunday hat. She would no longer be able to wear them. She packed only a few of her work clothes that were also suitable for riding. Marylou left the room and went to get fresh water to wash.

Even if her stepdaughter was expelled from the house, she should at least leave the house in clean clothes and washed. When Louisa was alone with Isabella, she put aside the bag, which was now packed and took her in her arms. Immediately Isabella started sobbing.

"Oh Louisa, why is he doing this to me?"

"Your father is a proud man and has been deeply hurt. Give him time to think, maybe then he can forgive."

"He never will. He hates Chágha tho. He never gave him a real chance."

"Do you love him?"

"Yes, I love him with all my heart but he will hate me

from today. He has been forced to do something he never wanted to do. How can I go with him when he despises me? He didn't even look at me in the office. Louisa, I don't know what to do?"

Tenderly she stroked her hair. She did not know how she should answer her. She herself had strong fears that it could end badly with Isabella, since she could not judge Chágha tho. What would the Indian do with her? She knew Isabella was facing difficult and uncertain times and so she hugged her tightly and then said, "Give him some time too and let me know where you are when you know where you are going to stay. Promise me that, Isabella, because otherwise I won't be able to find any peace. And now come. Cheer up. Marylou comes with fresh water. Wash up, put on some clean clothes and then show your father he can't keep a Hunt down."

Yes, Louisa was right. Her father might have won today, but she would show him that she could get along without him and then one day he would be the loser. With courage, she sent the two women out of the room and got ready to face her new life.

An hour later, Chágha tho was sitting on his black mustang and waited for Isabella. He was still wearing the light blue shirt they had given him before the wedding ceremony, with the words" so that he does not look completely like a savage". In addition, his leggings, which were soot-stained, and moccasins. Malcolm had also given him back his amulet and his weapons. Now he came from the ruins of the fire and held out his leather shirt to Chágha tho.

"Here, I found this in the house. It's dirty, but it does not seem to have any burn marks. I'm sure you'll still be able to use it."

"Thank you, Malcolm." Chágha tho stowed it in his pouch and turned his gaze back to the front door. Malcolm, on the other hand, continued.

"Listen, I'm sorry that it all turned out this way. Take good care of her, she means a lot to us."
Chágha tho looked down at Malcolm.

"Her father is making a big mistake, but I promise you, I will take good care of her. You have been a good friend, Malcolm."

Malcolm was honestly touched when Chágha tho said this to him, and was about to say something in reply when the door opened and Isabella, followed by Marylou, Louisa, and her grandfather stepped outside the door. She had changed her clothes and was now wearing her pretty dark green work dress.

Her hair was coiffed and tied in a knot at the back of her neck. In her hand she carried a rifle and her wide-brimmed hat. Marylou carried her bag and handed it to Malcolm, who fastened it to the saddle of Isabella's mare. Isabella looked up at Chágha tho, but he did not return her look with any expression. She had hoped to see some emotion in him, but he did not do her this favor. Sadly, she went to her horse and stowed the rifle in the holster.

With a heavy heart, she walked to Marylou, hugged her and said, "It's a pity we can't get to know each other better. We would have hit it off, I think. Take good care of father."

"I'll do that and you take care of yourself."

Then she went to Louisa and looked sadly at her surrogate mother.

"Here my child. These are some provisions for you. Take them with you. Oh my child. Come here and let me hug you once more."

She handed Malcolm the bag, stowing it by the saddle and took Isabella in her arms.

Tears welled up in both of their eyes. Would they ever see each other again? With a heavy heart, Isabella let go of her and turned to her grandfather, somewhat hesitantly. His reaction surprised her. He did not look angry, but his look was seized with sadness.

"I will miss you, my child."

"Grandfather, my father didn't even come to say goodbye."

Her eyes gleamed moistly, and even in her grandfather's eyes, too, she could see the emerging tears.

"I know. I'm sorry," and turning to Chágha tho he said, "Take care of her."

The Indian nodded, turned his horse in the direction he was to ride, indicating to Isabella that it was time to go. She hugged Malcolm tightly once more, then allowed herself to be helped into the saddle and waved goodbye. Chágha tho slowly set his horse in motion and left Isabella to follow him.

Isabella trotted along behind him. Again and again she turned and glanced back at the four people who were important to her. She tried to memorize everything. This would be the last time she would see her home. Never again would she see her grandfather, Louisa, Malcolm, and even Marylou, who she had grown fond of in that short time. This was the end of her as she knew it.

She had often wished that she could be independent. Make her own decisions. But now that she could, it hurt to leave. Her heart grew heavier with every yard between her and her home. The four outlines that continued to appear on the porch grew smaller and smaller and then were suddenly gone. Sadly, she turned and saw that Chágha tho was walking at a pace, but her horse was far behind him. She was about to catch up, when her eyes fell on the small hill to her left. Individual tombstones perched on top. It was the small cemetery that the ranch had and where her grandmother and mother were buried. Without a word she steered her mare up the hill and dismounted in front of the small fence. She wanted to say goodbye here, too.

At the graves of the two, she knelt down, looked at the fresh prairie flowers that she had recently brought here and began to cry. She had tried to hold back the tears. Bravely she had made it this far, but now, at the sight of these gravestones, there was no stopping her. Chágha tho looked around because he could no longer hear her horse behind him, and discovered her on the hill. He pulled his horse around and galloped back. Arriving at the fence, he could see Isabella sitting in the grass and heard her sobbing. His heart tightened.

Slowly he got off his horse and went to her. She didn't seem to have heard him, because when he now tenderly put his hands on her shoulders, she was startled. Quickly she tried to dry her eyes with the sleeves of her dress. It seemed to be unpleasant for her that he saw her crying.

"Come on, we should get a few more miles today before it gets dark."

She just nodded and he helped her stand up. He put lovingly his arm around her and took her to her horse. When he put her in the saddle, he swung onto his own horse and trotted off.

Isabella took one last look at the graves and the ranch in the distance, which had once been her home, and defiantly looked ahead. The past was behind her. Ahead of her lay an uncertain future, but it was in her hands to make the best of it. And that was exactly what she intended to do. She kicked her heels into the belly of her horse and galloped after Chágha tho.

Chapter 27

The Sun was already setting and it would not be long before it was dark. They had not gone far today and were still on the grounds of the Hunts. Chágha tho had not quite known which way to turn. To the north the terrain became difficult to access, to the west it was too uncertain, because of the Sioux, who had their territories there. Thus, he had chosen the way in the southern direction to get away from the house, and then turned east. Further to the south he didn't want to go either, because Laramie was there and he wanted to avoid the town. The east seemed to him, for the moment, the best direction. They went to the river which ran through the area and stopped there.

For tonight this was a good place to camp and tomorrow they would get further. So he made a halt at the bank of the river that had become the doom for them both.

"We'll camp here tonight. It's about to get dark soon and I do not want to be with you in the night on the road."

Isabella looked around. It was a good place, even if it was only three hours from her father's house. Chágha tho helped her to unsaddle her horse and then released both animals so that they could quench their thirst in the river.

A little later, when they were both sitting silently around the small campfire and ate some of Louisa's supplies, the

221

silence between them was unbearable. The few words that Chágha tho had exchanged with her since they had left the ranch had been only instructions.

The informality between them until the night of the fire had disappeared. Chágha tho avoided her wherever he could, and Isabella was afraid to speak to him. She secretly blamed herself for everything. Chágha tho, however, struggled with himself.

On the one hand he was angry at himself for not being able to keep his hands off her. If he had been able to control himself, it would never have come to this. Because of him, Isabella had lost her home. On the other hand, he had no regrets, because this woman got under his skin. She had become in the short time the most important person in his life and he wanted to be near her. He wanted to touch her and feel her, wanted to hold her in his arms and fall asleep with her every night, wake up with her in the morning.

Actually, he had gotten exactly this today, and yet he did not feel happy with the solution. The sadness that her whole body radiated, made him keep him away from her. Maybe she just needed some distance from what had happened today.

He decided that it would be probably better if he left her alone for today, and so he put his blanket at a distance from her by the fire. Isabella, felt a stab in the heart, when she saw Chágha tho spreading his blanket away from her and laying down on it.

She felt so unspeakably lonely. Left alone by everyone, even by him. She had thought that he would take her in his arms and comfort her, but he had so far avoided touching her. Disappointed and sad, she lay down on her blanket and watched him furtively over the fire. He was lying on his belly and it did not seem to be very comfortable. Suddenly it shot her inevitably through the head, that he could be in pain.

How had she forgotten? She had been much too selfish and had not thought for a minute about the fact that he was hurt. Ashamed she got up, went to his saddle and found the bag with the herbs. Then she knelt down next to him. He straightened up with a questioning look, but she put her hands reassuringly on his shoulders and gently pushed him back down on the blanket.

"I'm sorry. I've been so selfish. Take off your shirt. I'm going to take a look at your back."

A little puzzled, he looked at her, but did what she said and took off her father's shirt. The white bandage Marylou had tied around him was bloody in places. Carefully, she removed it and indicated to him to lie down on his stomach again. In the light of the fire, she saw for the first time the full extent of her father's punishment. Horrified, she bit her lips and put her hand in front of her mouth so that he could not hear the horrified scream that she had wanted to let out.

What had her father done to him. Even if all the wounds healed, he was marked for life. Some of the red welts were so deep and had torn the skin to such an extent that he would be left with scars from them.

She fetched some water from the river, tore off a piece of fabric from her petticoat and carefully began to clean the wounds. Gently she ran over his battered back and noticed a small birthmark, which he wore on the right shoulder blade.

Actually, it was nothing special, but the shape of it had caught her attention. She paused to look at it more closely. A slight smile played around the corners of her mouth. Chágha tho wore the symbol of love on his shoulder, for the birthmark was clearly visible in the form of a heart. Isabella, however, did not allow herself to be distracted by that mark and soaked the herbs a little before puting them on his back again. Then she let it dry and in the meantime she tore the fabric of her petticoat again. She needed new bandages and she would not need her petticoat anymore anyway.

Chágha tho lay still on his blanket and let everything happen to him without comment. He watched every movement of her. The light touches of her hands on his skin excited him. No matter what was between them, his body still longed for her.

When Isabella had re-bandaged him she hastily turned away. She had avoided looking him in the eye and did not want him to notice that she was in tears. She didn't want to cry, but somehow she could not hold it back and so she walked toward the river, turned her back to him and stared thoughtfully into the water.

What was she supposed to do? Suddenly she felt him close behind her. He pulled her to his chest and embraced her shoulders. Without being aware of it, she let him have his way. He did not say a word, but the tender gesture was expression enough. The closeness to him gave her strength. Isabella closed her eyes for a moment to experience the moment of security that suddenly surrounded her.

Chágha tho enjoyed it when her body snuggled against his, but he sensed that her thoughts were not with him. Softly, he murmured his words in her ear, "Isabella, do not be sad."

Her body stiffened and immediately Chágha tho let go of her. Isabella turned and stepped back to take a distance from him. Waiting to see what would happen next, he watched her. Isabella turned to face him, saw his incredibly blue eyes fixed on her and she knew she owed him an explanation.

"I can't do this."

"Can't do what?"

"I had no idea what my father had done to you. Your back...those injuries...All of this," she made a sweeping motion with her hands. "He forced you to marry me! I will therefore free you again. You can go wherever you like. I will ride on alone tomorrow. Far away, somewhere where no one knows me. Maybe I'll go to Boston. I'm sure I can find a teaching job there. I could pretend to be a widow, then no one would ask why I was traveling alone."

Chágha tho was surprised and horrified at the same time, at what he was hearing. Why did she suddenly come up with the idea of wanting to go on alone. Had she no idea of the dangers that were lurking out here for a woman traveling alone? Besides, he had thought that she would not mind going with him.

After all, a few days ago she had begged him to take her with him, and he no longer wanted her to go. His feelings towards her went much deeper than that he wanted to lose her now.

"You can't be serious!"

Exasperated, he put his hands on his hips.

"Yes, I am! I've never been so sure of anything as I am right now. I've always dreamed of one day, wearing a beautiful dress, being in a church, to marry a man I love and who loves me. Unfortunately my father ruined all that when he forced us to get married and I don't know if I can ever forgive him for that. He forced you into a union you didn't want, and I'm going to break it again. I've had a lot of time to think in the last two days and I've come to realize that you were right when you said that you would never be recognized."

Isabella came closer, placed her hands on his bandaged chest and continued desperately.

"They would have hanged you. With or without evidence, it didn't matter to them. They didn't care, and it was only because you weren't white. I don't want to put you in any more danger when you are with me. Go and ride where you can be free, where no one will judge you on account of your origin."

Tears welled up from her eyes and ran down her face. Her heart was as heavy as lead. She loved him so much, wished for a future with him, but she saw that it was not to be. Nor did she want him to stay with her out of a misconceived sense of duty. Chágha tho pulled her close to him and held her tightly in his arms. He did not want to let this woman go.

"Isabella, your father may have put a gun to my head, but he could never have forced me to marry you. If I hadn't wanted it myself at that moment, it would have come to a fight. You can believe that."

She pressed her hands to his chest to get distance from him. Chágha tho, however, held her at arm's length. Distraught, she looked at him. She had heard his words, but she had not understood them.

"Then why were you so angry?"

"I don't like having guns pointed at me and your father was lucky that I had been outnumbered at that moment, or I would have taken my chances in a fight. It was the situation that made me angry, but it had nothing to do with my feelings for you. I, too, have had more than enough time to think about us. I know Manitou led me to you and it was all supposed to happen the way it did. I have now realized that, and if I would have the choice again, I would do everything exactly the same, if it would bring me to you. Isabella, I am right now where I want to be. With you!"

Isabella looked into those magical blue eyes, that were looking lovingly at her. How would she have liked it to just let herself fall. It was so tempting, to believe his words, but were they really true?

"I can't ask you to stay with me."

"Isabella listen to me. I can't offer you a ranch. I can't even put a roof over your head. All I can give you is my deep love for you, my faithfulness, my loyalty and my muscle power, with which we will build something for ourselves. I will protect you with my life if it has to be. Let's make a new start together. We will settle down somewhere to have our own little farm. I won't leave you alone. I swear to you as I stand here. I love you."

Gently, he pulled her into his arms once again and closed her mouth with a kiss. She moaned as she felt the rising reaction of her body to his touch.

"I love you, Chágha tho."

She returned his kiss with passion. He loved her, as she loved him. Her heart leapt with joy and relief. She let herself fall into a new life with him and he would catch her, hold her, and protect her. He was the man she loved, and with him she would spend her life.

Chapter 28

The next morning Isabella awoke in the arms of her husband. Tightly embraced, he held her against his body to give her warmth. It had become cool overnight and the fire was only glowing. It was the first time that she was with him in the morning and she was happy that it would be like this every day from now on. He was her husband and she had never used this word for him before. Everything was still strange to her, but she would surely get used to this thought.

Isabella looked up at the sky, which was overcast, and she hoped that it would not start to rain, as she had no real protection from it. Actually, she should get up and put some more wood in the fire so that the fire could get going again, but she just couldn't bring herself to do it. It was much too tempting to continue to lie in the arms of her husband, to feel his security and to listen to his regular heartbeats.

He seemed to be still asleep and she did not want to wake him, so she remained very still. Isabella listened to the sounds of nature, which, like her, was just awakening. The horses were grazing nearby, blowing their breath audibly through their nostrils.

An eagle screeched in the sky and drew her attention. With large wings, it swooped down on a smaller bird, which desperately tried to escape the eagle's attack. This cruel game held her captive and she flinched when she heard a cracking sound in the nearby undergrowth. Unconsciously, Chágha tho strengthened his embrace.

"Don't be afraid. It was probably just a squirrel. Did you sleep well?"

He released his arms to give her room to turn around. Isabella turned to face him, nodded and kissed him. Immediately he was seized by an indescribable longing for her. How gladly he would have liked to take time for his wife and love her now, but it was not the right place for it. The weather had changed, which can happen quickly in the high altitudes of Wyoming, and it had turned bitterly cold.

"We should see that we get out of here. There could be rain or even a storm could come and we don't have the protection we need from it."

"Yes, unfortunately. I could otherwise still lie here and stay."

He rose and pulled Isabella to her feet with him. They gathered their belongings, packed the horses and continued on their way to the east. While they let their horses go at a walk, they nibbled on the beef jerky and bread that Louisa had packed for them.

"We need money, Chágha tho. I have the jewelry my grandmother left me. We could pawn it in the town and get money that way. It will not be enough to buy land but we could buy provisions and go to Boston."

"I don't like the idea of giving away your family's memories."

He reached for his amulet, which hung around his neck, and thought that it was probably the last thing he had left of his family.

"There must be another solution. Are there other ranches around? I could offer my help there, as I did with your father."

She thought for a moment, then she said:

"Yes, that's it! In the northeastern direction lies, about two days' ride from here, the MacIntyre Ranch. The owner is an old lady and our direct neighbor. Unlike us, she has a horse breeding farm and supplies the entire area and also the fort with good horses. The ranch is huge, much bigger than ours. Every summer she holds a festival for everyone from the surrounding area. The festival goes on for two days. There is barbecue, dance evenings, children play and you're just happy to meet the other families."

Isabella went into raptures. In the last years, she had always looked forward to this. It had given her the opportunity to chat with other young ladies, to wear her most beautiful dresses and to dance. But that now belonged to her past, she quickly continued to speak, in order to rid herself of the sad thoughts that wanted to take possession of her.

"Last year, Mrs. MacIntyre asked me if I would give the children and her workers teaching classes in reading, writing and arithmetic. But I could not accept the offer, since I had just started the small school on our ranch. If she still needs help, I could do that now and I'm sure she'll find work for you, too. A man who's as good with horses as you are, I'm sure she wouldn't want to do without. We would then earn money and if we save well, maybe in a few years we could afford something small to call our own."

Isabella looked at Chágha tho expectantly. He saw a gleam in her eyes and inevitably had to smile. Isabella didn't seem to notice how she had become more and more excited and enterprising while telling the story. She was literally bubbling over with thirst for action. There she was again, the old Isabella, with her pugnacious nature, which had already impressed him first time they had met.

"Can you teach me that, too?"

"What?" abruptly she stopped her horse and looked him inquiringly. Chágha tho reined in his stallion, brought him next to Isabella's mare and bent close to her. He stole a kiss, grinned at his wife's surprised look on her face and then casually said:
"Reading and writing and all that."
"Are you serious?"
"Yeah, I want to be able to do that, too. Can you teach me?"
"Of course!"

Only now did she realize that her husband could not do things that she had long taken for granted. He had never had the opportunity to go to school. But if they wanted to live among whites it was better if he mastered these things. She would try to fulfill his wish as soon as possible. Also another thing occurred to her. It would be better if his appearance would change a little.

She loved him the way he was and the way he acted, but in her world his appearance was not accepted. She could get him different clothes, but his long hair still made him look too Indian. But for right now she said nothing. When the time came, she would have to bring up this subject.
"We're going to start doing that right now tonight."
"Then we'll be on our way to that ranch."

A good two days later, they arrived at the first fences, which told them that it was not far any longer. They had talked about how they were going to proceed in the last couple days.

After initial reservations on the part of Chágha tho, Isabella had prevailed and had declared that she would ride to the ranch alone to speak with the owner. Isabella had thought it would be easier because the lady knew her well. So they build their camp, a half an hour's ride from the ranch house of the MacIntyres, in the shelter of a small grove. The next day she wanted to go and put in a good word for them with the old lady.

The sun was already high in the sky when Isabella passed the main gate to the ranch. Since the last time she had been here, it had been almost a year ago, nothing seemed to have changed.

The gate through which she was riding was adorned with the name of the ranch. It was made of three large logs and spanned the road. To the right and left of it lined huge pastures, where horses grazed in several groups along the way. She knew from her past visits that it was still a while until the first huts were to be seen. First she would pass two large elongated buildings that were the quarters of the single cowboys.

A little further on, log cabins came in sight where the cowboys, who had families of their own, lived. Then there were barns and pantries, and even an ice house, where food could be stored in a cool place. As Isabella rode on, she felt as though she was entering a small town of her own. There was a hustle and bustle. Cowboys with and without horses crossed her path, lifted their hats in greeting and let her move on.

Carts with hay drove to the detached paddocks behind, where more horses could be seen. Some cowboys were busy lassoing them. Others were standing in line with their horse at their own farrier's. Isabella was amazed at how many people seemed to be working on the ranch, and was not sure anymore if they would really find work.

What should they do if the old lady didn't need any more help? But then she saw the children, helping their mothers in the small front gardens, weeding, hanging out the laundry, or chopping wood. Everyone who saw her greeted her kindly, and Isabella greeted back.

All these children she could teach. With renewed courage, she trotted towards the largest building, which was now directly in front of her. It was an imposing impression every time, when she rode up to the large, two-story wooden house. The house had been built from mighty logs that had withstood every storm and blizzard so far. She knew that the huge fireplace inside warmed the house wonderfully, even in the winter.

A large, wide porch ran around the entire house and was now decorated with inviting flower boxes. She had always wondered where Mrs. MacIntyre had gotten these flowers from, until last year when she had taken her to the adjoining garden at the back of the house.

Mrs. MacIntyre had shown her that she grew those flowers there which now graced her porch in the spring. The first seeds of the hardy plants she had brought with her from Scotland. Furthermore, the veranda was furnished with a swing, a small sitting area and several rocking chairs. In front of the house Isabella reined in her horse and dismounted. She tied it up to the stake and went up the three steps to the front door. Without hesistation she knocked and it was not long before the door opened and Felicitas, the housekeeper, appeared.

"Oh, Miss Hunt, it's good to see you. Mrs. MacIntyre didn't tell me you were coming over today."

"Hello Felicitas, how are you? I'm afraid I'm not registered, but I need to talk to her."

"She's out back in the garden, I'll tell her you're here. Why don't you come in first?"

Felicitas stepped aside and let Isabella enter. Then she went forward, indicated to her to wait in the parlor and disappeared into the back part of the house. Curious, Isabella looked around. She had already been in this room once before and had admired the elegant furnishings. Two windows gave the room the light it needed, to create a cozy atmosphere. Floor-length, heavy velvet curtains in a royal blue hung along the sides. In front of one of the windows stood a small white secretary, with an upholstered chair in front of it, which wore the same color as the curtains.

A little further along the wall was a glass display case in which Isabella discovered a small tea set made of precious porcelain. A small sideboard stood on the opposite side of the room, on which stood a vase of fresh meadow flowers. The walls were adorned with paintings of hunting scenes from Scotland.

In the middle of the room there was a small seating area with four armchairs, also with blue upholstery and a small side table. The floor was covered by a large round blue carpet with beige fringes. Isabella had always secretly referred to this room as the blue salon. She was just about to sit in one of the armchairs, when the door behind her opened and a sprightly old lady with gray hair and watchful green eyes appeared in the doorway. She was wearing a green dress that was trimmed with lace at the collar and sleeves.

Isabella knew that Elisabeth MacIntyre, despite her age, was a lady who had a firm grip on all the reins here at the ranch and that had always impressed her. Now she joyfully approached her with her arms outstretched.

"Isabella, my child. Well, this is a surprise. Where have you left your father and grandfather?"

"Good afternoon, Mrs. MacIntyre. I apologize for coming here unannounced, but I thought you might be able to help me."

"Help? Yes, for heaven's sake, has something happened? Is your father or grandfather not well?"

"Yes, yes, they are both very well. My father recently remarried and will introduce his wife to you at the summer party and grandfather is also looking

234

forward to seeing you again. But I have come alone because I want to talk to you."

"Then please take a seat."

Mrs. MacIntyre gestured toward one of the chairs.

"May I offer you something to eat or a cup of tea?"

"I'm not hungry, but a cup of tea, would be very nice. Thank you."

Mrs. MacIntyre nodded, turned briefly toward the hallway and called out, "Felicitas, would you bring us a cup of tea in the drawing room and if you have any of your delicious oatmeal cookies left, you're welcome to some of those too."

Without waiting for a response, she closed the door and sat down across from Isabella in one of the other armchairs.

"So my child, why don't you tell me how I can help you?"

On her way here, Isabella had been thinking about what she should tell the old lady. How much of what had happened in the last weeks, she had to reveal. In her mind it had been much easier to open up to her. But now that she was facing this strong woman, looking at her with an expectant look, she lost her courage. Elisabeth MacIntyre must have sensed this, too, because she smiled encouragingly at Isabella.

"Is it so bad what you want to tell me?"

"I confess that before I came here, it seemed very easy for me to talk about it. But now I don't know where to begin."

"It's best to start at the beginning. Take the time you need, I will listen to you."

There now came a knock at the door, and Felicitas appeared with a tray filled with oatmeal cookies, teacups, milk and sugar, and a delightfully fragrant teapot.

"Thank you Felicitas. I'll pour it myself. Please do

prepare the guest room for Miss. Hunt."

"Oh, no. Thank you very much Mrs. MacIntyre, but I can't stay the night."

"No? Surely you can't ride back in the night. Even just coming here was very reckless."

"I am not alone. I'm expected."

Mrs. MacIntyre looked at Isabella in astonishment, but said nothing. She sent Felicitas thankfully out of the room, poured tea for them both and handed Isabella the plate with the cookies. Whereupon she helped herself. She ate the cookie and drank the tea and then slumped back in the armchair. Slowly she began to tell her story.

"Well, it all started a few weeks ago, when I went for a ride..."

Isabella told about the attack of the cougar and how Chágha tho had suddenly appeared and saved her life. How he had appeared at the ranch and from that day on he had been working there. She told the lady that she had fallen in love with the Indian, and that they had been able to keep it a secret until the day of the fire. She also told her about the tensions that had existed between Carl and Chágha tho and his false accusations that had been made after the fire.

Elisabeth MacIntyre listened attentively and interrupted Isabella only when she had a question or something seemed unclear to her.

"...Then three days ago my father cast Chágha tho and me off the ranch. Since I do not have any riches, we need to earn money."

It was quiet for a while. Isabella hoped for a gracious reply from Mrs. MacIntyre, but she seemed to need a little more time to think. After a while, which seemed like an eternity to Isabella, she said to her:

"I see. This is really a somewhat precarious situation. I'll be honest with you. I can understand your father's anger and I can't absolve the young man that he has put you in a very awkward position. Also, of course, you should never have given yourself to him like that. But since we were all young once and made mistakes, I will blame youth. Also that your father had shown something of an explosive nature with the wedding.

I do not want to approve of the fact that your father married you against your will, but the law was on his side. Your father is a proud man, and I guess the whole affair has affected him deeply. As for everything else, I can say little about it, but I hope that with time, your relationship with each other will be fine. As for the young man, I hope that he is decent to you and treats you well?"

"Oh, yes. He has never treated me badly. He and I love each other."

"Mmmh. It will not be easy for you two and you will be exposed to hostility. You have to be aware of the fact that society doesn't like to see white and red mixing."

Isabella had feared that the old lady might so rule, and it was visibly leaving her the hope of help. But Elizabeth was not stupid and she saw the disappointment and hopelessness in the young woman's eyes. She bent over and patted Isabella's knee with her fingers.

"Well, in spite of everything, it was good that you came here. I will help you. As you may remember, a year and a half ago I had a small schoolhouse built, because I was expecting a teacher from Boston. Last year, I told you that unfortunately, the matter had fallen through and that I would have liked to have you for the post. I would like to repeat this offer now. The school building has a small living area in the back. It is nothing huge and probably not what you have been used to, but it has a place to sleep, a small cooking area with a table and chair, and a fireplace that heats the entire house.

It certainly still needs to be made homely, but with a good broom and a couple of buckets of water, you should be able to get it done. I offer you to move in as a teacher. I would pay you a small salary plus free housing. What do you say?"

Isabella couldn't believe her ears. This was more than she had hoped for. She jumped up and spontaneously hugged the old lady.

"Oh, Mrs. MacIntyre thank you so much. I don't even know what to say."

Somewhat touched, the lady replied, "Well then, just say, yes."

„Yes, yes. I'll tell my husband the good news right away."

"There is one more thing."

"Yes?"

"If your husband really is as good with horses as you've just told me," she said, then I'm sure my foreman can put him to good use. Have him report to John Kendall tomorrow afternoon. I will inform my foreman."

Isabella once again took hold of Elizabeth's hands and held them tightly.

"Thank you very, very much. I have known that you are a kind woman. I'm sure you won't regret your decision."

When Isabella arrived some time later at the campsite in the forest, she could already smell the delicious roast hare roasting on the fire. The water ran together in her mouth at the smell. She had not even noticed how hungry she had become in the meantime, but that had to wait. First she wanted to tell the good news to Chágha tho. Unfortunately, he was nowhere to be seen.

She dismounted, tended her horse and looked around to see if she could spot him anywhere. She had just made a few steps away from the campsite, when suddenly two arms wrapped around her and held her tight. Immediately she felt his lips on her neck. After the initial shock she laughed.

„How do you manage to sneak up on me so quietly every time that I don't notice you?"

He turned her around and held her in his arms, smiling. Astonished and surprised at the same time she looked at him, but before she could say anything, he closed her mouth with a kiss. Involuntarily, the fire in her burned and she returned his kiss with an unbridled passion. When she had to catch her breath for a moment, she looked at him in disbelief.

"Why did you do that?"

Isabella ran her hands through his now short black hair.

"I thought it was the right thing to do. Do you like it?"

"Well it's unusual and it changes your face a lot. But yes, I like it."

Joyfully he pulled her close and kissed her again. Isabella could not help herself, she ran her fingers over and over through his short, full hair. Lovingly she played with the strands and ruffled them.

If he had looked good before, the short haircut gave him a breathtaking appearance. His high cheekbones and energetic chin now stood out as well as the narrow nose, which gave him an aristocratic look.

His long black eyelashes also stood out which brought the incredibly blue eyes well to bear. If no one knew him, Chágha tho would no longer be recognized as an Indian. He was the best looking man she had ever seen, and with pride she said to herself that he belonged to her. Chágha tho lifted Isabella up in his arms and carried her over to the campfire.

He settled down with her on a blanket, quickly turned over the roasting hare once more and devoted himself entirely to the lovemaking, which had begun with a harmless kiss. Later, as they leaned together against a tree and ate their dinner, Chágha tho addressed her.

"Now tell me. What do you have to report."

"Starting tomorrow, we'll have a roof over our heads. I'm so happy that she hired us. It takes away a big burden and I'm sure you'll like it there. Tomorrow a new life starts for us."

Chapter 29

A few days had passed since then and Isabella and Chágha tho had settled in well in their new quarters.

On the first day he had reported to the foreman, while Isabella had spruced up the small schoolhouse. Now they had been at the ranch for almost a week and she had started the schooling of her small class.

During the day she taught her twelve students, who ranged in age from six and fourteen years old, and in the evenings she taught Chágha tho reading, writing and arithmetic. She was pleased with the progress everyone was making. Her students seemed to be eager to learn and participated joyfully in her lessons.

But most of all she was pleased with her husband, who, when he came home from a hard day's work in the evening, spent two hours after dinner writing words, solving arithmetic problems or reading to her from a book. In the short time he had made good progress. When they were in bed at night, after they had made love, he told her about his days.

About how he had only done menial work in the first few days, but soon was given the same tasks as everyone else. Isabella was glad that Chágha tho seemed to enjoy the work.

He had already seen with her father how hard work was necessary to run such a ranch economically, but here it was something else. Here he stood in wage and bread and had to prove every day that he also deserved it. She knew that there were no such fixed structures with the Indians and had feared that he would not be able to cope with it. So she was all the more pleased that he seemed to fit effortlessly into the team of cowboys and that they accepted him as one of them.

In addition, it came clear that he had changed optically very much with the short hair and thus not immediately reognized as an Indian. Something had to be done about his clothes as soon as possible, she thought, since all he had was her father's old blue shirt and his leggings with the fringes. His embroidered suede shirt hung washed in the closet, but he didn't want to wear it anymore because it was too Indian for him. She knew he was trying to hide his heritage.

This time they were to judge him by what he did and not by what he was, he told her when she asked him why he had cut off his hair. It must not have been easy for him to take this step since she knew that for Indians long hair had a spiritual meaning. With the hair, he had also cut off his roots. Isabella fervently hoped that they would both be happy here on the ranch.

Sometimes, she thought about her father and grandfather and all the dear people she had left behind. She missed them, but she also knew that there was no going back. She had promised Louisa to send her a few lines when she knew where they had found a place to stay. Isabella had the opportunity a few days ago to take a letter for Louisa to a messenger who was on his way to Laramie. He would deliver it to the reverend and ask him to give it to Louisa the next time he visited the ranch. With that, she made good on her promise and hoped that one day they would see each other again.

In the meantime, almost two weeks had passed since Isabella and Chágha tho had come to the ranch and Elisabeth had made up her mind to have a look at her new residents. As she often did when the weather was nice, she hitched up her carriage and drove it across the pastures to watch the cowboys at work and to discuss new tasks with her foreman.

She knew that she could rely on him completely. He had been working for her for a long time and had never been anything to complain about. John had his men well under control, even if there was a friction between them. Today she enjoyed the warm weather.

A light breeze blew over the land and as far as one could see, the lush green covered the pastures. It had become summer and it would not be long before they would be able to prepare for the highlight of each year, her summer party.

It was a wonderful time when all the neighbors came to see her. Suddenly, Elisabeth was brought out of her thoughts by a cawing. She glanced up at the almost cloudless blue sky, and spotted a few vultures in the distance. This did not bode well, and so she gave her horse the reins and let it trot forward in the direction of the birds. The closer she came to the spot, the clearer she could see the small group of people who were standing with their horses a little away from the herd of mares. Something was lying there in the grass, and she hoped that it was not what she feared. When she spotted John, she stopped her car and called him over.

"John, what happened here? I saw the vultures."

With quick steps, he approached her.

"Yes, a cougar unfortunately killed one of the new foals. I will assign some men to find the cougar and finish him off, because if he's still around, he might come back and try to get another one. I will also have the pasture guarded for the next few nights."

"This is not good news. Pull the measures, I also think they are absolutely necessary. We can't take the risk of him doing any more damage. Who do you think you're going to get to do the search for the cougar? He should have some experience."

"I was thinking of Chágha tho. He has agreed to hunt the puma, and I think he has the best qualifications for it. The others will stand guard here tonight."

"How is he doing? Can you use him? You know I usually only hire people who come highly recommended. But I made an exception with him."

"Well I'm pleased with him. Quite a pleasant fellow so far. He works hard and does not grumble when it comes to the distribution of work. However, I have a feeling he's hiding something."

"What do you mean by that? Do you think he's got something the sheriff might be interested in him?"

"No, I think it has something to do with himself. I've had to deal with so many cowboys, you get a feel for it. There are blowhards who think they can do everything and then it quickly turns out they just know how to put the saddle on. And then there are those who observe and wait. They are often the ones you should be wary of who are often underestimated.

I believe that Chágha tho belongs to those ones and that he is more experienced than he currently wants me to know. If he feels unobserved, then one can see how he communicates with the horses only by hand signals. Strange horses follow him by the word. His own horse is so fantastically trained, it parries on voice and signs. He seems to have an unbelievable feeling for these creatures and I have never seen anything like it. But he holds back this knowledge and at the moment I don't know why he is doing it. With your permission I would like to have him look at the mare that is destined for the Colonel.

The animal is somehow disturbed and so can not be sold to him. Unfortunately, the Colonel of all people, has set his mind on this animal, because his wife liked it so much."

"That sounds interesting. Isabella told me that on her father's ranch he worked with a horse who wouldn't let anyone get close to it. There are people out there like that, who have this gift. My husband and also my son could do something like that. It is a pity that you were not allowed to get to know either of them. Is Chágha tho here now? I would like to have a look at him, he's made me curious."

"Yes, he's standing over there with the others. It's the tall young man with the jet-black hair and the blue shirt."

Elizabeth followed with her gaze the outstretched arm of her foreman and froze. Although this man was facing her at the moment only with his back, his slim, tall and muscular stature, the color of his hair and his supple movements, reminded her inevitably of her late son.

Was this all just a wicked play of her imagination or could there really be so much resemblance. She hoped he would turn to her, but he did not do her that favor.

Of course, she could have called him to her or gone there herself, but something prevented her from doing so. Maybe she didn't want to destroy the illusion, that his face was different than she wanted to see in him.

"Mrs. MacIntyre is something wrong?"

John had seen his boss's petrified face as she had looked over at Chágha tho. He, too, had followed the look, but had not seen what had frightened the old lady so much.

"Mrs. MacIntyre? Is everything all right with you?"

"I beg your pardon? Oh, yes, yes. Everything is fine. I was just thinking for a moment of someone else. John, I have to get back. Please take care of the cougar, and, of course, I'll give you all the freedom you need

with the mare. Please keep me informed."
"Yes of course."

Elisabeth slowly turned her cart around and let her horse trot off. John took off his hat, scratched the back of his head and looked after her thoughtfully, then he put his hat back on and joined his men.

Arriving at the ranch house, she tied her horse in front of the house and walked quickly to the upper floor. Once there, she opened the former room of her son. Devoutly she stopped briefly in the open doorway and breathed in audibly. How long had it been since she had entered it for the last time. A pain of loss ran through her, as it always did, when she was in here.

Ever since her son had left the ranch and had gone to Scotland, nothing in this room had been changed. Everything was still as if he would appear any moment in the doorway, but she knew that this would never happen again. Even his bed was still made and on the bedside table stood the small oil lamp and laid the book in which he had last read. At the only window stood a small desk, on which paper and pencil lay.

On the right wall stood an armoire, which she now went to and opened it. She knew that there were still some of Robert's clothes hanging in it, that he had not taken with him, because they would not have been society in Scotland.

Elisabeth let her fingers run thoughtfully over the pants and shirts, then took a few of them out and spreat them on the bed. She picked out several pairs of work pants and shirts, stopped in front of the black cloth trousers and the elegant white shirt. She thought briefly, put these things on the bed with the others and was pleased with the idea that had come to her.

Quickly she put all the things together and made her way back to her one-horse carriage. It was already late afternoon when Elisabeth drove up to the small school building. Her eyes fell on the small garden in front of it and she had to acknowledge that Isabella had taken care of it and cleared it of the weeds.

The ground had been freshly dug up. She would soon give her some flower seeds, so that the most beautiful flowers could bloom there next spring. After she had tied her horse to a tree, she went to the door. She knocked and listened to the the quick footsteps that sounded from inside.

"Mrs. MacIntyre! What a lovely surprise. Do come in."

Isabella stepped aside and let her enter. Elisabeth let her gaze wander over the clean windows, over the floor, which was also clean, and saw a slate and chalk on each small desk. The textbooks were on her desk, which stood in front of a large blackboard. She was very pleased with what she saw. Her decision to take Isabella as her teacher had been the right one.

She had been told by the parents of her students that the children liked Isabella and enjoyed coming to school. Elisabeth was very happy about that and wanted to tell the young woman today.

Isabella led her further into the living area. Here, too, everything was clean and tidy. On the stove a delicious smelling soup was simmering. The furnishings were spartan and simple, as Elisabeth knew, but she admired the fact that Isabella had created a cozy atmosphere out of the little she had.

"May I offer you a cup of coffee or tea?"

"A tea would be nice. You've done a really good job in such a short time."

"Well, I wish I could have brought more from home, then I would have had other options, but that's the way it goes."

Isabella put water on the stove and prepared a pot of tea leaves.

"Isabella have you heard anything from your father?"

"No, he doesn't know I'm here and I want to keep it that way. He doesn't want me near him anymore and I have to accept that, even if it's hard for me."

"I'm sure everything will work out with time."

"I don't think so. By getting involved with Chágha tho, I died to him. He never really gave him a chance. From the very first day he was against him. He could have taken the stars from the sky and it would not have been enough. He has always seen the Indian in him and never the man. But I don't want to bore you with my problems. Chágha tho and I are so grateful to you for giving us this chance and I hope that you will be satisfied with us."

"That's exactly what I wanted to talk to you about. I saw that you had cleared the garden of weeds. If you would like, I can give you some flower and vegetable seeds, so that next year something can grow."

"That would be very nice. I would like to grow some vegetables."

„Do you enjoy teaching?"

"Oh yes - very much! The children learn quickly and I think they like the lessons, too."

As she spoke, she poured the water into the teapot and placed the pot with cups on the only table there was in her little kingdom. Elizabeth took a seat on one of the two chairs.

"It's the first time I've taught so many children at once," she said," but it's going well."

"That makes me happy, especially since I can also report to you that the parents have been equally positive about you. I saw your husband today from a distance. Unfortunately, I have not met him yet, but I would like to change that. In two days I get a visit from an old friend of the family. He is passing through on his way to Laramie and will be staying overnight. I would like to have you both for dinner at my house. It would be a very good opportunity in an informal setting."

Isabella didn't answer right away. She did not know how to turn her down.There was no way she could attend a dinner with Chágha tho. She knew that Elisabeth came from a very fine family and attached importance to proper etiquette in her house.

Under no circumstances did she want to show Chágha tho up and expose him to ridicule, and that would inevitably happen since he did not even have the right clothes.

"Mrs. MacIntyre, it is quite charming that you want to invite us but I'm afraid I'm going to have to refuse."

"But why my child? It's only a casual dinner."

"I can't tell you why, it would be too embarrassing."

"Oh I see, it was silly of me not to come right out with it. Well, I already told you that I saw your husband today and I noticed that he's about the same size as my late son. I have outside in my carriage some pants and shirts that I'd like him to have. Why should my son's clothes be left in the closet for the moths, when your husband could use them?"

"I cannot accept that; you have already given us so much that it would not be right to take any more."

"That is nonsense. I insist. I have them hanging around uselessly , and your husband needs a pair of pants. Isabella, I know you're a proud woman. You want to prove to yourself and to others that you can manage your life on your own. Nevertheless, you are allowed to accept help from time to time. We women have to stick together. The next town is far away and you have to save every cent if you want to build something of your own one day. I, on the other hand, have these old pants that probably don't even fit fashion anymore, and I would be happy to turn them over to you. Do me the favor and take them and then you attend dinner at seven o'clock on Saturday."

Isabella nodded and agreed. She couldn't refuse the old lady and accompanied Mrs. MacIntyre to her carriage and took the package of clothes.

Chapter 30

When Isabella heard a noise behind her, she turned around and looked into the blue eyes of her husband. What a transformation. She could hardly believe it herself, but tonight nothing reminded her of the Indian in him. He looked like an elegant gentleman. His long, slender legs were tucked into the black cloth trousers, which fit him perfectly.

He wore black boots that Frank had given him for work and had polished to a shine. The muscular torso was covered with the white linen shirt and its long sleeves. Around his neck he should have worn a matching collar and a vest or jacket, but those things he did not have, and so he had loosely left open the first button on his shirt. His black hair shone like velvet and fell lightly on the collar at the nape of his neck.

Perhaps she should have cut his hair a little more accurately but the way it was, it gave him a bold expression which she liked immensely. If she had not already fallen madly in love with him, today she would have. He looked breathtaking, however, he himself did not seem to be sure of his effect on her and looked a little uncertain.

"You look great. I love you!"

"You really think so. The clothes are unfamiliar. I'd feel more comfortable if I didn't have to dress up like this."

Isabella gave him an encouraging kiss.

"I know, but it's the appropriate attire for the evening. Let's go, or we'll be very late."

Chágha tho took Isabella's hand, pulled her to him and kissed her. She looked beautiful. She was wearing an elegant, dark green dress, which Louisa had wisely smuggled into her garment bag and the color reminded him of her eyes when she was full of passion. He could not let his thoughts drift any further in this direction, because otherwise she might not get out of the house. So he detached himself from her and together they went over to the main house.

Felicitas opened the door and led them into the large dining room in the back of the house. She knocked on the door and entered as Mrs. MacIntyre's voice sounded from inside. Chágha tho let his wife go first and stayed back a little. Immediately, Elizabeth came toward her with open arms.

"Good evening my dear, you look lovely. May I introduce Mr. George Franklin to you. George, this is Mrs. Isabella Hunt. Perhaps you remember her. She's the daughter of James Hunt, our next-door neighbor, and she's been here two weeks with her husband. I have been able to get her to teach at the school."

"Oh, yes. Good evening, Mrs. Hunt."

Mr. Franklin took the hand offered to him, bent forward and indicated a kiss on the hand.

"It is an honor."

Elizabeth, looked around for Chágha tho but he had not yet entered the room. Somewhat confused, she turned to Isabella.

"Isabella, where did you leave your husband? Didn't he come with you?"

At that moment, however, the young man entered the room and stood rooted to the spot in the doorway. He had never seen such splendor. Since he had entered the house, he could no longer come out of the amazement. He had already thought the Hunts' ranch was huge, but this house was in comparison much larger and more elegantly furnished.

This room alone could easily accommodate half the tribe of his father. Everywhere he looked, there was classy looking furniture in the room and on the walls. The chairs in the room were covered with fabric, the table in the middle of the room had been set for four at one end, while the rest of the long table was left empty. A silver candlestick stood in the center.

On the windows hung heavy red curtains and on the walls hung some portraits. What was he doing here? It was not his world. He didn't know his way around here. He didn't know how he should behave. He would have liked to turn on his heel and flee from the house, but then he felt Isabella taking his arm encouragingly and step next to him. She was trying to make him feel safe, and as long as she stayed with him, all was well.

"Mrs. MacIntyre. May I introduce my husband Chágha tho to you?"

Elizabeth had stopped moving the moment Chágha tho had entered the room. As if petrified, she stood before him and stared at him.

"My God, Robert!" she whispered, barely audible. All color had drained from her face. She swayed a little, and immediately Mr. Franklin and Isabella came anxiously to her aid.

George hurriedly pulled out a chair and sat the old lady down on it. Isabella poured a glass from the water carafe that stood on the table and handed it to her.

"Elisabeth, are you not well? Shall I tell Felicitas to take you upstairs? Maybe you should get some rest?"

In a strong voice, she replied, "No, I'm fine."

She gratefully accepted the glass of water from Isabella, drank it down and then rose slowly under the watchful gaze of George and Isabella. She walked directly toward Chágha tho and held out her hand in greeting.

"I'm sorry for my appearance, I didn't mean to frighten you. But the way you appeared in the doorway, I saw my deceased son in front of me. You have a lot of resemblance to him."

„ I'm sorry if I frightened you."

"No, you didn't. It was foolish of me, I just wasn't prepared for it. Please come in. I am glad to finally meet you and I hope that you like it here as much as your wife."

After the initial shock, everyone sat down at the table. Isabella took a seat next to Chágha tho, while Elisabeth sat at the end of the table and George to her left. A little later Felicitas brought in the food and left the small society to itself.

It was supposed to be an informal dinner, but the evening turned out to be difficult. While Elizabeth, George and Isabella tried to keep a conversation going, Chágha tho had become increasingly silent.

In the beginning, he answered questions, but then his answers had become more and more monosyllabic, until he barely followed the conversation. Something seemed to be preoccupying him. Isabella sensed how Chágha tho was becoming more and more distant from this place. The other two noticed it, too, but they politely ignored the bad behavior.

Isabella, on the other hand, would have liked to have jumped up and set his head straight. She knew that he was not a man of big words, but this behavior was embarrassing for her. How could he do this to her? Chágha tho, however, did not seem to notice anything amiss and stared with a blank look at a certain point on the wall behind Elisabeth. Just as Elisabeth was about to say something, Chágha tho rose without a word and went directly to the wall behind her.

Three pairs of eyes followed him with curiosity and Elisabeth paused in what she wanted to say. It had become quiet in the room. She turned around and saw him standing right in front of a portrait, which showed her husband and her son back then at the age of eighteen. "Who are these two men?"

Chágha tho had addressed this question more to himself than to anyone in the room, but Elizabeth had risen and was now standing beside him.

"This is my husband Kieran with our son Robert. How old are you?"

"I don't know exactly, Madam. Maybe twenty or twenty-one."

Elisabeth had had a feeling ever since she saw him in the pasture, and it had grown stronger tonight. For fifteen years she had hung on to a hope that had never left her. Could it be possible that God finally had heard her? She had to find out more about this young, silent man. It was hard for her to keep her excitement in check, but she didn't want to scare him off.

He was just beginning to open up a little to her. Elisabeth had completely forgotten the two others in the room. At the moment, only Chágha tho mattered, and she did not want to destroy this moment.

"Chágha tho, do you want to tell me how you grew up?"

Somewhat puzzled, he looked at her, but something about that question told him that it was important for both of them to answer it.

"I was adopted by Chief Kitchi Honovi as a boy. He was the Chief of the Cheyenne. Until a few months ago I didn't know that I was adopted and thought that I was his legal son. But on his deathbed, he told me that I came to him from the Sioux when I was a little boy. Since then I've been trying to find out more about my past."

Elizabeth's heart leapt. It would all fit. The pieces of the puzzle were slowly coming together.

"Would you follow me for a moment, please? I would like to show you something."

Chágha tho, who had apparently become aware again that there were others in the room, sought Isabella's gaze and saw that she nodded to him. Elizabeth, meanwhile, was already at the door to the hallway. Curious, she was followed by not only Chágha tho, but also Isabella and George.

They found her in her writing room. There, on the secretary, stood a framed photograph. She took it in her hand and handed it to Chágha tho. In a trembling voice she asked him, "Do you recognize anyone in the photograph?"

Chágha tho took the photograph in his hands and stared at it for a long time. Something touched him, but he could not see it clearly. He closed his eyes and tried to concentrate. He noticed how the sounds around him became different. He heard screams and horses.

People screaming in pain and others, who seemed to be shouting for joy. He saw Indians in their war paint and saw a frightened face of a white woman holding a small child close to her. Words came to him. Words of love of a mother for her child.

He recognized in her the lady from the photograph. But then he looked into the empty eyes of this woman and knew that she was dead. Unconsciously, Chágha tho reached for the amulet which he always wore around his neck and held it tightly. Elizabeth saw in Chágha tho's face, the agonies that the child's soul must have gone through on that past day and it almost tore her heart apart. Isabella saw the wildly throbbing vein in his neck and the pain in his face. She wanted to help him, but Elisabeth held her back.

"Please don't, he has to remember. I need answers and he needs certainty."

She didn't understand exactly what was going on and George was also looking on, stunned.

All at once Chágha tho startled and let the picture slip out of his hand. Isabella was just able to catch it before it fell to the floor. She glanced at it and knew all at once what Elisabeth was getting at. The man in the photo looked like the one in the portrait in the dining room and had an egregious resemblance to Chágha tho.

Just when she was about to give the picture back to Elisabeth, her eyes fell on the lady in the picture. She looked closer, could it really be? She looked up and noticed that Elisabeth was again completely focused on Chágha tho, who seemed to have calmed down and was now also staring at her with open eyes.

With astonishment she noticed that her husband had watery eyes, but Elisabeth also seemed to be on the verge of bursting into tears. What was happening right now?

"What did you just see?", Elisabeth wanted to know with a faltering breath. Slowly and noticeably struggling for composure the Indian answered her.

"The woman and the man from the photo....many Indians in war paint and everywhere dead.... and screams, terrible screams of death. A massacre."

Isabella had now stepped forward and held out the photo to the old Lady.

"Mrs. MacIntyre. What does all this mean? I don't quite understand what's going on here."

Elizabeth slapped her hands in front of her face, closed her eyes and took two deep breaths before opening her eyes again and making a statement.

"This photograph shows my son Robert and his wife Moira with their son Cameron, just before their trip to visit us. My son had been in Scotland for several years to take care of our property. He met his wife in Scotland and had my grandson. They were all on their way to us when this attack happened. He had sent this photograph together with a letter announcing his visit to us before they went on the trip. How happy we were.

After the long time we wanted to finally embrace the family in our arms. My husband and I were so excited to have our grandchild here that we could hardly wait. But then we got the bad news, that the wagon train he had joined had been attacked by Indians shortly before their arrival.

The soldiers of the Fort had ridden to look after the trek when it was overdue and had not arrived. The picture for them must have been terrible, because they never released a lot of information about it. The fact that there were no survivors and that all of them had been bestially murdered, hit us with unimaginable force.

The strange thing, however, was that among the dead, none of the children had been found. At first there was hope that at least they would be found, but with each passing day, without any trace of them being found, hope was lost. Soldiers who had seen several massacres in their lives had told us what Indians like to do with captured children. Any death, on the other hand, would have been a salvation and so there was a time when we pleaded with God that our grandson would hopefully be spared that. My husband set up a small cemetery behind the house, three crosses with their names on it.

The graves are empty, because the soldiers buried all of them on the spot, but it gave us a place to feel close to them. Despite the cross for my grandson and that I was told that he could not possibly be alive, I never stopped believing that one day a miracle might happen and he would come to us. My husband often got angry with me because I simply did not want to let go. Unfortunately, a few years after this tragedy he died. I think he was heartbroken."

Elisabeth paused for a moment and looked into the

moved faces of Isabella and Chágha tho.

George, who as a friend of the family back then could apparently still remember the terrible time well, for he nodded mutely. Elizabeth walked toward Chágha tho, looked him firmly in his blue eyes, as if she wanted to make sure one last time before she spoke again.

"Chágha tho, after what you have told me today and after what I have seen with my own eyes, I firmly believe that you...that you are my grandson Cameron."

Chágha tho looked at her in horror. He had indeed understood what she had said to him, but he had not realized it. What was happening here right now? Was his memory playing tricks on him? He had to think, he wanted to be alone. Never before in his life had he felt so confused. But before he could escape from it all, George walked toward Elizabeth. He knew how she had longed for this moment for fifteen years, but was it really Chágha tho? Could it be? After all these years?

"Elisabeth are you absolutely sure about this?"

"George, you can see it for yourself. The size, the look, these movements and the blue eyes. He's the spitting image of Robert. On top of that, my foreman and Isabella told me independently of each other that he is particularly good with horses. These are the skills that all MacIntyre men have had in recent generations. I'm not gullible, but this is enough evidence for me."

"Isn't there perhaps more?"

"Oh, yes. There is something else."

All eyes were on Isabella. She walked past Elisabeth, took the photograph in her hand once more and pointed her finger at the lady in the picture.

"Do you see that necklace there? Chágha tho has a necklace that looks just like that."

Immediately, all eyes turned to him, who slowly took the necklace from under his shirt, took it off and handed it to Elisabeth.

"Where did you get this necklace?" asked George.

"My foster father gave it to me on his deathbed. Said that it had been around my neck when I came to him."

Elizabeth looked at it closely and knew immediately, that it could be opened.

"George, this necklace is my mother's. It was part of our family jewelry. Robert must have given it to his wife Moira, who in turn gave the necklace to Cameron. Inside are two photographs. Unfortunately, you can't make out their faces anymore but, they look like they could be Moira and Robert."

George, who still did not seem to be one hundred percent convinced, said nothing. Isabella looked at Chágha tho who stood there with a petrified face. She would have given a lot if she knew what he was thinking at that moment, but she could not see any movement in his face. Elisabeth, on the other hand, made one last attempt to convince everyone involved of what she had long since known with her heart.

"There's something else that all the MacIntyre men have had. My father-in-law had it, my husband had it, and even Robert had it. It's a little birthmark that has a heart shape and was on the right shoulder blade. Chágha tho, do you have such a birthmark?"

Isabella remembered the birthmark that she had seen when she had treated his wounds on his back and nodded immediately.

Elizabeth, overhearing this, turned to Chágha tho.

"Would you please take off your shirt for us so that we can see this birthmark?"

George had come closer and was now standing next to Elizabeth. Elisabeth, George and Isabella stood and waited anxiously for him to deliver the proof and on the other side stood Chágha tho, who gave the impression as if he wanted to escape from this situation. Isabella felt sorry for him.

She saw the harried look in his eyes. Chágha tho felt like a predator in his cage. He no longer understood his world. He was supposed to be the grandson of this lady? Without a word, Chágha tho unbuttoned his shirt and took it off. Then he turned around to show his back. Horrified Elisabeth put her hands over her mouth and George was startled. The birthmark was almost forgotten, because now the red welts of the whip were clearly seen.

"He has been whipped," whispered George more to himself and Elizabeth asked:

"Who did this to you?"

Isabella was embarrassed and was about to say something, when Chágha tho annoyed and angry

replied," That doesn't matter here. The birthmark is here on the right shoulder."

He turned his right shoulder toward them and all of them could clearly see the heart-shaped mark.

This was proof enough. Chágha tho put his shirt back on and turned around. Elisabeth's tears were running down her cheek. It was real. She wanted to take her grandson in her arms and hold him tight forever, but she recognized the young man's dismissive attitude that it was too early for that. She tried to keep her distance from him and said to everyone present in this room:

"Chágha tho is clearly my grandson Cameron. To be more precise: Lord Cameron MacIntyre."

Chágha tho saw the joy and surprise in the faces of the others. He probably should have felt the same. But somehow he could not. The only thing he knew was that he wanted to get out of here as fast as possible. He couldn't stand the house and its inhabitants at the moment and so he turned without a word and left the room with hurried steps. He did not notice the surprised shouts behind him. Elisabeth wanted to follow him, but Isabella held her back.

"I think it's better if I go and see him."

"Yes, perhaps it is better. I didn't want to scare him off. I'm sorry."

Isabella just nodded, thanked her out of politeness for the dinner and followed her husband. Elisabeth struggled with herself. For fifteen years she had hoped and prayed for this day to come, and now that it was actually here, she had done everything wrong.

She had pushed and forced Chágha tho and in the end she had put him to flee like a hunted animal. If she lost him again now, when she did not even know him well, she would never forgive herself.

"George, I'm such a fool. I wish Kieran had lived to see this day, he would have known what to do. I, on the other hand, did everything wrong. I should have been more attentive to him, taken things slower.

Instead, I assaulted him with my impatience. He probably does not understand a lot of what I said and I would like to explain it to him, but now I might not have the opportunity to do so. George, what am I going to do? I'm afraid of losing him again."

George took Elizabeth's hands and added encouragingly," I don't think he's going to run away. Give him a little time to calm down and think things over, and I'm sure everything will work out."

"I hope you are right. One request I have for you. What has been spoken here tonight remains among us. No one should know yet that he is my grandson."

"You can count on me."

She found him outside, not far from the house, with his back to her leaning against a tree. The bright moonlight made his white shirt shine in the night.

Actually, she felt the need to take him in her arms and hold him tight, but the closer she came, the more she had the feeling, that he wanted to be alone. She was just about to turn, when she heard his words:

"Don't go!"

He didn't have to tell her twice. She threw herself into his arms, nestled up against him and held him as tight as she could. He wrapped his arms around her and enjoyed how the warmth of her body flowed into him and touched his heart. His chin rested on the top of her head.

"I need you," he whispered to her. "I need you so damn much."

Isabella said nothing, letting him speak. She could tell how he was troubled inside. Lovingly she stroked his back.

"Is the old lady upset that I just left? I just couldn't stand it in there anymore."

"I know. Your grandmother is not upset, maybe disappointed. She didn't expect your reaction. I told her that I would follow you."

Chágha tho broke away from Isabella and walked two steps, then he turned around and replied resolutely:

"I'm not going back in there, you don't even have to try." He made a sweeping motion.

"All of this. This isn't me. I can't do this, Isabella. She puts expectations on me, that I can't live up to. The old lady in there," he pointed his finger at the big house, "sees in me only her son, which I am not. I can't replace him, I don't even know what he was like. For God's sake, I don't even know who I really am! My whole life just got turned upside down in there!"

Isabella walked up to him and tenderly took his face in her hands.

"No one expects anything from you. All your grandmother wants is to talk to you. She knows you're not her son. So give her a chance to get to know her grandson. Give her a chance to get to know you better. Give you both the time. Talk to her - not today but in the next few days. She can answer your questions and you can show her what a great grandson she has. She is your family."

Chágha tho looked at his wife thoughtfully. The moonlight reflected in her green eyes. She looked so lovely. Isabella had found her way effortlessly in this environment. He, on the other hand, had not felt at ease. The clothes that were not his, the elegant house, which had literally slain him, and then the truth about himself. He was about to run away from it, but the more he calmed down, the more he realized that Isabella was right. Maybe he would talk to the lady again, but not today. Now he just wanted to get away from here. His gaze wandered upward. He saw the starry sky.

The moon shone and he thought that it was probably the most beautiful night he had ever spent with Isabella, if it had not been for this. Slowly he bent his head down and kissed Isabella passionately. When she returned his kiss, he said, "Let's go home."

Chapter 31

Two long days had passed since the dinner and Elizabeth had not yet seen Chágha tho again.She knew that he was still there, but he seemed to be avoiding her. How much more time would he need?

She tried to exercise patience and occupied herself with her garden as a distraction. It was a very beautiful mild day in July and in her garden flowers, herbs and vegetables were growing. She was just keeping the weeds in check when she heard a familiar voice behind her.

"What was my father like?"

Elisabeth was startled and saw the tall figure of her grandson in broad sunlight in front of her. Sitting on his horse in his Indian dress. How long he had been watching her from there, she could not say, but as relaxed as horse and rider were standing, it must have been quite a while. She did not answer immediately, but looked at him from top to bottom.

Did he want to scare her or why had he put on his Indian clothes? She admitted to herself that the sight had its effect. What else had her foreman told her about him?

That the calm impression should not be underestimated? That this impression should not hide the fact that he could be very dangerous. Yes, she believed him on his word. She tried not to be intimidated further and went through the small garden gate towards him. When he made no effort to dismount, she put her hand on his arm and looked up into his face and said.

"It is warm and my bones are old. Let's go into the shade and have a glass of water."

Thereupon she walked away towards the house and left him to follow her. She stepped out onto the porch and sat down in one of the chairs that stood in the shade. Chágha tho followed with his horse, slid down and tied it to a post. He followed her and sat down in the chair next to her. Without paying any further attention to him she began to talk.

"Robert was my only child, and he was a horse lover, like his father and grandfather. He was strong, brave and smart. Together with his father, he made this ranch what it is today. He loved this country, didn't want to go. But when my brother died overseas and left everything to me, he was immediately ready to manage the estates in Scotland. At first it was only to be for a year or two, but then he met his wife and you came and finally his stay was prolonged, extended again and again. That's why we were so happy when he finally wanted to come with you. Unfortunately, fate played nasty tricks on us."

Elisabeth stopped talking and an oppressive silence took place. She had the feeling that Chágha tho wanted to say something, but he remained silent. For quite a while they sat like this side by side and looked into the distance, but then Chágha tho said to her.:

"I will never replace your son."

Elizabeth listened. Was this what seemed to be tormenting him? Had she given him the wrong impression?

"Is that why you came in your Indian clothes to prove it to me?"

Chágha tho owed her an answer, but she looked at him and knew she had hit the nail on the head.

"What does it mean, Chágha tho?"

"It is the word in the Cheyenne language for 'ice blue' and refers to the color of my eyes."

"A truly fitting name - the eyes were the first thing I noticed about your grandfather. He also had these bright blue eyes. A special Macintyre characteristic. Oh, if only he were here now. He was so looking forward to seeing you then. For weeks, he talked about nothing but the things he was going to show his grandson. He even had a little pony picked out for you."

Elisabeth had to fight for her composure. Tears welled up in her eyes, when she thought back to that time.

"Chágha tho, if it were within my power to turn back time and make everything undone, I would not hesitate for a second. I cannot undo the suffering that has happened to you, and I have long struggled with God as to why He has done this to us. Your grandfather became a broken man and died two years later.

I lost everything that was ever dear to me, but I am infinitely happy that fate has brought you here. You are a young man and have your life ahead of you. You can go wherever you want and make your own decisions. I demand nothing from you and presuppose nothing. I would just be happy if you would give us a little time to get to know each other better.

I would like to know more about you. Would like to know something about your life, know your thoughts, understand you better. Maybe you feel the same. You said that the chief died, is his wife still alive? Did you have brothers and sisters?"

Chágha tho had become very thoughtful during the narration of her. That what she had told him touched him. This attack had more victims than he could imagine. He himself could not remember the first years of his life and he had almost no memory of the attack. It was probably better that way. He did not want to imagine what the Sioux had done to him and the other children, because he knew what they were capable of. His luck had probably been that he had come to the Cheyenne. When the chief had summoned him months ago to tell him the truth, a desire had arisen in him to find out his truth. Now that his search was over, he did not know how to deal with the facts.

Actually, his grandmother only wanted the same thing as he did, so why did he have such a hard time with it. He gave himself a push and began to speak.

"The chief and his wife could not have children, so they ransomed me from the Sioux. He made me into who I am today. My mother, I mean, my Foster mother, is still alive. I don't have any brothers or sisters."

"Are you going to go back to them?"

"No. I've said goodbye forever. It would be no life for Isabella, either."

"You could stay here. It could become your home. One day, all of this will be yours."

"I don't know anything about running a ranch."

"This can all be learned and I could teach you everything I know. It would be worth a try if you want and I know you are good with horses. So you bring the best prerequisites already. You do not need to make any commitments. If you decide to change your mind and want to leave some day, I will accept that. What do you think?"

Chágha tho considered for a moment. Nothing would change for him for the time being. Isabella would continue to teach the children and he would do his work on the ranch. It gave him time to come to terms with the new situation. Quickly he agreed.

"I have one condition, though. I want you to call me Cameron from now on. Chágha tho belongs to the past. Starting today."
Joyfully, his grandmother agreed.

Chapter 32

Six weeks had passed since Cameron had sat on the porch with his grandmother. Things had changed since then. The relationship between grandmother and grandson had visibly improved. They often sat together with Isabella in the evening on the veranda and talked.

The quiet, taciturn Indian had turned into a young man who had worked hard to earn the respect of the cowboys and her foreman. Unlike on the ranch of James Hunt, the men had accepted him as one of them, even before they had learned that he was the prodigal grandson of the owner and thus stood before them.

Elizabeth had understood the need to give him the chance to earn his own position on the ranch, which he had made good use of. He had developed a good relationship with her foreman and worked hand in hand with him. Meanwhile, she left it up to him to make his own decisions.

She trusted his abilities and saw that he was not afraid to ask her for help or advice when it was needed. She was also pleased that she could observe how much Cameron loved Isabella. When they thought they were alone, they exchanged kisses or caresses with each other. Who would have thought six weeks ago that everything would work out so well. Robert and his grandfather would be proud of him if they could see him today.

The only downer was that he still refused to move into their house. He still lived with Isabella in the small schoolhouse. An accommodation that was absolutely unworthy of a Scottish-born Lord, but she did not want to discuss this subject with either of them.

At the moment, she could not devote time to this topic, because the annual summer festival was coming up. She had been busy for two weeks making all the preparations. In two days, the neighbors would show up and until then there was still a lot to do. Isabella was a good help, although Elisabeth noticed that the young woman had been looking very pale in the last few days and she was a little worried about her.

Just as she thought of her, the door opened and Isabella came into the large dining room with an armful of tablecloths.

"Here are the tablecloths I was supposed to bring. Now we can set up the table that's already done."

"Yes, let's do it then."

Suddenly Isabella swayed and held on to the edge of the table. When Elisabeth saw this, she rushed over and pushed Isabella down on a chair.

"Aren't you feeling well?"

"Oh I don't know. For a few days now I've been feeling dizzy a lot, and I don't really have much of an appetite. Yesterday morning I couldn't keep my food down."

"Does Cameron know about this?"

"No, I didn't want to worry him, and he's often gone by the time I get up in the morning. But there's something wrong with me."

"You have been very pale for a few days. When did the complaints start?"

"Maybe a week ago? It's often only in the morning. I'm really starting to worry, what could it be."

Elisabeth felt Isabella's forehead.

"You don't have a fever. I think you could be in other circumstances."

"A child? Are you sure about that?"

"Well, I'm not a hundred percent sure, you need to wait a little longer, but from your description everything points to it. I think you should not worry too much. If it is the morning ailment, it will soon pass. Oh, a child! That would be a joy!"

Elisabeth clapped her hands.

"What is Cameron going to say about that. We never talked about kids. Maybe he doesn't like kids."

"Oh, poppycock. He'll be thrilled and he'll be a great father."

Not quite as convinced that he would share his grandmother's enthusiasm, Isabella replied, "I certainly hope so."

"The best thing you can do is go and tell him."

With that, Elisabeth pulled Isabella to her feet and gently pushed her out of the room.

But that evening, when Cameron had come home, she had not found a suitable moment to tell him about his grandmother's suspicions. She had been at the hearth and had been preparing dinner, when he had come in. His cowboy hat, which he always wore now, was placed on a hook on the wall and he stepped behind her. Tenderly he had taken her in his arms and kissed her. Immediately the passion grew between them, as it happened every time he touched or kissed her.

She only had to take one look at him and she was instantly hooked. He still exerted a magical attraction over her. Memories of places where they had made love appeared before her eyes and she noticed herself blushing. Cameron, pulled the fragrant pot from the stove, slipped the latch over the fire and lifted his wife up on his arm. Surprised, she wanted to say something in return, but he closed her mouth with a kiss. "I'm hungry for something else now."

He didn't need to say more. He brought her over to the bed and began to slowly, and with pleasure, peel her out of her clothes. With impatient hands Isabella tugged at his shirt. He laughed and pulled it over his head. Finally she could nestle against his strong chest. She loved to slide her hands over his hard muscles; running her fingers through his soft, raven hair, while he kissed her. In the arms of this man she was like soft butter. She could no longer think clearly and only wanted him to give her fulfillment.

He also wanted to fulfill her wish and so it was quite late when they had their dinner. Since Cameron usually diligently practiced reading and writing with Isabella for an hour or two after supper, she wanted to get out the reading book for him, but he held her back.

"Let it go for today. I am no longer in the condition to remember anything in my head."

He grinned as she looked at him inquiringly, and pulled her onto his lap.

"We need to talk about something important."

"Oh yeah, what?"

"Your father will be here in two days. So what are we going to do?"

"Honestly, I have no idea. My first thought was to stay out of his sight while he's here, but that's not possible. However, I don't want to spoil the feast by having a fight with my father."

Cameron tenderly stroked her cheek.

"You don't have to be afraid of your father. He can't hurt you here."

"I know, but the situation still weighs on me. I wish he could forgive me."

James sat moping in front of the house and smoking his cigarette as he had so many times in the past. Next to him on a small table sat an empty bottle of brandy and a glass. When the front door opened and Louisa appeared, he called out to her.

"Bring out another bottle of brandy before you go."

Louisa, who could no longer bear the misery that had been going on for two months, went angrily toward him.

"With respect, sir, I won't do that. I think you've had enough."

James, who thought he had misheard, rose from his chair and stood in front of Louisa with a threatening finger.

"Who gives you the right to talk to me like that?"

Louisa, who had been working at the Hunts' ranch for a very long time, was not afraid of her boss and so she answered him in a firm voice.

"It's about time someone told you what everyone here is thinking. Since the day you expelled Isabella from the ranch, you're no longer yourself. You don't care about the ranch anymore. You left it to your father, who, at his age, really can't do everything alone, nor do you take care of your young wife.

Marylou doesn't deserve to be treated so dismissively. In general, there is no air to breathe in this house anymore. Everybody tries to sneak around on cat's paws and give a wide berth to you and your moods. No friendly word comes from your lips, as it used to.

No more laughter sounds in this house and the name of Isabella may only be mentioned behind closed doors. You should see yourself once. You try to soothe your conscience with alcohol and sinking into pity, that has never helped anyone."

"Oh, go to hell and leave me alone."

James turned away and wanted to enter the house but he was too drunk and lost his balance. Louisa tried to support him, but he withdrew his arm from her.

"No I won't do that. You miss her as much as the rest of us. Get her back. No mistake in the world is worth banishing your only child. I admit that at first I also wronged Chágha tho. I was just as suspicious of him as everyone else here. Malcolm was always different, he liked him from the first moment.

I've changed my mind about him, too, because he saved my and Malcolm's life, and anyone who does this can't be that bad. Besides, you should have seen the loving look he gave your daughter the day they left. They love each other. Give yourself a break and make up with Isabella."

James seemed to have become thoughtful, because he leaned against the wall of the house and let the admonishing words come over him. Louisa hooked her arm under his and pulled him into the house with her. James let it happen, but when he reached the stairs to the upper floor, he turned to her, "Even if I wanted to, I wouldn't know where she is. How am I ever going to find her again?"

"If you really want to do it, I can tell you where she is."

Abruptly he stopped.

"You know where she is, and you haven't told me all this time?"

"She made me promise that I wouldn't tell anyone, especially not you. But I believe that I can reconcile it with my conscience if I tell you now. It serves a good cause, the preservation of this family."

"Where is she?"

"She was at the MacIntyres ranch two months ago. Whether she's still there, I don't know. She hasn't been heard from since. But since you're going there tomorrow, you will find out soon. Can you make it up the stairs alone or should I call Marylou?"

"I'll make it on my own."

Louisa nodded and was about to turn away to finally go home, when James grabbed her by the arm.

"Thank you, for setting me straight", was all James could say to her then he climbed the stairs with heavy legs.

Chapter 33

One by one the guests arrived at the home of the MacIntyres, took up their quarters for the next two days and met each other downstairs in the festive drawing room. Elisabeth, who wore a dream of a dress in dark red muslin, greeted her guests effusively. Most of them had known each other for years and took advantage of the annual feast to keep up their friendships.

Felicitas and a few other employees provided the guests with drinks. As was the custom, the ladies had gathered and were chatting about fashion, children, and the latest gossip from Laramie, while the men, with their whiskey glasses in hand, were talking about cattle, horses, and the latest political developments in Washington. In all this crowd, James looked for the familiar face of his daughter, but he did not find her.

He had introduced his new wife to everyone and now saw her standing among the ladies. His father, on the other hand, was talking with a man James knew by sight, but did not know his name. Just as he made out a movement to his right, Elisabeth asked her guests for some attention.

"My dear friends, I want to thank you, for accepting my invitation again this year and that you have attended in such great numbers. It is always something very special when we conclude our summer with a meet here.

A whole year with many events is behind us and it is a very special pleasure this year to introduce you to someone who is very close to my heart."

Elisabeth made an effective pause, looked behind her and signaled. A murmur went through the room and James tried to see from his back seat what was going on there in the front.

Elisabeth continued: "Some of you have known me and my husband for a very long time and therefore, know that our son and daughter-in-law were killed in an Indian attack many years ago. Since then, our grandson was considered missing. Miraculously, I got my grandson back two months ago. My friends, I would like to introduce my grandson Cameron MacIntyre and his wife Isabella to you. Some of you will recognize her already. Isabella, is the daughter of James Hunt."

Robert's son had reappeared? Was that really possible? James tried to push his way forward, but everyone present, were now crowded tightly around Elizabeth, Cameron and Isabella and bombarded them with questions. This was definitely the most interesting and exciting thing that had happened all year and would now spread like wildfire.

This event would be told even in the coming year at many small parties. James, on the other hand, still could not understand what had happened. Isabella had been married to Chágha tho, why did she appear here as the wife of this Cameron? Just then he caught a glimpse of the young man and was horrified to discover that he was the spitting image of his friend Robert.
Then he heard Elisabeth next to him say: "A nice couple aren't they James?"
"I don't quite understand what's going on here."

"May I have a word with you? It would be best if we went to my office. It's quieter there."
In the writing room, Elizabeth offered James a seat in

one of the armchairs.

"You must be surprised to see your daughter here with me. I know of her situation and I just wanted to inform you briefly about what has happened in the meantime. She came two months ago with her Indian husband and asked for a job. I hired her and him. When I saw Chágha tho for the first time, I almost fainted.

He is the spitting image of Robert, as you could see for yourself. It turned out that he was not an Indian at all, but my grandson Cameron, who was presumed dead. Since then, we have been trying together to make up for some of the lost time. I know this all comes as a little surprising for you, but I am telling you this because I think that it might help to get things back on track. Maybe you can find a way to reconcile with them."

James couldn't believe what he was hearing. Chágha tho was not an Indian? He was supposed to be Robert's son? He had been Robert's best friend, and had not recognized his son? And if all this was indeed true, then he had sinned against the young man. He could never have imagined that one day he would be able to harm his best friend's child, and yet he had done it.

He had beaten him almost to death. Ashamed of this fact, he did not know how to answer Elisabeth. How could he now still step under the eyes of the young man.
"Elisabeth, there is something I have to tell you. I have sinned gravely. I had no idea that Chágha tho was your grandson and with his long hair, he really looked like an Indian. So I had absolutely no reason not to believe what he seemed to be. In addition, he didn't speak a word of English when he came to us."

Elizabeth, suspected there was more going on between James and her grandson than just the fact that he loved Isabella and so she asked:
„What else happened?"
Breathing heavily, he opened to her:" I have punished

Chágha tho severely for having my daughter. I whipped him."

"It was you? How could you do that to him? I saw his back. He will be scarred for the rest of his life."

"Didn't he tell you about that?"

"No. He never talked to me about what offense had led to such a punishment. Oh, James, why did you do that?

"Elisabeth, you have to believe me, I was furious...with rage. He had just been accused of arson and then my daughter told me that she had spent the night with him. I was not able to think straight. I'm sorry and I wish I could undo it."

"Well, I can't forgive you for anything. If you want forgiveness, you're going to have to look for it with Cameron and Isabella. I hope for your sake that you will find it."

James hoped the same for himself.

A little later, the two rejoined the others, who continued to talk magnificently. James saw that neither his father nor Marylou seemed to have missed him, so he tried to see his daughter for the second time that evening. He caught sight of her at the other end of the salon where she stood together with Cameron and two gentlemen he knew as father and son named Hampton. They had a ranch a day's ride west of here.

The four of them seemed to be having a great time, because they didn't realize that he was coming toward them. Suddenly the door opened behind them and John, the foreman, marched into the room. He searched the the room with his eyes and seemed relieved when he found the man he was looking for right in front of him. James could see John walking up to Cameron, whispered something in his ear, and the latter's expression darkened. It didn't seem to be good news he was getting. Cameron spoke briefly to John, then took Isabella's hand and excused them both to the Hamptons. When he left the room with Isabella, James wondered what it had been that the foreman told him.

Now that he had once again missed another chance to make contact with his daughter, he joined the other gentlemen. Until dinner he did not get another opportunity. Cameron did not show up again and Isabella did not return to the salon until shortly before dinner. James was talking with Elisabeth, but this time on business matters, when he saw Isabella approaching them. She faltered when she caught sight of him and seemed to think briefly about what to do, but then decided to continue on her way in their direction.

"Excuse me, father, but I must urgently speak with Elisabeth."

She didn't look at him further, and it stung his heart that she seemed to be able to ignore him effortlessly. Elisabeth, on the other hand, looked worried at Isabella's announcement.

"What's so important?"

"Cameron wanted me to tell you that he unfortunately had to leave. John informed him that the cougar has already torn another foal. He is off with him and they want to finally hunt down the animal so that it can't do any more damage."

"Mmh, that's really annoying. Of all things today. Thanks for letting me know. Since now a place at the table remains empty, I want to talk to Felicitas right away, to see if we can change the seating arrangement a little. Will you excuse me?"

With this clever move Elisabeth quickly departed and left Isabella in the care of her father. James would not get a better chance to talk to his daughter today. He hoped that he could do this for himself. But Isabella didn't want to be alone with her father. The contemptuous words he had hurled at her in her room were still too deep. She was just about to turn away to leave again, when her father's hand held her tightly. Immediately she stiffened, but James spoke to her calmly.

"Please stay for a while. I would like to have a talk with you."

Isabella looked at him, trying to fathom his gaze, but she could not guess his state of mind.

"Are you all right?"

"Yes, father."

"It was a surprise for me to see you here. But I am very glad about it."

"Really?"

"Yes, Grandfather and Marylou would also be happy if you'd say hello to them."

James was beating around the bush and he knew it. He didn't know how to start the conversation with his daughter. He couldn't think of the right words to describe his state of mind. It hurt him that his otherwise so empathetic daughter was reserved and dismissive. But he had to blame himself for that. He had cast her out of the family.

"Father, what do you want?"

"Just to talk to you. To tell you that I'm sorry and that I wish many things had not happened."

Isabella glared angrily at him. How could her father think that all he had to do was come here and everything would be all right again.

"No one can change what has happened. You wouldn't listen to me then, so why should I try to talk to you about it now."

"Because I'm telling you I'm sorry, and that is not easy for me to say."

"I didn't ask for an apology, father. I hoped that you would give me a chance to explain, but you didn't. You didn't even try."

"Then I'll try it now! Please Isabella."

She was willing to just leave her father standing in that room with all those people, like he had done when he locked her in her room that time, but when she looked into her father's distraught face, she couldn't be that heartless.

"Actually, there's not much to say other than I love Chágha tho. I have found in him the person who makes me happy. I have only followed my heart. What kind of offense is that when two people love each other? Why couldn't you give him a chance?

All we wanted was to get to know each other better. That we would both fall in love with each other, neither he nor I had planned it. It just happened. As you must have heard earlier, Chágha tho is not an Indian, but Elisabeth's grandson Cameron. This realization was not easy for any of us, but it was especially hard for my husband. His whole life broke apart. Since then, he has tried to fight for his place in society.

He has gotton something here that he never had gotten on our ranch. He got a chance to prove what kind of man he is. He was able to gain recognition with his skills, his diligence and his will and I'm so proud of him. Maybe he doesn't see it that way yet, but I hope that one day he will see this ranch for what it is. His home.

So you can see father, we've been getting along fine so far. I've taken your expulsion as an opportunity to take my life into my own hands and to make my own decisions. My place from now on is at my husband's side. You can accept that, which would make me very happy, or you can refuse it, in which case we would have nothing more to say to each other."

Isabella tried to calm down again. This speech had upset

her more than she had thought. Her father on the other hand, seemed to let the words resonate.

"I'm glad if you're happy with him, that's all that matters to me now, and it takes a burden from my heart. I'd still like to speak with Cameron because I want to ask for forgiveness."

"You'll have to wait until he gets back. Maybe he'll give you the opportunity to speak to him but I'll be honest with you. I don't know if he can ever forgive you. It is up to him."

The dinner and the hours afterwards went harmoniously. Elisabeth was a skillful hostess and knew how to entertain her guests. Since Cameron did not come to dinner and the place remained empty, Elisabeth had quickly placed Isabella between her grandfather and Marylou. Her father sat on the other side of his wife. Through this seating arrangement Isabella, William and Marylou had the opportunity to get acquainted with each other again, which all three enthusiastically did.

Since the conversation of the other guests never ran out, the meal dragged on. At the end of the first day the ladies had their little evening drink in front of the fireplace in the blue salon, while the gentlemen went out to the veranda for a cigarette or cigar. It was already shortly before midnight when the last guests went to bed. William and Marylou had already said good night to Elizabeth. Only James was still there. Just as he was about to retire as well the door of the room opened and Isabella appeared.

"Felicitas and I have prepared everything for tomorrow. I'll go now and come back tomorrow early enough to help you with the breakfast preparations or do you still need help?"

"No thank you Isabella. We are going to bed too. See you tomorrow."

James stood up and walked toward his daughter.

"Wait, I'll take you home. I think a thunderstorm is on its way. It's already flashing and the thunder is coming closer and you shouldn't be out in the dark."

"It's not far father. You don't have to come with me."

"But I would feel better if I knew you were safe at home."

Isabella agreed and together they left the house in the direction of the schoolhouse. They could see the lightning flashing in the night sky. The thunder rumbled in the distance from the hills, but with every minute it seemed to be closer. Never before had she gone home so late in the evening. Until now Cameron had always been there. Everyone seemed already asleep, every hut they passed was already dark. Isabella shivered a little. Even if at first she had found it ridiculous, that her father wanted to take her home, she was now glad not to have to go the way alone.

"I hope Cameron and Frank don't get wet and finally catch the cougar. It is the second foal he's snatched in a short time. That animal is smart, it can't be caught. I hope nothing happens to either of them."

"He'll be fine. Don't worry about it. He'll probably be back in the morning. Are you really happy with him?"

"Yes. I love him with all my heart and I know that he loves me too. Please, Dad, give him a chance.He's a good man."

Isabella had stopped and put her hand on her father's arm who, now grasped her hand and held it tightly.

"As soon as he's back, I'll try to straighten everything out. Satisfied?"

"Yes, Dad."

At that moment, a dazzling flash of lightning illuminated the surroundings and a loud thunder followed at the same time. The thunderstorm was almost upon them. They hurried on.

"It's probably just one of those thunderstorms that don't carry rain. But the lightning gets more violent and so does the thunder."

"We're almost there. Thank you, for coming with me."

Suddenly another flash of lightning twitched through the night and the thunder that followed was much louder than it had been before. Isabella was startled and quickened her pace as her father suddenly collapsed next to her and went to ground. Afraid that he might have stumbled, she rushed to him.

"Father, what happened? Did you hurt yourself?"

But there was no answer. The fear crept up in her when she felt her father lying on the ground and tried to talk to him. But no sound came from him. She shook him, but nothing happened.

With another flash of lightning coming and in the bright glow she could see the red spot on the ground next to her father.

"Oh my God! That's blood!"

That was as far as she got. She realized the danger too late and could no longer avoid it. She felt the blow of the butt on her temple and fainted on the ground.

Chapter 34

John and Cameron had been on the road for hours, but it had been worth it. They finally found the beast and were able to kill it. Satisfied with themselves, they rode towards the ranch and were both looking forward to a hot bath and a good meal. The night had been anything but comfortable. First, they had to deal with the threat of a storm and at dawn they had finally discovered the cougar. Now it was already afternoon, the weather had calmed down again and a gentle breeze was blowing when the first cabins appeared in the distance.

Nowhere did they see cowboys working in the pastures. Not a soul was to be seen. Everything was eerily quiet, much too quiet for the fact that countless people were working on this ranch and, in addition, there were guests staying in the house. Cameron and John threw worried glances at each other. It didn't take words between them to know that they were both thinking the same thing. Something had happened here.

Cameron pulled his rifle out of the holster and spurred his horse. John followed him with his rifle ready to fire. Even as they rode up to the main house nobody showed up. Before his horse came to a stop in front of it, Cameron had jumped off and rushed up to the door. He held his rifle in his hand, ready to fire as he pressed down the doorknob with his hand and pushed the door open with his foot. Rushing in, he stopped, as if rooted to the spot, when he saw the crowd of people standing in the house, now turned in his direction in horror.

He quickly put the rifle down and made his way through the silent crowd. They let him pass until he reached a lifeless body lying on one of the long tables in the middle of the room. Around it a weeping Marylou, holding her husband's hand.

He saw William, who looked distraught and his grandmother, who came toward him with a face full of concern.

"Oh Cameron, it's good to have you back. Something terrible has happened."

"What's going on? What happened to James?"

"We don't know. We found him this morning lying outside by your house. He'd been shot and lost a lot of blood. We could patch him up but..."

"Is he dead?"

"No, but he's unconscious. He was just taking Isabella home last night. That he, himself, did not come home we only found out this morning through Marylou. Cameron - Isabella has disappeared!"

"What do you mean disappeared? She can't be gone."

"We searched everywhere for her, but we couldn't find her anywhere. Unfortunately, James hasn't been able to tell us anything either."

At that moment, James seemed to regain consciousness again, because he let out a groan.

It seemed he wanted to say something. Immediately, Cameron rushed to him and bent over to be closer to James. But because he was so weak, the words would not quite pass his lips. James tried to summon up all his strength. He had to tell Cameron who it had been. Just before he had fainted, he had recognized the guy who had shot him. In a shaky voice, he spoke the words.

"It was Carl!"

"Carl? Are you sure about that?"

James nodded. Cameron looked at the surrounding faces. When he saw John, he called him.

"John feed my horse and give him enough to drink. I'm going to head right back out after that son of a bitch."

"You got it. Shall I round up some men?"

"No. I'll ride alone. I have a score to settle with him and I won't rest until I've caught him. I'll get him."

Even before Cameron was about to set off, a surprisingly firm hand held him by the arm. He looked down at the man who looked at him pleadingly.

"Please Cameron, bring her back, she's my daughter."

"I intend to, because she is my wife."

Isabella gradually became aware of her surroundings again. It was still dark and lightning continued to flash, but the thunder died away in the distance.

The thunderstorm was passing. But where was she? Her head felt as if it were about to explode, and she felt nauseous. She tried to move, but her hands and feet were tied. She was hanging upside down over the neck of a horse. What had happened? She had been on her way home with her father when he suddenly collapsed. Blood, there had been blood everywhere.

Someone had shot her father. With this certainty, fear came up in her and with the fear, her nausea increased. The rocking of the horse increased the pressure on her rebelling stomach. Somehow she had to get off the horse, no matter how, she knew that she was about to throw up. Isabella began to kick and wriggle. The horse immediately reacted to her surprisingly violent movements and mounted. Isabella plopped hard to the ground and the rider of the horse cursed as he tried to get the animal under control again. Isabella, however, crawled on all fours on the ground and gave in to her gag reflex.

"You stupid bitch, don't try that again. You almost broke both our necks."

Furious, Carl pulled Isabella back to her feet. All of her limbs ached.

"Carl!"

"Yes it's me. Did you think I was going to let you slip through my fingers?"

He yanked her to him, took his knife from his belt and slit the skirt of the horrified Isabella. From now on she would sit astride on the horse. He loosened the shackles then he lifted her up and mounted himself. He tied her hands to the saddle horn. Then he rode on. Desperately Isabella tried to think. What was he up to?

"What do you want from me?"

"Can't you guess? I'm just getting what's rightfully mine."

"I don't belong to anyone!"

"Oh yes, you do, you belong to me. Your father promised to give you to me as my wife, but he broke his word and that's why I took what was mine tonight."

"You shot my father," she yelled at him and tried to free herself from her shackles.

"Give it a rest, or I'll give you a second blow. It's your father's own fault. If he had kept his word, I wouldn't have had to shoot him. At least not right away, but actually, it simplifies things immensely." Carl started to laugh. Isabella didn't understand what he meant, and the more she tried to think about it, the more her head hurt.

"What do you want from me."

"You are now the inheritress to the ranch because your father has said that he will not change the line of succession despite his marriage to Marylou. That means you'll be my wife and bear me a son.

After that, I'll see what I will do with you."
"I will never become your wife and what about my grandfather and Marylou? Do you think they're going to stand by and let you take over the ranch?"
Carl laughed out.

"You're really cute when you act so naive. I'll take care of Marylou and your grandfather when the time calls for it. There are a lot of accidents these days. All I need is a legal marriage with you, and that's why we're riding to the nearest town."

Isabella heard what he said, and was horrified. How had Carl become such a criminal, or had he always been like that only no one had noticed? Carl did not know that she was already married to Cameron. Should she point that out to him? No, it would be better for her if he remained in the belief that he could marry her. That would give her time to find a way to escape.

Did the others already find her father and know that she had been kidnapped? But since it was still nighttime, it was more likely that by morning no one would have any idea what had happened last night.
And Cameron? He was out here somewhere looking for the cougar. Nobody knew how long he'd be gone. Isabella didn't hold out much hope that help was near. She had to come up with something herself and wait for a good opportunity. Maybe it was good if she could try to stall for time.
"Can't we take a little rest? I don't feel well."
"I can't take that into consideration right now. I want to cover a great distance by tomorrow morning."
He pulled her to him and immediately Isabella's stiffened her back. Carl just laughed.

"You'll see what pleasures I can give you," and to punctuate that, he breathed a kiss on her temple. Isabella resisted and inwardly she shuddered at the thought that Carl wanted more from her. How was she going to protect herself from Carl's advances? The last time Cameron had come to her rescue, but this time he would not be there.

For two days now, Cameron had been following Carl and he didn't really feel like he was catching up to him. That afternoon when he had returned to the ranch with John, he had only allowed himself as much time as it had taken to get into his Indian clothes, to grab his bow and arrows, tuck his hunting knife into his belt and fetch his rifle. Felicitas, at the behest of his grandmother, had packed him a bag with some provisions and John had brought him his freshly supplied horse.

Elizabeth had expressed surprise that he was wearing his old clothes, but he had explained to her that for this mission these things were advantageous and one traveled more silently with the moccasins than with the heavy work boots.

"Be careful Cameron and come back safely."

He had seen the fear in his grandmother's eyes and for the first time, he had the feeling of wanting to kiss the old woman on the forehead. Elisabeth was moved by this gesture and her eyes shimmered with moisture.

"I will come back and bring Isabella with me, no matter how long it takes."

With those words he had left everyone behind and had ridden his horse back to the schoolhouse to begin his search from there. As Cameron continued to ride his horse, he thought about the past two days. Carl had been good, he had to give him that, because it had taken him some effort to discover any trace of him at all. A few times he even thought that he had lost them, but he found the trace each time again. Carl had taken great pains to cover his tracks, but in the loose soil, he had not succeeded very well and Cameron had seen the heavy prints of his horse. That's how he knew he was heading northeast and towards the rocky massif.

The first night he had had particular difficulty in following the trail further. He had arrived at the rock massif at dusk and had lost his tracks there. As much as he had searched the ground, nowhere had he been able to discover anything. But giving up had not been an option and so he had thought. Carl's horse was shod and it carried double the load. In the loose soil, the hoof prints had been deep. Here on the rocky ground, the animal must have sought special footing. Cameron had made a torch out of brushwood lying around and lit it.

With this light source he had searched the ground and after a while he found what he was looking for. On some stones scratches had been discovered, which had arisen from an iron hoof. He had pointed his torch in the direction, in which the stones with the scratches had lain. It had satisfied him, what he had seen. You won't escape me that fast had been his thoughts and he had seen the path in front of him again. Quickly he swung himself back onto his horse and pushed on. Now on the second day of his search he was again in the open and apparently Carl was no longer afraid of pursuers, or he had simply become too careless. The hoof prints of the horse had been clearly recognizable and so he was able to make up for the lost time in the mountains.

Towards the end of the afternoon he passed a place that had served as Carl's night camp. Around the cold fireplace the grass was flattened and the lower branches of the trees standing closer were bare. Underneath, he found hoof prints of a single horse. Here the horse had grazed and plucked the leaves from the trees. Cameron allowed himself no rest and continued his pursuit.

On the morning of day three he and his horse were so exhausted that both definitely needed a break, but the concern for Isabella drove him on relentlessly. Cameron demanded a great deal of himself and his horse, and he was glad that his horse had such stamina so far. Somehow it seemed to sense that it was not allowed to slacken now. A little later, he found another spot where they had camped and the fireplace was still warm. So he was getting closer to him.

This camp had been left no more than two hours ago. The realization of it released the adrenaline in his veins and suddenly his tiredness was gone. He spoke well to his horse in Indian words, and as if the horse had understood, it set off on a gallop across the prairie. Towards afternoon the terrain changed again. After coming from the pastures of the ranch into rocky terrain, then riding across the wide plains of the prairie, the terrain now became more hillier and more overgrown. Larger bushes and scattered cedars grew in a terrain that was becoming more and more rocky.

A little later he came across a river, which on his side was densely overgrown with bushes and on the other side was held in check by rocks. The current of the river was strong and he saw no opportunity to cross the water with the horse. Also Carl had ridden his horse further downstream and so Cameron continued to follow the trail. He had been following the river for quite some time when he stopped abruptly.

Not far from him, on the other side of the river, he saw a small clearing where he found the ones he was looking for. Apparently Carl had found the only spot where he could cross the water and Cameron could observe from the distance that he started to set up his camp for the night. A small fire was already lit. The place Carl had chosen for the night was good.

He wouldn't have done it any other way. To the rear were the rock walls, which gave him protection and no rider could get through from the sides.

The only way to get to him was from the river side, but Carl would have shot him before he had reached the riverbank. Cameron turned his horse around and rode back upstream quite a distance, where he dismounted and tied his horse to the bank in such a way that it could still drink. While he knelt down by the water and quenched his thirst, he tried feverishly to find a plan for how he could free Isabella.

He had to do it here and now, because with another day of pursuit without rest, his horse would not survive. The only possibility he saw was to try it on foot. He had to get to the other side somehow and sneak between the bushes to the campground. Cameron took a closer look at the river, guessing how many strong strokes it would take to get him to the other side.

Under normal circumstances, it would not be a problem for him but with such a strong current, it would be difficult and not without danger to cross it. Nevertheless, Cameron was determined to give it a try. He took off his shirt. Left the bow and the rifle with his horse and climbed only armed with his hunting knife into the cold water of the river. He was not quite comfortable having to leave his weapons here, but the bow and the rifle would hinder his swimming and he needed to have his hands free to make powerful moves. Slowly he let himself slide deeper into the water.

As soon as he was able to swim, he dove under and began to move forward with powerful strokes. The current caught him and carried him along. In order not to get too far downstream he fought against it and he was once again glad that he was a good swimmer. He surfaced briefly, the approaching shore in front of him, and took another deep breath, then disappeared under the water again. With a few more strokes he reached the other side. Cautiously, he peeked out of the water to see where he landed. When he saw nothing but bushes in front of him, he crept quietly out of the water and carefully walked between the bushes further downstream.

Chapter 35

Isabella was cowering, tied hand and foot, on the ground. This way she could not run away.

Carl approached her with an armful of firewood, knelt down and added some wood to the fire. Although it was still summer, the nights could get quite cool and the last two nights he had been glad to have a good fire at night. He looked to Isabella and an idea ripened in him that he immediately wanted to put into action. Isabella looked up when she saw Carl step up beside her. The lecherous look in his eyes did not give her a good feeling and immediately she braced herself for what was to come.

Carl sat down close to Isabella, who immediately tried to crawl away from him, but he held her back.

"Where do you want to go? We're going to make ourselves a little comfortable now."

He pulled her to him and tried to kiss her, but Isabella put her bound hands against his chest and turned her face away so that he only met her cheek. Carl laughed derisively.

"You don't have to be so coy in front of me. For three days now your little bottom has been rubbing against my loins and I have been very reserved, but now I think you could be nice to me."

"Let go of me Carl, go away."

Isabella tried desperately to keep him at a distance but the more she tried, the stronger Carl's grip became.

"I know you are not a virgin anymore, so your behavior is completely out of place here. I've been watching you and that redskin in the woods and I know what you've been up to. So don't make a fuss, I just want the same thing that he got and as my soon to be wife, it is also mine to have."

To emphasize his words, he shifted his weight and pushed Isabella to the ground. Isabella began to struggle violently. She tried to kick and scratch him, but all the struggling didn't help, Carl was heavy and too strong and so it happened that he tore her top, revealing the base of her breast.

Isabella cried out in fear, but Carl only had eyes for the soft hills in front of him. He grabbed her neckline with one hand and embraced her breast, while the second hand tried to lift her skirt.

With gasping breath he lay on top of her and could barely keep his excitement in check. Under him, Isabella desperately tried to escape from his attack, but the more she squirmed, the more aroused he became.

"Now don't be so coy. I know that you love it. I've seen and heard you enjoy making your legs wide. So stop it if you don't want me to be violent with you."

Carl glared wickedly at Isabella. She knew she was doomed. Who was going to come to her rescue now. In the last days she had tried to find a way to escape, but Carl had always had her tied to the saddle horn and even at night, she had been tied with a rope to Carl, so that he would wake up immediately if she had tried to escape. Until now, she had hope of escaping the inevitable - somehow, but the situation was coming to a head and there would be no stopping him now.

He would rape her. No matter how hard she tried to fight him off, she couldn't. He was too heavy and held her firmly on the ground. Tears of despair ran down her face. How was she ever going to get through this and would she ever see Cameron again? She was sure that as soon as he heard about the kidnapping he would come after her. But he would not be able to prevent this rape and how could she ever come under his eyes again?

She thought of the unborn child growing inside her. Cameron's child. One thing seemed clear to her, if she continued to struggle, Carl would do worse to her than the pain she was already suffering. So she decided inwardly to meet her fate and gave up the resistance. Somehow she would endure the act and then hope that he would let go of her. Stiff as a stick she lay under him and disgustedly allowed him to touch her breasts and feel his hand on her naked thigh.

His breath disgusted her, she put her head to one side to avoid his kisses, and looked over across the fire. All at once she thought she could not trust her eyes. Was it possible? Yes. The rescue was approaching, but Carl was not allowed to notice.

"What's the matter? Don't you like what I'm doing?"

Carl laughed and tried to kiss her again. Then he suddenly stopped. Something in her gaze made him pause. He took his hand from her bosom and also from her thigh and slowly reached for his revolver. Then he jumped up as fast as lightning, turned around and fired a bullet from his revolver. Cameron, who was standing a few yards behind Carl, was able to escape the deadly bullet by diving to the side, but a glaring pain in his upper left arm told him that the bullet had struck him. Despite the graze, he intercepted his jump and at the same moment threw his knife in Carl's direction.

The latter cried out in pain when he saw the knife stuck in his thigh. The revolver slipped from his hand and fell to the ground. Before Carl could even pull the knife out of his thigh, Cameron was on him in one leap, throwing himself on top of him. Isabella cried out in horror. She gathered up her top and crawled away from the struggling men. Somehow she had to get rid of her bonds and help Cameron. She got hold of a stone and tried to rub her bonds on it. Cameron, however, grabbed Carl by the throat with one hand, keeping him down, while his other hand pulled the knife out of Carl's thigh. Carl cried out in pain and tried to shake him off.

When Carl got one arm free, he slammed his fist into Cameron's side, who lost his balance. Carl got his second arm free and quickly grabbed Cameron's wrist with both hands to prevent Cameron from plunging the knife into his throat. With a drawn foot he kicked Cameron in the hip, sending him backwards to the ground. The knife flew out of his hand. Immediately Cameron picked himself up again and lunged at Carl, who was just trying to get up.

The two men wedged together across the dusty ground and beat at each other with their fists. Two equally strong opponents faced each other. Carl was older and not as nimble and quick as young Cameron, but he was as strong as a bull and could defend himself well against the young man's attack. Just then Carl had the upper hand as he sat on Cameron's chest and tried to squeeze his throat. Cameron, who was having trouble shaking him off, quickly drew his legs up and wrapped them around Carl's torso, throwing him to the side.

Then he rolled on top of him and punched his fist in his face. He felt Carl's bones crack and the back of his own hand became bloody. His whole body ached and his left arm gradually lost strength due to blood loss from the graze. But he could not take all that into account. Here it was a matter of life and death.

One of them would not finish this day alive. This seemed to be clear to Carl as well, because he developed immense strength despite the thigh wound. Where he got it from, after all the punches and kicks, was a mystery to Cameron, but he had no time to think about it, because the next attack from Carl followed immediately. Again the two men rolled across the ground and tried to defeat the other somehow.

When it seemed that both of them were losing strength and the punches and blows were becoming more sluggish, both fought dangerously close to the river bank. Cameron, who had the upper hand this time, pulled Carl to his feet by his shirt collar. Standing on wobbly legs in front of him, he swung a quick right punch, sending Carl to the ground. The latter got a thick branch and knocked Cameron's feet out from under him so that he fell backwards into the water.

Before Cameron could even get out, Carl sat on him and pushed his face under the water. Finally, he had reached the position that would bring the end for the Indian, Carl thought. He could kick under him as he wished. Carl sat on his arms and chest, slowly pushing the air out of the redskin's throat with his hands under the water. Grinning maliciously, he looked through the water at his opponent eyes. Cameron tried feverishly to free himself. He was running out of air and just couldn't get his arms or legs free.

Carl had too good a position. Was this the end now? Was he going to drown miserably here? He had to use his last reserves of air well and gather all his strength, once again, to make a last defensive attempt. Isabella had watched the never-ending fight with horror.

She feverishly rubbed her hands on the stone to get rid of the shackles. Her skin already bloody. Suddenly the rope gave way and she was able to free her hands. Her eyes fell on the two fighters. In shock she realized that Carl was holding Cameron trapped in the water below him. From her position, she could only see Carl's back and the legs of her husband kicking underneath. How long had Cameron been under water? She had to rush to his aid.

Isabella looked around and spotted a thick branch. Armed with this she crept up to Carl as quietly as she could and just as she was about to give him a strong blow to the head, Carl heard a noise from behind. He moved around, recognized the danger and dodged it. The fatal blow hit only his shoulder and made him cry out in pain. In his rage he rose and struck Isabella violently in the face with his fist.

She lost her balance and staggered backwards. When she tripped over something she fell on her back, hit her head on something hard and remained motionless. The second Carl had moved, it had been enough for Cameron to shake Carl off and get out of the water. He dragged himself coughing and gasping for breath to the shore. There in front of him he saw his knife in the grass. With his last strength he crawled forward, got the wooden handle of his knife when he heard the trigger of the revolver behind him.

He had no time to think. At that moment, he only reacted. He grabbed the knife, rolled onto his back in a flash, and shot forward with his upper body throwing the knife in the direction where Carl was standing with his revolver drawn and ready to fire.

The latter looked with astonishment at Cameron, who was still sitting on the grass. Then he looked down at himself and the knife stuck deep in his chest. Cameron looked into Carl's surprised eyes and saw how astonished Carl became when he realized that he was now going to die. Carl's hand went limp and the revolver fell to the floor, he staggered backward a few steps and then fell dead into the river. The strong current swept him downstream.

Cameron dropped back to the ground for a moment. It was over. For a few seconds he closed his eyes and tried to get his heavily breathing body, pumped full of adrenaline, back under control.

His muscles trembled and would not obey him. He took a few deep breaths, then rose and looked for Isabella. With his eyes filled with shock, he saw her lifeless body lying on the ground. He ran to her and dropped into the dust in front of her. With trembling hands, he pulled her into his lap, called her name and cradled her like a small child, but she gave no sign of life and fear grew in him.

"No!"

Cameron shouted out his desperation and from the rock face around him the echo came down. In his fear of having lost Isabella, he tried to find the fatal injury. He felt the thick bump on the back of her head and saw the bloody film trickling down her temple, but he could not see any other injury. Enormous anger spread through him. He did not want to accept what seemed to be reality. Had it all been in vain in the end? Had he lost her forever? Was his life with her already over, even before it had begun? He could not and would not accept this end.

Firmly he held her to his wildly throbbing chest, stroked her cheek affectionately, and called her name again and again. But nothing stirred in her. Isabella did not know exactly how long she had been unconscious but when she heard her name she slowly opened her eyes. Her gaze fell on Cameron who held her in his arm with his filthy face and body. Even if it seemed crazy, it was the most beautiful sight she had ever enjoyed. Cameron was alive and she was in his arms, that was all that mattered.

Softly she whispered his name and immediately their eyes met. His face lit up and his eyes shone in such an intense blue, as she had never seen before. A heavy burden fell from him and relieved, he pressed her against him and kissed her.

„What about Carl?" asked Isabella, still a little dazed and

worried, because she couldn't see him anywhere.

"He'll never be able to hurt you again. Are you okay? Does anything hurt you?"

"My head feels like it's going to split."

"You've got a nasty bump on the back of your head and a cut on your forehead."

"I got that bump from Carl's rifle butt when he attacked me and my father", horrified she pulled up and began to cry. "Cameron, he shot and killed my father."

Isabella let her tears run freely, but Cameron pulled her to his chest and tried to reassure her.

"No, he didn't. Your father is alive."

"He's alive?" Isabella looked at him hopefully.

"Yes, he's hurt but he's alive. He's going to be okay."

Relieved by his words, she snuggled up to him and could have sat there forever. She listened to his now calm heartbeat and her eyes fell on his arm. She sat up abruptly.

"You're hurt!"

"Just a graze. It's not bad."

Saying, "This needs to be bandaged," Isabella set about tearing her cut petticoat into bandages. Cameron rose to his feet.

"I'm going to take Carl's horse and ride over to get mine. We will spend the night here, as it will soon be getting dark and we need a rest. Tomorrow we will ride back. Can you manage on your own for a while?"

Isabella looked up at him and nodded. A while later, the two of them lay nestled together in front of the warm fire and fell asleep on the spot. When Cameron awoke at dawn, Isabella was still sleeping blissfully next to him. He for his part had desperately needed this restful sleep. How exhausted he had been, he had noticed since he had fallen asleep immediately.

The insane worry about Isabella had driven him almost out of his mind, and when he had seen Carl was about to pounce on her, he had no time to lose. He had left his cover and launched an attack. There went his plan to take Carl out quickly and without a fight. All this had sapped his strength and he was now glad to feel that some of his spirits had returned. He felt Isabella's soft skin against his body and immediately his body began to respond to her. Carefully, he leaned on his arm and stroked her long, soft hair out of her neck.

With little teasing kisses on her neck and shoulders, he slowly brought her out of her sleep. Comfortable like a little kitten, she began to purr and move. But with every new movement she excited him more. His blood started to boil and his kisses were more demanding. Isabella, now fully awake, turned over and looked at him with her green eyes encouragingly. She wrapped her arms around his neck and pulled him on top of her.

"Love me!"

That's all she needed to say. In the silence of dawn they made wild and passionate love. Their bodies ached for each other, as if each had to make sure that the other was alive and actually together. As fulfillment approached, their bodies reared up and their names echoed off the rocks. Happy and exhausted, Isabella dozed off at Cameron's side. He was leaning on his arm again and looked down a little worriedly at his wife. He had not exactly been tender with her and blamed himself for it.

"Is everything okay?"

Isabella, who saw the concern in Cameron's eyes, realizing what he meant, only replied,

"Yes, I've never felt so alive. It's all right, except my head still hurts."

Somewhat embarrassed that he had completely disregarded her injury, he kissed her tenderly. Suddenly, Isabella's facial expression changed and all cheerfulness disappeared from her face. Worry lines appeared on her forehead. Concerned Cameron looked at her.

"What's wrong?"

"All these days, the stress, the excitement. I hope the child continues to do well."

Cameron looked at her in disbelief. Had he just misheard her?

"The child?"

Isabella sat up and looked at him uncertainly.

"Yes, I'm expecting a child. Your child! I wanted to tell you a few days ago, but somehow it never worked out, and then this thing came up."

Cameron had gone quiet. His child! He was going to be a father. Panic crept up. Was he really ready for this? He had no idea what a father had to do. On the other hand, it could not be changed and the thought that his flesh and blood was growing inside her, he liked it more and more. He would have his own little family. Then he remembered that he had just really rough sex with her and feared that he might have hurt her or the little creature inside her and it made him deeply ashamed. Isabella finding his silence frightening, took control. She tenderly put her hand on his arm and stroked his cheek with the other.

"I know this all comes as a surprise and at first I reacted just as you did. I didn't even know what was going on until Elisabeth told me."

"She knows?"

"Yes, she is so excited already and I am also looking forward to the child, and if it is a boy, I hope he will look like you, because then I will have the two best looking men around me."

"I wasn't very restrained just now, did I hurt you two?"

"No!"

Laughing, she threw herself into his arms and kissed him. Cameron could not help himself, he returned her kiss and threw away his dull thoughts. A child - what better way to crown their love for each other? They both sat wrapped in their blankets by the campfire for a while and watched the sun as it rose in the east and greeted the new day. Cameron silently thanked Manitou, God, or whoever else was up there watching over them that he had gotten Isabella back safe and that Carl was now a thing of the past. From now on they could both look forward. But where did his future lie?

Was it really with his grandmother on her ranch? Cameron let pass the last weeks and months in his mind. Since he had left the Cheyenne, he had rediscovered what he had been looking for at his grandmother's place. At the ranch, he could use his skills and he enjoyed working with the horses. The people had accepted him and trusted him and Frank had become a good friend. But what about Isabella? Would she want to stay? Without looking at her, he voiced the question.

"Do you still want to go to Boston?"

Isabella looked at him in wonder.

"I never wanted to go to Boston. That was my father's idea and when he kicked me out I thought it would be a solution. But I love this country and I don't want to leave here. But also my place is at your side and I'll go with you where you're happy, even if it's to the end of the world."

Happy and relieved at her words, he took her in his arms.

"Then, Mrs. MacIntytre, let us start on our way home. The others at the ranch have been worried. Let's pack and ride home."

Isabella's heart leapt with joy. It was the first time he had called his grandmother's ranch home.

"Yes, let's ride home!"

Epilogue

Wyoming 1878

It was a fairly warm spring day and the sun was shining down a cloudless sky. The harsh winter was over, although in the distance on the peaks of the mountains, the remaining white of the last snow could still be seen. The nights were not yet frost-free, but as soon as the sun showed itself during the day, it warmed the ground and with it the wildflowers, which made the prairie glow in bright colors.

On this seventh day in May, the big house of the MacIntyre Ranch was filled with life. Shortly the large salon had been converted into a kind of chapel. Isabella stood near a baptismal font with a small bundle in her arms and a loving smile on her face. Cameron stood beside her with Reverend Charles Duncan on his side, who now addressed his small congregation.
"We are gathered here to welcome this new inhabitant of the earth into our congregation."

Charles paused for a moment and looked into the happy faces of those present. They had all come. William and James Hunt with his wife Marylou, who sat next to Elizabeth. Malcolm and Louisa sat in the second row with Frank and his family in the second row. Who would have thought months ago that everything would take this turn. He was glad that his help with the marriage had come to such a good and happy end.

The Reverend now gave Isabella a sign to step closer to the basin and hold the little head above it. Then he took a few drops of water and wetted the child's scalp with it.

"I hereby baptize you by the name of Robert James MacIntyre. In the name of the Father, the Son and the Holy Spirit. Amen."

Cameron grinned as his son started to cry loudly against the wet drops. He was a healthy boy and had been keeping his young parents on their toes for four weeks. Tenderly, he put his arms around his beautiful wife and gave his son a kiss on the forehead. A little later, as the congregation sat at the table, Charles Duncan raised his wine glass.

"To the new Lord in the MacIntyre line. To little Robert James."

Everyone toasted him and it became a happy day. In the evening, when the guests had gone to bed, Cameron was sitting on the porch in front of the house. In his arms and wrapped thickly in a blanket so that his son would not get cold, he watched the dark starry sky. Blissfully, he looked at the little creature in his strong arms. His son looked at him from the same bright blue eyes that his great-grandfather had had, and gurgled to himself. Also the small heart-shaped birthmark had prevailed in this generation.

A small black fuzz on the head of the boy suggested that he, too, would get the black MacIntyre hair. Proud of his son, he pressed him affectionately against him and looked again into the night sky.

What had not happened since the summer festival. His grandmother had been pleased about his decision to stay with her. Lately she had kept more and more out of the management of the ranch and had left the decisions to him. Cameron, on the other hand, continued to involve her in his plans and discussed important things with her. One day he would be the new owner of this ranch and there was still a lot for him to learn. Isabella helped him with the bookkeeping and on the days when she gave lessons to her students, Elisabeth lovingly took care of her great-grandson. Cameron listened to the sounds of the night and rocked his son to sleep. In the pasture with the other horses stood Black Storm. James had brought the Stallion to him one day with the words:

"I think he missed you. Since the day you left, he hasn't let anyone get close to him. Apparently, you're the only one who can ride him."

Cameron had to smile when he thought back to that day. The animal had seen him and had joyfully approached him. He had never had any problems with him after that and rode him regularly ever since. Black Storm was only one reason for James to approach Cameron. After he had returned his daughter back safe and sound and had learned from Isabella what Carl had been up to, James could not help but see the good in Cameron. Twice he had saved his daughter's life and he had witnessed how much the two of them loved each other. He had taken Cameron aside and Cameron still remembered the words of that time.

"I know I have no right to ask you for anything. Not after what I did to you. I was your father's best friend and his death affected me deeply at the time. If I had ever had the slightest idea that you were Robert's son, things would have been different. Not that it excuses my behavior towards you. Even as an Indian, I should never have treated you the way I did. I don't know what got into me at the time. I suppose I wanted to punish you becauce Isabella stood by you and disobeyed me. I'm sorry, and if I could undo it, I would not hesitate. Your father and I had always thought that one day we would merge our parents' ranches with our children. He would probably be happy today to see that fate has indeed worked out that way."

James had held out his hand to him, with the words, "I ask for your forgiveness."

Cameron had not hesitated to agree and forgive James. It belonged all in the past and somehow he had come out of it all right. He had the love of his life by his side and the bliss in his hands, what could be more beautiful? Cameron looked up as he spotted a movement at the end of the porch and saw two shadows standing close together also looking at the starry sky.

A smile played around his lips, for he knew, that William and his grandmother were standing there. In the last few months, the two seemed to have become a little closer, because William had conspicuously visited often in recent times. Quietly, not to disturb the two, he rose from his rocking chair and went into the house. Upstairs in the bedroom the oil lamp burned on a small flame. Isabella was already asleep and so he quietly put his now sleeping son into his crib. He took off his clothes and crawled under the blankets. Isabella, awakened by the movement, turned to him and snuggled into his arms.

"Are you happy, Cameron?"

"Yes, I have you and my son. We are a family. That's more than I could have dreamed of a year ago. You have helped me and stood by me and I thank you for that. I love you, Isabella."

"You are my life. I love you!"

He pulled her close, kissed her, turned out the light and let night fall around them.

Read another Novel from Barbara Eckhoff

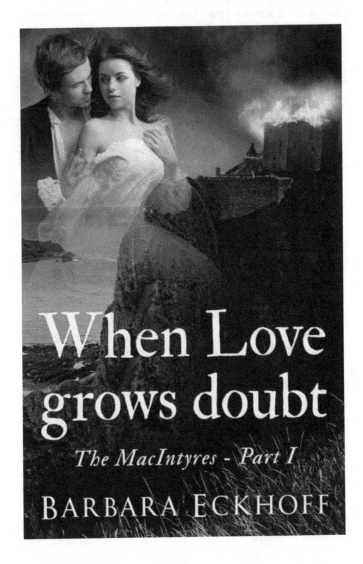

When Love grows doubt

The MacIntyres - Part I

BARBARA ECKHOFF

The wind swept icily over the freshly covered grave. Despite the noon hour, it was gloomy outside and the sky held ominously dark-looking clouds. The mourners had long since retreated into the warmth, but the small, delicate figure standing over the grave with a flowing cloak was oblivious to all this. Despite the warm winter cape with the fur-lined hood, she stood trembling in front of the mound covered with flowers. Her quiet tears were quickly dried by the wind, leaving red cheeks on her face. Now everything was over. She had just buried her last hope. Who could help her now?

"Moira!"

She was startled when she felt a hand on her shoulder and heard the priest's voice.

"Moira, there is nothing more you can do for him! You will catch your death if you don't get warm. Come my child, Martha has a cup of hot tea ready, it will warm you up again."

With these words he put his arm around her shoulders and gently led her away from the grave towards the rectory. Moira silently let herself be guided. Inside the house, a comforting warmth from the heated fireplace welcomed her. Martha, the priest's housekeeper, handed her a hot cup of tea with a good shot of rum in it.

"This will warm you right up, my dear. You're half frozen!"

Gratefully, Moira accepted the cup, only now realizing how cold she was. Her hands and feet began to tingle as the warmth flooded her body. She looked out the window and saw that a storm was brewing outside. Perhaps she had better start on her way, so that she was home before the expected rain.

"I thank you for your hospitality, but I think I should be heading home now."

"You should have gone back with one of the others earlier, then you wouldn't have to go all the way alone. Oh, it's a shame. I remember when you used to drive up with your parents in the carriage. You should have kept it for yourself so you wouldn't have to walk home."

Moira had to think back to the time the priest was talking about. Yes, things had been different before. It seemed like an eternity when she could go through life without a care. When her father knew her so well, he could read her mind through the eyes of a parent and had promised her a rosy and secure future. But that was long ago. That time would never come back. She was in trouble and the only one who could have helped her was now lying in the cold grave. Moira tried to suppress the tears that were welling up inside her again, but nodded and quickly said goodbye to the priest and Martha and headed back out into the horrible weather.

A gust of wind caught her. She quickly held her cloak tighter to her body and hurried away with quick steps towards the village. Normally she would have walked the path by the cliffs to her home. This was a shortcut, but in this weather it was not advisable.

The narrow trail, which on sunny days gave a breathtaking view of the sea below, lined with warped trees and hedges on the landward side of the path, was now soggy and slippery in the rainy and windy weather. Thus, there was an easy danger of losing one's footing due to the strong gusts and falling down the cliffs.

This had already happened in the past and for this reason Moira chose the longer, but safer way through the village. She had just heard the rumble of thunder in the distance. How unusual at these temperatures, she thought, and took another step faster. In the village she saw no one on the street and so she hurried on in the direction of her home.

As the first drops fell from the sky, she came down the long driveway. She paused for a brief moment in front of the burnt ruins of the large two-story brick house that had once been her home. Then hurried past the ruins, over to a much smaller house whose lighted windows and smoke from the chimney seemed to invite her in. Just as the sky opened up and heavy rain dropped down on her, she reached the heavy wooden door and entered the comforting warmth of the house.

A few months later

"**M**oira! You have to come right away."

"What's so important?"

She was just checking her expense book when the door to the small room opened and Eileen, her only employee and friend at the same time, entered excitedly.

"Sir Dumfrey is driving up now. You should go greet him."

Moira pursed her mouth and heaved a sigh, but she rose from her chair and marched past Eileen, saying, "That's all I need."

She opened the front door just as Sir Dumfrey raised his hand to pull the bell rope. With a sugary voice and a beaming smile, Moira welcomed her uninvited guest.

"Sir Dumfrey, this is quite a surprise. You should have announced your visit, then I could have prepared something to eat. Unfortunately I can only offer you a cup of tea with some pastries."

Sir Dumfrey enclosed Moira's hand with his wet fingers and pressed a slippery kiss on it. Disgusted, she let it wash over her.

"My dear- Moira, you needn't trouble yourself. You know how you could make me happy."

Moira shuddered inwardly. Charles Dumfrey had paid his respects to her several times in the past months, and each time his visits had been accompanied by lewd innuendos. Twice he had already proposed to her and twice she had made him understand that she was not willing to marry him. So what more did he want from her? Politeness dictated that she invite her guest in anyway, and so she led him into the small sitting room and asked Eileen to bring them a cup of tea.

Charles Dumfrey took a seat in one of the four small armchairs covered with dark red velvet and watched as Moira turned to Eileen. The young lady was beautiful. Her petite figure was in a light blue muslin dress. Her slender waist was accentuated with a yellow belt, and with it she wore a white blouse and a tight, light blue jacket that stopped below her breast line.

She had twisted her long brown hair into a bun. The rose complexion of her skin made her green eyes stand out. She was young, just eighteen and actually too young for him, but he liked young, inexperienced women whom he could still mold to his liking and who were capable of satisfying his particular preferences. Moira had already turned down his marriage proposal twice, and perhaps it was time to show her that she had no choice. When she turned back to him and approached him, he began to speak.

"Moira, it always shocks me what poor conditions you must live in here. This," he made a sweeping motion with his hands, "is not worthy of you. Have you thought about my offer?"

Moira took a seat in the opposite armchair and let her thoughts run free.

"If by that you mean your marriage proposal, I'm afraid I'll have to turn you down again. I do not love you and I will not marry you."

"I am not asking you to love me either. Let's call it an agreement. I offer you a life at my side in my castle with all the luxury you deserve, and in return you give me the rights to your property. At the moment it lies fallow and decaying. Your house is in ruins and you have to live in a house which is not more than a barn."

"If my land is not worth much, why are you so interested in it? You are a rich man and don't need the house."

"Well, I was a good acquaintance of your parents, and it's just a shame how the property deteriorated after they died. Not that it's your fault. You are young and inexperienced and forgive me for saying so, but you are a woman and this is more of a man's business after all."

Moira was about to protest when Sir Dumfrey raised his hand placatingly and continued,

"I would like to have the fields tilled again and the house rebuilt so that everything is restored to its former glory. Now what do you think of my offer?"

Silently, she sat there for a while. It was a tempting offer, of course. How happy she would be if her home was rebuilt and the farmers could return.

If everything would be like it used to be. But the price she would have to pay seemed too high. She looked in Sir Dumfrey's watery brown eyes. He was at least in his mid-forties, was not much taller than herself, and had a bulging belly. His formerly black hair was streaked with silver and he wore a cologne that weighed too heavily on him and hung in her nose.

His beige pantaloons were from an expensive tailor and the brocade vests he always wore were also made of fine fabrics; yet all his luxury could not hide the fact that she did not trust him. His eyes always seemed to be on the lurk and something about him inwardly warned her to be careful. No, she would not sell herself for possessions. There had to be another solution for her to keep her land, and so she turned back to him.

"Sir Dumfrey, I am flattered that you seem to be considering only me for your wife, but unfortunately I must again decline. Acceptance of this offer does not seem right to me and I ask you not to pursue me further."

"Well my dear. Your answer is unfortunate because I have thus granted you an opportunity to distance yourself from the debts of your parents. However, since you are still unwilling to consent to a marriage with me, I must inform you that I will demand from you the amount your parents owed me."

Moira thought she had misheard. What debt was he talking about? Her parents had been wealthy and had had no debts. There had to be some mistake.

"My parents had no debts, I would have known."

"I have with me the promissory bill that your father signed shortly before he died. He borrowed the sum of ten thousand pounds."

"Ten thousand pounds! That's impossible."

She was horrified. Why had her father needed so much money, and where had all the money gone? It could only be a mistake.

"May I see this document?"

"Certainly."

Sir Dumfrey pulled out a folded piece of paper from his vest pocket and handed it to Moira. She saw the incredible sum written on it and her father's signature. The date was a day, two weeks before the fire. She stared at the letter. "I see you confirm the authenticity of the signature and I'm willing to give you the option of paying me back the amount in installments. Every month from now on you will pay me the sum of one hundred pounds."

"That...I can't do. Where am I going to get that much money. I don't even have enough to keep the orphanage open."

"You had a choice. With marriage, you would have gotten rid of the debt all at once, so now it's your problem how to get the money together. You could, of course, transfer the land to me as compensation."

"Never!"

Annoyed, she jumped up. Sir Dumfrey rose slowly, came menacingly close to her, and said, "Then we have nothing more to say to each other, and I expect the payments on the first of each month."

With these words he bowed and marched out of the room. Eileen, who had just come in with the tea, looked at him in surprise.

"Don't bother, I'll see myself out."

Feeling very pleased with himself, he boarded his waiting carriage, leaving two distraught women in the house.

When Love grows doubt

Now Available

Barbara Eckhoff

Born near Hannover/ Germany in 1968, she was drawn to faraway places at an early age.

As a hotel manageress, she worked in hotels all over Germany and spent a year in Canada as an au pair, before settling down with her husband and the two daughters in a small village in Schleswig-Holstein. In 2013, she emigrated with her family to Florida/USA. It was there, when she began to get more serious about writing. In the meantime, more books have been published in German and English. Today, she lives with her husband and their Golden Retriever in the beautiful Shenandoah Valley in Virginia/USA and runs a Bed & Breakfast.

For more Infos:

www.barbaraeckhoff.com

www.brierleyhill.com

Wind of Fate